The sacrifice

BY
Mark Bouton

Oak Tree Press  Taylorville, IL

Oak Tree Press

Oak Tree Press books may be purchased for educational, business or sales promotional purposes. Contact Publisher for quantity discounts

First Edition, July 2012

Cover by Reese-Winslow Designs
Interior Page Layout by Kalpart (www.kalpart.com)

ISBN 978-1-61009-197-8
LCCN 2012939147

Although this book was reviewed and approved for publication by representatives of the Federal Bureau of Investigation, Washington, D.C., the ideas and opinions expressed herein are strictly those of the author.

Dedication

This book is dedicated to my grandkids,
Christopher, Jaclyn, Will and Abby.
You guys are the absolute best, and I love
you all very much.

Acknowledgments

Many thanks go to the members of my writing critique group, The Write Stuff, including Evie Green, Pat Bonine, Dennis Smirl, Patsie Sweeden, Phil Morris, Steve Laird, Lee Goldstein, Dr. Bob Conroy, Elizabeth de Ford, Sheila Dalrymple, Gwen Funston, Kris Polansky, Judie Miller, Sam Pierson, Randall Martin, Agnes Kazminski, Lee Anne Lichte, George Paris, and Ellen Jones for their encouragement, suggestions, and corrections of my work. Special thanks also to Dr. Bob Conroy, Anna McClure, and Chad Bouton for their help with technical and practical considerations concerning the operations of a hospital. I'm grateful to Billie Johnson, Publisher, Oak Tree Press, for her support; Sunny Frazier, for editorial assistance; Suzi Yazell for facilitation of publication and promotional support and assistance; and Jeana Thompson for her promotional efforts.

Thanks also to my writing groups, the Kansas Authors' Club and Kansas Writers', Ink, for their encouragement and help in preparing the book. And my heartfelt appreciation and thanks to my encouraging and helpful agent, Kirsten Neuhaus of the Kirsten Neuhaus Literary Agency, New York, NY, for her invaluable input on the book.

And thank you to the brave men and women of the FBI, whose efforts each day help make the United States a safer and better place for our children and adults.

Deuteronomy 32:17
They sacrificed unto devils, not to God;

King James version of The Holy Bible, published 1611.

1

Lyn jerked upright in bed and stared at the wall in drowsy confusion, then it hit her—this was the day—and, for an awful moment, her heart froze. She clenched her fists and rocked, saying, "Ah, crap." She'd feared this morning for months, often getting a nervous stomach and dull headaches that lasted for hours. Then last night he'd said, "Don't fail us," his dark eyes peering into her soul, and she knew if she did, she'd have hell to pay.

She stood up and shook her head, trying to clear her foggy mind from the lousy night's sleep. The pinewood floor felt cool and gritty beneath her bare feet. Through a broken slat in the mini-blinds she stared at the slate-colored dawn, thinking it matched her mood.

She showered, then padded back into the bedroom, toweling dry. She put on some beige panties and a bra, and from beneath her tee shirts, she pulled out the blue outfit and slipped it on. She added the last part of the costume, then, after a quick check in the closet door mirror, she nodded, thinking that she looked the part. Pacing to the kitchen, she poured a glass of juice. She managed to force down half of it, but her stomach was too jittery for more.

She put the glass in the fridge, then she opened a drawer beside the sink. Tearing a section of aluminum foil from a roll, she folded it lengthwise, then doubled it over and stuck it in her pocket. She was ready. Time to *get on with it.*

As she left the house, with the screen door screeching open, then slamming with a clattery *bang* behind her, a breath of misty air brushed her face. Hurrying toward her car in the driveway, she was startled by a clap of thunder. She cursed the developing foul weather and slid into the car with foreboding.

Twenty minutes and several miles later, as the stoplight turned green, she squealed away, roaring down the street in her rattletrap Chevy, her breathing uneven and her hands clammy on the wheel. The skies had darkened, and a steady sprinkle dampened the roads to a sinister sheen. A wreck on the freeway tangled traffic, making her run late.

Her brow furrowed as she studied a fierce bank of clouds, blacker than hate, moving in fast from the west. The wind gusted, and scraps of paper skittered along the pavement like wild street boys. She shook her head, doubtful and shaky, wondering if she could really pull it off.

The speeding car hit a pothole, the thud jarring her bones. But she clenched her teeth and stomped the pedal, lurching ahead faster. Lightning glared, followed by an ominous *boom,* and her knuckles went white as she gripped the wheel.

She checked her watch and grimaced. If she didn't get there soon, they'd be madder than rabid dogs. She sped ahead as fast as she dared, and within minutes she careened into the side parking lot of a looming hospital, nosed into an empty space, and pumped the spongy brake. As she killed the engine, a driving rain cut loose, pounding the roof in a clamor.

"My friggin' luck," she said. *It was fifty yards to the building in this soaker, with no umbrella, no raincoat, and no time to wait it out.* She flung open the door and ran toward a side entrance of the tall, imposing edifice. A flash lit up her pale blue scrubs, and then *ka-wham!* Her insides twisted like cheap rope.

She blew out a breath as she reached the shelter of the building's overhang, finally escaping the downpour. Pausing by a stucco-covered pillar near an outside door, she studied the trimmed hedge that bordered the building's concrete apron. She glanced back toward the parking lot, and then peered up and down the stretch of sidewalk.

Seeing no one, she bent down, reached beneath the hedge, and retrieved a rock. She juggled the rough, gray stone in her palm, studying it. Then she gripped the rock with both hands and twisted it in half. Plucking a key from the plastic fake, she moved to the door. With a trembling hand, she shoved the key into the lock, turned it, then opened the sturdy lever handle. Ah, *the first hurdle down.*

She pushed inside, and the heavy door swung shut behind her with a metallic *thunk.* There wasn't a soul on the staircase, which was good. She took a deep breath and let it escape, forcing herself to relax.

Rainwater dripped from her hair. She shook it out, and

then skimmed the clammy wetness off her arms. It felt colder than summer rain ought to. Or maybe it was being in the A/C. Anyway, it was time to move. She looked up the staircase, and her mouth twisted as she thought over the situation. The staff ought to be drinking coffee or doing stuff at the nurses' station. She just hoped there was no one in the halls to mess with her.

Up the stairs she went, her wet shoes squeaking with every step, wobbly as a colt. Her hand shook on the railing, but she kept moving, reviewing her instructions, not wanting to screw it up. At the top of the stairs she hesitated, her heart hammering to mimic the outside thunder.

She pushed open the door a stingy few inches and peered down the corridor. No one was there, and her shoulders slumped in relief. Her nerves crackled with electricity, but she sucked in a deep breath and whispered to herself, "Okay, gal, you can do it."

* * * * *

Booming thunder awakened Trisha. She blinked, then turned her head to peer out of a spacious window. In the murky sky, lightning flared, glow-white and jagged, followed by a menacing rumble. A gusting wind hurled sheets of water against the plate glass window to course down in crooked rivulets. She studied the cloudburst for several moments. Then she smiled, thinking about her situation. She and April were safe and warm in the best hospital in San Antonio, so heck, let it pour.

After the feeding, April had fallen asleep right away. Now her head listed, and her Cupid's bow mouth hung open. Trisha smiled. What a perfect moment.

There was a bump at the door, and in came a nurse pushing a portable isolette. "How's the little one doing?" she asked, moving to the bed. Her glistening black hair framed a plain face.

Trisha gazed at April, smiling. "She's full, and she's taking a nap." She turned back to the nurse, noting her scrubs were soaked—the woman smelled of dampness. "Oh, dear, you're so wet."

"Well, I left my umbrella here at the hospital, which didn't help none outside. But I won't melt." Then she patted April's bottom, saying, "What a doll."

Nodding, Trisha said, "Thank you. We think so, but, of

course, we're prejudiced. She's our first."

"Oh, there's none sweeter," the woman said, lifting the baby and swaying it in her arms. "I'll take her back to the nursery. You best get yourself some rest. You look tuckered out."

Trisha stretched out a hand and touched the hem of the swaddling, worried the woman might get April wet—but no, the fluffy pink blanket should keep her dry, protect her. She glanced at the nurse's name tag. "Thanks, Mary, I am pretty beat this morning." She rose up on one elbow for a last look at her beautiful baby, wincing from the slash of pain across her middle. "Ooh, I suppose I'd better lie still."

"You done your mommy duty. Now take a break." She laid the newborn in the isolette, rolled it into the hallway, and closed the door with a click.

Trisha stared at the ceiling, marveling at the recent miracle. She adjusted herself to favor her sore, split abdomen. The C-section had been a last minute surprise from her concerned doctor, but at least April arrived unharmed and healthy. Everything was fine now. Trisha's eyelids began to droop as a wave of exhaustion moved through her body. Sleep came to her right away.

* * * * *

Outside Trisha's room, Lyn stood as still as a deer, checking up and down the hall, listening for voices or footsteps. There was only the murmur of conversation in the distance, but then a young, blonde candy striper rounded the corner. Damn it, why now? Lyn stood there rigid and unsure as cold creek water flushed through her veins.

The girl stopped, looked at a note in her hand, and then entered a patient's room.

Had the young 'un paid her any mind? She didn't seem to, but was it worth the risk? Lyn stared at a security camera on the opposite wall, thinking it over.

Then, with her heart thumping like a jackrabbit's, she wheeled the isolette and paced down the hallway. Moments later she stopped and looked back, seeing nothing and no one. She pulled the folded aluminum foil from her pocket and wrapped it around the baby's hospital ID bracelet. Then she snatched up the baby and her blanket, held the child close, and leaned a shoulder into the door beneath the red exit sign.

Down the stairs she hurtled, her footfalls pounding in her ears, then she barged through the door and marched out into the pouring rain. As she hurried toward her car, a brilliant fork of lightning zipped across the sky. She jerked open the passenger door and laid the baby into an infant car bed. As she tugged the blanket over the child, a thunderclap shook the Cavalier's tinny frame.

She dashed around to the driver's side, climbed in, and slammed the door. Panting from the effort, for several moments she studied the sleeping infant as she collected herself. Then she snatched open the glove box and tugged at a black velvet cloth that covered a silver athame. The baby jerked at the sudden noise, and her eyes fluttered open.

The dagger felt slippery in Lyn's damp hand. She reached over and pulled the foil off the baby's ankle. Then she slid the blade under the hospital bracelet, cut it in half, and placed the plastic strip and the foil into her purse.

Now she stared at the baby with purpose. Holding her breath, she placed the sharp point against the child's forehead and slashed a vertical line. The baby let go a loud shriek, shaking her small hands and kicking her feet in protest. Quickly, Lyn re-gripped the knife and sliced again, from left to right.

She surveyed her work. *It was done good,* she thought . . . *no one could bitch about it.* Wiping the point of the athame with a tissue, she gave a weary smile, then shoved the blade back into the glove box.

She cranked the ignition, then glanced again at the wailing kid. Another flash of lightning lit up the tiny face. The bloody cross on her forehead shone like fire.

* * * * *

More than an hour before the rain started, Jack Ransom had rolled out of bed, his back feeling as stiff as a frozen steak. "Unh," he said, striking a pose like the Greek discus thrower, and then he straightened up and twisted his torso left and right, making vertebrae crack like gunshots. Hmmm, that sounded *like Chiquita with her castanets.*

She'd done a strip act in Matamoros years before. The girl provided more sizzle than a **jalapeño** pepper. But he supposed he'd lost a beat in his salsa rhythm since then.

Snapping out of his stupor, he hobbled toward the bathroom, his legs feeling like wood. He began to doubt the wisdom of jogging *fifteen miles in the Hill Country on Saturday.* Now facing another ten on this Monday morning, he grumbled, "I must be going middle age crazy."

He flushed the toilet, washed his hands, then splashed cold water on his face and toweled dry. Back in the bedroom, he pulled on some running shorts. More and more he was coming to realize that training for a marathon at his age might be an irrational act.

Not that he was old, and he did keep in shape. Running, some racquetball, pushups and a few sets with dumbbells. But being in his late thirties meant that the big four-o was on the horizon. And the days kept zinging by.

He yanked the shoelaces of his Reeboks into tight knots. Standing, he leaned over to pull his Glock pistol from the drawer. As always, it felt solid—and deadly. He stepped over to the closet and shoved the black matte weapon to the back of the shelf. There were no kids around now, but it never hurt to be safe.

As he pushed open the front door, a chill morning breeze brushed his face. Lightning glowed in a bank of angry clouds to the west. "Damn, it's going to rain?" he asked aloud, remembering the sunny forecast.

Whatever, he thought he had time to make his run before it hit. He walked across the apartment parking lot, then broke into a slow lope down the road. As he jogged along the blacktop, past stands of Swamp Ash and Texas Mulberry, his muscles began to loosen. Even if he weren't training for the marathon, he thought he'd still run often. It was a good way to relax his mind, as well as his body. Besides, he could think things over and analyze them, as his legs pumped automatically in the repetitive jogging motions.

He'd do no running tomorrow, and then he'd start tapering his mileage and doing some carbo-loading. The Alamo City Marathon was a week from Saturday. No chance he'd win the event, but he did hope to finish.

* * * * *

As she awoke, Kathy Devereaux flipped a tickling strand of crimson hair off her forehead, blinked to clear her eyes, and for half a minute contemplated the meaning of life. She shrugged, then heaved herself up and crossed the room to click on a small TV. She climbed aboard her stationary bike and set the timer, then watched the news as she pumped.

During a commercial, she glanced down, studying her leg muscles as they flexed. They were sturdy, but cut with good definition. Hey, *not bad stems for an old maid.*

But then, her early twenties had been easier, when she kept in shape by dancing all night to a feisty Cajun band. Altogether, life was *tres confortable* then. There were no difficult duties or tricky responsibilities to handle, and there'd been no life or death decisions to make, as she had to do now.

Yes, now she worked hard at everything. For the past six years, she'd busted her butt to build up both her strength and endurance. Because she knew the FBI didn't cotton to wimps.

She glanced at her credentials and badge lying on the dresser. She knew that if *she lost a pissing contest with bad guys, she could end up good and dead.* She'd be just another half-breed shipped back to Louisiana in a body bag. And as she had no husband or kids, there would be only her momma and daddy and brother to note her passing.

She pedaled harder. Sweat trickled down between her breasts. In training school she'd tugged on boxing gloves and duked it out with fellow trainees, dishing out black eyes and busted lips, and catching some painful punches to her gut and cheeks. But, of course, in the real world, the street pukes went at it bare knuckles, or they whipped out a nine or an AK-47.

She grinned to herself, because it was fine with her to get it on with weapons. She thought back to training school at Quantico. She'd been the best in her class with firearms—pistols, shotguns, and MP-5 submachine guns—and she figured in a shootout she could hold her own, probably come out on top. So bring it on, bad boys.

* * * * *

When Ransom returned from his run and opened the door to his apartment, he felt a yawning emptiness. There was no one there to welcome him back, to ask how his run was, to care if he'd dropped dead on the road of a coronary. The furniture, done in tones of russet and forest green, neat and functional, made the room look like a picture in a Sears ad. There were just a few knick knacks, a couple of personal photos, and several porcelain or pewter beer mugs, mementos of offices he'd worked in, scattered here and there. His barbells and a bench were set up behind the sofa.

But then, he did have his freedom—and that was great, wasn't it?

After a quick breakfast of cinnamon toast, a banana, and a glass of milk, he showered, shaved, and dressed in a dark blue pin-striped suit. He grabbed his pistol and shoved it into the holster at his hip. Then he slipped his Bureau credentials, with the badge pinned on the front of the black leather case, into his jacket pocket. All good to go.

As he climbed into his Crown Vic, good-sized raindrops plopped on the hood. By the time he hit Loop 1604, there was a torrent. The Texas drivers began sliding into chaos, but he was lucky enough to dodge the pileups. Good thing it wasn't cold; those pickups and SUVs would look like the Ice Capades on wheels.

Arriving at the circular federal building, he inserted his electronic parking card, and then wheeled into the lot. The elevator was crowded and smelled like a wet dog. After escaping the confinement, he crossed the floor beneath the security cameras and punched in numbers on a cipher lock.

He retrieved his mail, and ambled down the linoleum pathway to the Violent Crime Task Force squad room. Hanging his suit jacket on a rack, he glanced about the cream-colored room favored by governmental architects, which was filled with cheap, functional desks and numerous blocky safe-cabinets for work files. A couple of dozen task force members, comprised of FBI agents and other federal agents or local cops or deputies, were all drinking coffee, yakking on the phone, or telling stories and laughing in small groups. They usually discussed cases or sports. He supposed that he was a different sort from many agents—interested in not just facts and crime, but in the metaphysical, the artistic, and the ethereal part of the world.

Well, it was time to get busy in the world of cruel reality. He winked at Kathy, said good morning to the others, and got himself a cup of java. Plopping down at his desk, he put his pistol into a drawer, locked it, then put on his reading glasses. He skimmed his mail, and then pulled a couple of folders from his safe cabinet that dealt with cases he wanted to investigate. As he studied the first one, the phone buzzed, startling him from his concentration.

"Agent Ransom."

"Jack, thank God you're there." He heard heavy breathing on the line. "It's Merle Owen."

Owen was the head of security at Metropolitan Hospital. He wasn't the type to hyperventilate. "Hi, Merle. What's up?"

"We got a baby missing from the neonatal ward. It's prob'bly some screwup, she's gotta be here somewhere, but it's been nearly an hour since her mom last saw her. She should be in the nursery, but when the dad came by looking, no one could find her."

"Who last saw the baby?"

"A woman came to the mother's room and said she'd take the baby to the nursery. But the nurse who brought the kid to the room says the mom never buzzed back. And no one else says they got her."

"You've checked all the rooms?"

"We just finished. No luck. And the kid's isolette was sitting at the end of the hall, empty. So I called you and the cops. Could you give us a hand?"

"Sure, I will, Merle. Listen, did you see a suspect on the security tapes?"

"Uh, we haven't had time to review them, Jack."

"Okay, we'll do that when I get there."

"Sure, but there's something else. We had a hitch with the door alarm. The baby had a security bracelet, and the alarm should have gone off when she went out the door."

Hmm. He wouldn't expect the hospital to foul up like that. "Okay, I'll be right there. We'll sort it all out."

"And there's . . . one other thing."

"What's that?"

"The baby is, uh . . . Senator Baldazar's kid."

"I see. I'm on my way." Ransom hung up, then sat motionless, thinking about the scenario. Baldazar had started his career as a defense attorney for dopers, and then he married into a rich Anglo family and became a state senator. That meant the media would be all over this, which was something to consider, as they could either help or seriously screw everything up.

Feeling a growing heat beneath his collar, Ransom unlocked his desk drawer and withdrew his pistol and a leather holder with two magazines. But, as he gripped the butt of his Glock, he realized he couldn't blow a hole in a shadow. Especially not while the shadow was holding a baby.

2

Ransom approached Kathy's desk. She tossed back her flaming hair, looking up with sky blue eyes the size of nickels. As she stared at him, he could swear she was reading his mind.

"*Hé, mon ami,*" she said, "you look tense."

"A baby's missing from Metro Hospital. I could use a hand to find out why. Are you busy?"

She leapt up like a cat. "Not anymore. Let's go."

They marched into the supervisor's office.

"Sonny" Jenkins sat leaned back in his leather chair, engrossed in reading a newspaper at his desk. Jenkins had long ago outgrown his nickname; frazzled wisps of gray hair snaked across his pinkish pate, and deep-set wrinkles fanned from beside his eyes. Brought up as a native New Yorker, he'd been assigned to several places in his Bureau career, including Mobile, Alabama; St. Louis, Missouri; and now San Antonio for the past three years. He glanced up from the *Express-News,* dropped the paper on his desk, and smacked his hand flat against his forehead.

"Uh oh, my horoscope warned me to watch out for wild, wanton women." Sonny was always quick with a quip. Ransom realized that New Yorkers knew few boundaries for their humorous targets.

Kathy rolled her blue orbs. "And *bonjour* to you, *chauve.*"

Studying her rigid posture, he said, "Is there something wrong? What's going on?"

"We've got a possible kidnapping, Sonny," Ransom said. "A baby's missing from Metro Hospital. They've got an empty isolette in the hall that the kid should be in."

"How sure are they? I mean, could they have misplaced him?"

"The baby's a female. Maybe so, but since it's Senator Baldazar's kid, he probably wants a definitive answer, and right now. We can't afford any mistakes, either."

Sonny's face reddened. "Ransom, you've got the ticket. You two run it out for the usual, and I'll round up reinforcements. Keep me advised of what's going on."

In two seconds, they were out of there. "So what'd you call him in there?" Ransom asked.

"*Chauve?* It means 'baldy.' But don't tell Sonny, he might assign me a ton of bullshit cases."

As rain drummed the car, Ransom told Kathy what details he knew about the missing baby. Her face flushed. He figured her Cajun blood was running hot.

* * * * *

Minutes later Ransom killed the engine, and they entered the imposing building. Pastel art and stylish furniture greeted them inside. But the place still smelled of chemicals, disinfectant, and fear.

Ransom reached the security department and walked straight down the hallway to Owen's office, with Kathy right behind. He rapped several times on the door, then stuck his head inside the airless room. Owen sat straight and rigid at his desk, his complexion ash gray, his forehead damp. The man glanced up with vacant eyes, but recognition seemed to infuse him with hope.

"Jack! Come on in." He rose with a spring unexpected in such a burly man, motioning to two scarred wooden chairs that hugged the wall.

"Merle, this is Kathy Devereaux. She's with the Bureau."

Owen nodded to Kathy, mumbling a greeting. She held out her hand and he shook it briefly.

They settled onto the hard seats. Dover took a breath. "Is there any new information about the baby?" he asked.

"Hell, Ransom, I'm afraid not. We're checking storage, the boiler room, even broom closets. We have guards posted at the exits, for all the good that'll do now." He picked at a cuticle on his thumb.

"What are the usual security precautions for babies?"

Owen winced as he yanked off a hunk of skin. "The mothers and the babies wear matching plastic ID bracelets. There's a chip in them so that an alarm will sound if they don't leave together, but apparently it didn't work."

"That's an RFID system?" Ransom asked.

"Right. Also, babies are footprinted right away, and they're kept in their own private isolettes. Our nurses are told to be alert for people on the floor who don't seem to belong there." He shrugged. "We also do a head count of the babies when each new shift comes on. And there are security cameras in the hallways that are monitored by our security guards. I guess that's about it."

"I understand," Ransom said, rubbing his chin. "Have you set up the tapes?"

"The security guys are running them now. They'll call me if they see a suspect."

"Okay, good. So, what's the baby's description?"

Owen shuffled papers, some anchored by a brass paperweight made from a machine gun cartridge, silently observed by a silver-framed photo of a stocky woman and two moon-faced kids. Snatching up a computer printout, he said, "Here it is. April Bayless Baldazar, born two days ago, April twenty-third."

"An astrological soul mate to the Bard," Ransom said.

"Huh?" Owen glanced up.

"She was born on the birthday of William Shakespeare."

"Oh, sure, I didn't think of that."

"What else do you have?" Ransom shifted in the hard chair. As a runner, he didn't carry much padding on his butt.

Owen adjusted his bifocals. "She's seven pounds, three ounces. Nineteen inches long. Dark hair."

"And you said the child was footprinted?"

"Yes, a couple of hours after delivery."

"She have any birthmarks?"

"Just one. A strawberry mark on the back of her neck."

Kathy leaned forward. "How's her mom doing?"

"The poor woman's wound up like a cheap watch. And the Senator's in orbit."

Ransom considered the problem. Baldazar was used to people doing his bidding without question. But the FBI had its own way of operating. There could be trouble in dealing with him.

"Where's the baby's isolette?"

"We left it at the end of the hall down from her room," Owen said. "It hasn't been touched."

"Excellent," Ransom said. "Let's take a look."

The journey down sterile hallways was strained. When they arrived, they didn't have much to see. There was only an empty isolette on wheels, as forlorn as a tombstone.

Just then two agents strode down the hall. Hank

Atherton powered toward them like Maximus Prime from that *Transformers* movie. Six-feet-four-inches, with lumberjack shoulders, he carried a heavy evidence kit with ease. Beside him was an agent that everyone called Jester—a man with shiny mahogany skin, a gunfighter's gait, and known to be as tough as beef jerky.

Ransom briefed them on the situation. Atherton rocked back and forth on his heels, taking it in. Jester stood there like a cool chunk of marble, nodding.

"Hank, could you check the isolette there for latents?" Ransom asked. He studied the red sign over the exit. "Dust that door, too."

"You got it." And he knelt, studying the surfaces on the isolette.

"And the alarm on this door malfunctioned?" Ransom asked.

Owen nodded. "We don't know why it didn't sound. Maybe they cut off the baby's security bracelet or shielded it some way. Or it could be the alarm sensor just failed to pick up the signal. Someone's comin' from the alarm company to check it out."

Ransom pursed his lips. "Wouldn't your security system have caught it if someone cut the band?"

"It should have. There's supposed to be a secondary signal if the first one is compromised. As I said, we're still trying to figure out what happened."

Ransom frowned. The radio frequency ID system was a pretty sophisticated one. He didn't like the scenario. Either the alarm malfunctioned at just the wrong time, or else someone knew how to defeat it. Whichever happened, it was bad.

He pulled out a handkerchief and pushed open the door. Concrete stairs with metal railings descended. He and Kathy and Owen all headed down, avoiding touching the railing. At the landing shone another exit sign. Ransom peered at the security chief.

"It goes into a side parking lot," Owen said. "Employees use it as a shortcut."

"So, can anyone come in this door?"

"No, only employees have a key for it. Of course, anyone could go out of it."

Ransom's forehead wrinkled, then he pulled a penlight from his coat pocket and shined it at the bottom of the door. Some dust had gathered on the floor there, and he spotted a shoeprint. It was small, like a woman's or a child's. He could discern a zig-zag pattern to it. It had to be a sneaker or a walking shoe. He'd have Hank photograph it.

He opened the door and inhaled damp air. The rain had eased to a desultory patter; the sky remained murky. Far away, lightning flared.

There were probably a hundred cars in the lot. The booth for the attendant was sixty yards from the far side of the cars. Not a good vantage point for seeing anyone coming out this door with a baby.

"Jester, talk to the attendant. Tomorrow morning we'll check arrivals in the lot."

"Consider the dude debriefed," said Jester, squeezing by.

Ransom looked at Kathy. "Let's interview the mother."

A pained look creased her brow. "Jesus, Mary, and Joseph."

He nodded. "Some divine intervention couldn't hurt."

Owen huffed up the stairs and tugged open the door. Atherton squatted there dusting the isolette with deft brush strokes, dark powder drifting downward. At his shoulder, like a staff surgeon watching an intern, was Lieutenant Sanchez.

The swarthy man turned toward Ransom. "Hello, *amigo.*"

"*¿Como estas?*" Ransom asked, sticking out his hand.

Sanchez's grip was as solid as a bear trap. "I'm fine, man. And you're looking *muy bien.*" He glanced back at the isolette. "What's the situation?"

"We've got this empty portable isolette, no nurse on duty claimed to have picked up the baby, search of the hospital found *nada.*" He told him about the door alarm that didn't sound, and how someone was reviewing the security camera tapes.

"*That's bad about the alarm. Do you think someone sabotaged it?*"

"*I don't know. We'll see what the repair guy says. Right now, we're on our* way to talk to the mother."

"*Pues, vamos,*" Sanchez said, and they all paced down the hall.

* * * * *

The Senator opened the door. He was tall, with frizzy hair and an expensive suit. His tan face had somehow gone dark crimson.

Ransom introduced everyone, then said, "We need to talk to Mrs. Baldazar."

"Good, come in." But first he leaned toward Ransom, his eyes intent behind gold-rimmed glasses. "My wife is very upset. Please try to keep it brief."

Pink lambs and blue lambs cavorted on a stenciled border that accented sugar-white walls. The beige floor shined, and stainless equipment gleamed. The Senator's wife reclined against a jacked-up bed, her eyes red and wet.

"Mrs. Baldazar," Ransom said, moving to her side, "we're very sorry about this situation, but we know how to handle it. We'll do whatever it takes to find your baby right away."

She dissolved into tears, and the Senator moved to her side, gripping her shoulder and stroking her hair.

Ransom studied the man's hands. They were soft and unmarked, like two tawny Chihuahuas. The man had never picked any Ruby Red grapefruit in the Rio Grande Valley with those mitts. But the guy had the touch. His wife stopped crying, then she dabbed her eyes with a tissue.

Ransom said, "I know this is very difficult for you. But it's important that you tell us everything you can remember about the nurse who picked up April."

"I don't recall much about her. I guess I was focused on April." She searched Ransom's face. "Was the woman not a real nurse? How could I know that?" Now she looked desperate. "Do you think she has my baby?"

"I don't know, but we'll find out. First, just tell me what happened."

She told the story as she remembered it. Sometimes she paused to cry, but she pressed on. The minutes without her baby seemed to be crushing her.

Mrs. Baldazar knew the nurse who brought the child for its feeding, a woman named Sheila. But a new nurse, Mary, whom she'd not seen before, came to get April. Mary was Caucasian, medium height, average weight, short dark hair, not very attractive. Possibly wore glasses, maybe a watch and a gold wedding band. She might recall the woman if she were to see her again. Oh, and the woman's uniform was wet from the rain.

So, it was probably an outsider, thought Ransom. What they needed was a face. People remembered faces.

For a few moments, Ransom considered using the Facial Imaging computer software FACES, which they had at the office, to make a sketch of the phony nurse. But he knew Senator Baldazar would like something done now. Besides, he personally favored sketches done by artists from the FBI

Lab at Quantico over the computer-generated ones. If Mrs. Baldazar had a good memory, she might recall enough about the woman for an artist to do a helpful sketch.

Ransom asked Mrs. Baldazar if she'd like to try it. She agreed to review a Facial Identification catalog with Kathy shortly. They could then send the filled out form to the lab.

"One other thing," said Ransom, "did her nurses' outfit look different from what the others wear?"

She thought it over. "No, it seemed like the regular nurse scrubs."

"What about her name tag, did it look the same, too?"

"I think so. It had her name in black letters and some kind of purple insignia on it."

He closed his notepad. "Thanks, Mrs. Baldazar. And if you remember anything else, you or your husband should call me." He handed his card to the Senator. "Now we'll leave you alone. When we find out something, we'll let you know."

"That's it?" Baldazar said, inclining his head, his eyebrows arched.

"For now," Ransom said.

Kathy moved to the woman's side, squeezing her hand and murmuring something as the others started to leave. Trisha nodded and gave a tiny smile.

Down the hallway they discussed the situation, deciding that Ransom would check on the security tapes, then he and Kathy could talk to the nurse who first brought the baby to the room. Sanchez would speak with the mother's obstetrician. For now, Kathy would grab a Facial Identification catalog from the car and go over it with Mrs. Baldazar. The anxious woman would go through it, selecting noses, lips, hair styles, etc. from the catalog so an artist could meld the various descriptions into a complete face.

As they started to break up, Sanchez turned and stared at the room for a long moment. "Who would just march into a hospital and grab a baby?"

Ransom frowned. "Maybe it's like Shakespeare wrote: 'Lovers and madmen have such seething brains, such shaping fantasies that apprehend more than cool reason ever comprehends.'"

Sanchez said, "So you think it's a nut case?"

"You know anyone rational who'd cop a kid?"

* * * * *

22

During the time the agents talked with Mrs. Baldazar, and Atherton dusted the railings along the stairwell, a woman slipped into the bathroom at the end of the hall, across from where the isolette now sat in a corner. The room was empty, so she went straight to the paper towel dispenser and reached underneath it, searching with her fingertips. There it was. She pulled loose the tape, unstuck it from the key, then slid the key onto the ring with her others. Tossing the tape into the trash, she glanced into the mirror. She thought she looked calm and collected. All was going well.

* * * * *

Kathy had finished her interview with Mrs. Baldazar, and she'd filled out the form requesting a sketch to be done at Quantico. Ransom had looked at the security tape from the hallway in question. Now they sought the nurse who took April to her mother this morning. They found Sheila Pettijohn sorting various pills. She agreed to take time to speak with them. Down the hall, they found a private spot where they could talk.

Ransom surveyed the luxurious curves that expanded the nurse's tight scrubs. She looked to be in her mid-thirties, with long dark hair and creamy white skin. Her full lips were painted a candy apple red. An expensive perfume exuded from her pores. From her mouth purred a throaty voice which rose and fell in a sensual lilt. In short, she was hot.

She eased into a chair behind a Formica table in the nurses' break room, and Ransom and Kathy seated themselves opposite her. A refrigerator hummed, and the smell of fresh coffee filled the air. Nurse Pettijohn folded her hands on the table and waited for them to speak.

Ransom said, "I know this is difficult for you—"

"I *do* feel awful about the baby," she interrupted, "but I didn't violate any rules. I don't know what else I could have done."

"We're not saying you did anything wrong. But maybe you saw something that could help our investigation."

"What happened," Kathy said, "when you took April to the room?"

She glanced at Kathy, studied Ransom a moment, and then said, "There's not much to tell. It was time for the baby to be nursed, so I took her to Mrs. Baldazar. I left her there, and then I went to do some other things. I didn't hear from Mrs. Baldazar again, so I assumed that when she buzzed the beehive, someone else went to get the baby."

"The beehive?" asked Ransom.

"The nurses' station. There are usually several nurses hovering around it, busy as . . . well, you know."

"Sure, I get it. Was anyone in the hall when you took the baby to Mrs. Baldazar's room?"

"I don't think so. I mean, I didn't notice anyone. Besides, I'd have told Security if I'd seen anybody unusual."

Ah, the good citizen. Ransom glanced at her dove-white hands on the table. She wore a star-shaped ring on her right hand and a watch with a sweep second hand on her left wrist. Her left ring finger was bare. His guess was that she was probably divorced.

"Your scrubs look standard," Ransom said, eyeing them steadily.

"Yes, they're pretty plain. We use light blue ones. Some hospitals use green. But they're rather ordinary, no frills."

Kathy asked, "Where do you get them?"

"At uniform supply places."

"And can they be rented, like the old nurse uniforms used to be?"

Nurse Pettijohn gave Kathy a conspiratorial smile. "Yes, I think so."

Ransom was puzzled, but he forged ahead. "Are there any nurses here at the hospital named Mary?"

"No, there's no one like that."

"Anyone who matches this Mary's description?"

"What was it, again?"

"She's Caucasian, about 35, medium height and build, with short dark hair."

"That's not an especially unusual look."

Ransom shook his head. "I know. Well, if you think of anything else, please call."

He handed her his business card, which she slipped into her pocket as she stood.

Kathy said, "What's the purple insignia on your name tag?"

She looked down at her chest. "Oh, that's a caduceus." She apparently caught Ransom's blank look. "It's the symbol of the medical profession. Or, at least, the American version."

"What do you mean?" asked Ransom.

"Most of the world uses the staff of Asclepius, the god of Medicine in Greek and Roman mythology, which is a staff entwined by a single snake. In the U.S., we use the staff of Mercury, or Hermes, as the Greeks called him, which has wings at the top and two snakes entwined around the staff."

"Of course," he said. "Thanks for your help."

* * * * *

Lyn fingered her blonde bangs, staring in the dim light at the tiny form. Swaddled in a pink blanket, the baby breathed evenly in sleep. She's mighty peaceful now, she thought, studying the smooth cheeks, the puckered lips, the tiny balled fists. But with the graven cross on her forehead, the tot had learned a little about life's pain.

Lyn heard a noise behind her, turned, and put a finger to her lips.

Harvey froze in a hunched position. Then he tiptoed closer and peered over her shoulder at the still bundle. He hadn't touched the baby yet. Lyn knew he thought children came under the heading of "women's work."

She jerked her head toward the door, and they both crept out of the room. The floor in the hallway creaked as they walked past their framed wedding photo, with her looking much slimmer and more hopeful. She stopped and straightened the print of the Bavarian forest, ignoring the snapshot of Harvey's long-gone hunting dog.

In the kitchen she pushed aside a pile of crusty dishes and began fixing coffee. The robust aroma competed with the lingering odor of grease. She scuffed the toe of her shoe at a bit of bacon stuck to the linoleum.

"Are you doin' okay?" Harvey asked, staring at his boots.

"Of course, why wouldn't I be?"

"You know, goin' in the hospital and picking up that kid all by yourself. And with me hauling ass in my rig back from L.A. I wasn't even here to help you."

She peered at the forlorn figure as he scraped a fingernail along the stubble on his cheek. "Don't   worry about it. Everything's fine, Harvey. Do you want some coffee?"

He fumbled a pack of Pall Malls from his shirt pocket and smiled with stained teeth. "Did you ever know me to turn it down?"

She shook her head and poured the coffee. He lit up a smoke. They sat and drank the dark, steaming liquid.

"Think it'll rain tomorrow?" she asked. They seldom discussed anything meaningful. She'd quit trying.

"Nah, it looks to me like she'll clear up."

"When it dries out, you best cut the grass."

"Why? It'll just grow again."

She gave him a tired smile. "I guess I'll fix up some lunch. I sure hope that baby sleeps awhile, I got to get some rest."

He patted her hand. "Why don't you take it easy? Go in the bedroom and stretch out."

"But ain't you hungry?"

He grabbed his yellow ball cap. "Yep, I'm hungry as a starved dog, but I'll gas up the truck and then swing by Church's and get some chicken." He flipped on his cap, tugging down the brim.

She stared at the front of his ball cap, which said, "Heavy haulers do it better." She knew there had to be a catch to his offer. He'd been on the road a week. Then she realized what was going on. When he got back from a run, he was often nice to her. Until he got what he wanted.

* * * * *

"So what'd you get, Jester?" Ransom asked.

The agents had gathered in a small office in the hospital to discuss their progress in the case. Atherton said he found some latent fingerprints on the crib and some palm prints on the stairway railing. He also photographed the footprint by the lower level door. Of course, there was a lot of traffic in those areas, so the prints and photos might not mean a thing.

Jester said the parking lot attendant had been out to lunch. Oh, he'd been in the booth all morning, but he was always out to lunch. The guy didn't recall seeing anything or anyone unusual that morning. He saw no woman carrying out a baby. "Like my wife these days," Jester mused, "the guy was really spaced."

"How's Sharene doing?" Kathy asked.

"Just fine," Jester said. "She's getting as big as a house, but that's normal."

"One of the few chances a woman gets to eat enough."

Ransom eyed Kathy, but he kept his wisecrack to himself.

Sanchez walked up to the group. "What did you find out, Lieutenant?" asked Ransom.

Sanchez regarded his notepad. "Dr. Maxwell is the mother's obstetrician. He typically cares for a baby for the first few days, and then a pediatrician takes over. April was doing well, and she seemed healthy. She'd had all the tests done, and no defects were noted."

"So the baby's got no medical problems?" Kathy asked.

"Nothing specific that they found."

Ransom noted an uncertain tone in the man's voice. "Except?" he said.

"*Pues* . . . Dr. Maxwell said that babies can get dehydrated," said the Lieutenant. "Then they can incur trouble digesting their food. It's usually no problem when they're getting breast milk, but when you take away their normal supply . . . ."

"What happens?" asked Ransom, worried.

"Maybe nothing at all. Maybe the baby adjusts fine to cow's milk or formula. Or it doesn't do so well and gets diarrhea, colic, or whatever."

Kathy wrinkled her brow. "Can that be critical?"

"It could be nothing worse than a tummy ache and fussiness. Or sometimes a child will get diarrhea and die of dehydration. It happens a lot in poor countries."

Ransom glanced at the wooden faces of the agents. No one wanted to think about that kind of problem. It was too awful to consider.

"Let's plan how we're going to find this baby," said Ransom.

Sanchez sat down. "You tell us."

Ransom dropped into a swivel chair behind the desk and pulled out a pen.

"Okay, let's go over what we've done so far. We have a trap and trace on the parents' home line, the hospital line, and Baldazar's office line. We'll keep teams of two agents at each location, so if there's a ransom demand we can react right away."

Sanchez said, "We can put seven or eight detectives on this case."

"We'll do the same with our agents," said Ransom. "And we'll need a hot line at our office for tips being called in."

He tapped a pen against his cheek and looked around the group. "I watched the security tape," Ransom said. "I saw no sign of a woman with an isolette on it."

"How can that be?" asked Kathy.

"I'm not really sure," Ransom said. "Hank, do you have any ideas on the security tape or the alarm? What did you find out?"

"I talked with the security guards," Atherton said. "They said they didn't know why the tape for that hallway camera didn't show the woman with the baby."

"Could they have brought up the wrong tape?"

Atherton pursed his lips. "Well, I viewed the tape with Owen, and he thought it was kosher. He did see some regular employees, clean up people, and a doctor who was leaving after a delivery. But he thought those things probably happened after the baby was taken."

"So the alarm quit working when it might have helped us," Ransom said, "and the security camera didn't pick up a person with the baby?"

"That's about it, Jack." Hank shrugged. "And even stranger, the repairman couldn't find anything wrong with the alarm. So, he replaced it with a new one and took the original one back to the shop to study it some more. He'll try to find out if anyone might have tampered with it."

"Okay, that's important. Stay on top of it."

Ransom looked over his notes. "Let's divide up the list of nurses and other hospital staff for interviews. Jester and Atherton can deal with the alarm, and they'll also cover the patients and their visitors we haven't talked with yet. Lt. Sanchez, could you handle interviews with the candy stripers and cleaning people?"

Sanchez nodded and wrote on his notepad.

"So, Kathy and I will talk with the nurses and any doctors who were here this morning." Ransom put away his pen and said, "Let's do it."

As they were searching for the next nurse to interview, Ransom spotted a brightly lit candy machine stationed like a Buckingham Palace guard in a small alcove next to an equally stately Coke machine. He fed the candy machine some change and hit the buttons to order a Milky Way chocolate bar. He got one on the first try. Hey, he thought, it's my lucky day.

As he retrieved his prize from the machine's drawer, Kathy gave him a disparaging look. "If you keep that up, Jack, you're going to get as big as a float at *Mardi Gras.*"

"I've never seen one, but I'll bet they're huge."

"*Assure.* They're quite impressive."

"Did you ever ride on one of those bad boys?"

She gave him a wary look. "No, I just watched them drive by on the parade route."

"Ever cage any of those flashy beads? I've heard it takes

some bribery. Did you ever give the guys riding the float a quick flash?"

"If I did, when I was young, it doesn't concern you. But your professional appearance, or lack thereof, reflects on our whole organization."

What patronizing pap; she was jabbing him. Besides, chocolate was a balm to frayed nerves, and it gave him energy. Those were both things he'd need plenty of for this case. He stepped over to the pop machine and slid more silver down the coin slot for a Diet Coke. Aha, another instant winner.

Kathy ignored his latest purchase and gazed out the window.

He settled into a chair, munched on the bar, and stared at the machines. And just then he realized that this case had aroused in him a slow-burning rage. He felt his face and ears reddening from hot blood. His hand balled into a fist. Just imagine! How could anyone steal another person's kid?

Somewhere out there in the city, or maybe beyond, some jerk had the Baldazar's child. He had to find out who it was. And do it quick.

3

The agents finished their initial interviews at the hospital, but a glance outside revealed a gypsy-like encampment of news people staking out the front door. Oversized white panel trucks mounted with concave antennae dishes hunkered down chock-a-block, looking much like a scouting party for alien invaders. Trying to avoid a face-off with the eager-eyed cadre of microphone-wielding TV reporters, the agents sidled out different exits one or two at a time to avoid drawing attention. Then they all drove back to the office for the evening conference.

Sonny Jenkins marched into the bustling room that was filled with agents and half a dozen detectives from the San Antonio police department who were assigned to the task force. He pushed his errant silver strands back across his mottled scalp and cleared his voice. "All right, let's get started."

The room quieted by layers of sound as various groups ended their conversations. Sonny continued, "Now, everyone who hasn't already been working this case should have a handout. Basically, Senator Baldazar's newborn baby has been missing from Metro Hospital since a little after six this morning."

The detectives that had arrived with Lt. Sanchez leafed through the handout, but otherwise, the room was as silent as a church. Ransom looked over the group. The atmosphere was charged with anticipation, the excitement and pulsing adrenaline that came with working a new and crucial case rippled through the assemblage. But there was also a sense of gloom, a pervading heaviness of spirit that exuded from the men and women there who were burdened by the import of the situation, realizing how terrible the consequences could be if they didn't perform their work perfectly.

"The media is going crazy with this," Sonny continued.

"I've set up afternoon press conferences to placate them. But let's cover as many leads as we can right away before we get flooded with crank calls and worthless tips."

Atherton said, "Also, if the press splashes it too big, the people who grabbed the kid might get spooked and vanish."

"That's right. We want no leaks from anyone to the media." He scanned the group with laser eyes. "And gentlemen, we're going to find that baby." Looking at Ransom he said, "What've we got from your work at the hospital?"

Ransom stood up. "Our suspect is an unknown female who posed as a nurse. Her description is on the handout. So far, we haven't found any direct witnesses except for the mother."

"Did you do blanket interviews?" asked a young agent.

"We've interviewed a number of the nurses and other hospital staff, as well as patients from the other rooms on the maternity ward. We're trying to find out if anyone had an exchange with this 'Mary' who posed as a nurse."

He checked his notes. "In the morning we'll canvass people in the parking lot where the woman probably left with the baby. And teams will follow up on any calls about the baby that come into the hospital, parents' home, or Baldazar's office."

A round-faced, balding detective with a deep, raspy voice asked, "You didn't get anything on the hospital surveillance cameras?"

Sonny frowned. "The camera that should have caught the kidnapper didn't pick up anyone with the isolette or the baby."

There were some grumbles from the gathering.

"You think there was some inside help?" asked the detective.

"That's possible," said Sonny. "We're checking it out, and we'll let you know how it looks."

The detective cleared his throat. "Okay, and there've been no ransom demands?"

"Not a word," said Ransom. "But we do have trap and traces in place on the phones at the spots I just mentioned. And we'll have two teams of agents cruising the streets, ready to respond to any calls."

"What else might we try?" asked Jenkins.

"Interviews with the Baldazar's neighbors and friends might give us a line on a motive," Ransom added. "And we'll gather background info about hospital staff. Also we'll check out places where the woman might've rented or bought some light blue scrubs."

Kathy spoke up. "Jack, you wanted to set up a hot line to the office for tips. And remind everyone about the forms for computer entries."

Ransom crossed out the items in his notepad then stuffed it in his pocket. "Guess I don't need that with Kathy here."

He caged a few laughs. Any relief from the tension was welcome.

"Also, we're sending a teletype to other field offices," Ransom said. "We want them apprised of the situation in case we develop a hot lead that needs to be covered in their territory right away."

"What about Headquarters?" Jenkins asked.

"Give 'em my regards," Ransom said.

"I don't mean just notifying them and having them ride our backs, I think they might have some helpful input."

"Naturally, I'll cut them in. Hey, maybe all the brains in the FBI aren't in Texas."

From the back of the room came, "Or all the assholes, either."

* * * * *

Later that night, Ransom pulled on a pair of jeans, wandered into the kitchen and fixed a ham sandwich, then sat at the dining room table and washed it down with a cold beer. His mind roamed the black night in the Alamo City. He imagined the soaring Tower of the Americas building aglow in the center of town, the gold-domed bank building, and the meandering San Antonio River with strings of white lights tracking its course and tourists treading the walkways in search of fun.

He was trying to contemplate every nook and cranny in town where someone might hide a kidnapped baby. And he was also searching for a reason for the insanity. He tried to speculate who might have a motive for such a crime.

It could be for revenge. And that was a dangerous proposition. Or maybe it was a straightforward kidnapping for money. But why no ransom demand? Of course, it was still early in the process. Sometimes kidnappers waited a day or two, trying to come up with a plan to avoid capture. Or maybe they were making sure the baby was well-hidden. In the worst case scenario, they could be destroying the child and any evidence.

Sometimes crimes were done for love or other passions. But that wasn't likely in a kidnapping matter. Not unless someone was desperate to have a baby, which he'd seen happen several times before.

He tossed his paper plate into the trash. Then he crumpled the beer can and dropped it into a plastic sack in the pantry. Okay, environmental protection handled.

Moving into the living room, he noticed he felt tired and achy, probably from running. Plus there was the emotional strain of the day, which hadn't been your bankers' regular nine-to-five shift. But then, that's why he'd signed on with the outfit in the first place. Not just for the excitement, which was often thrilling, sometimes electrifying, and occasionally terrifying, but to do something that made a difference to other people in the world. At least, he hoped it did.

Now he stared at a filled-to-the-max bookcase, looking over the titles. The collection consisted mostly of paperbacks: mysteries and thrillers. Busman's holiday reading.

Though he did have one shelf bulging with more eclectic tomes. They covered subjects from psychology and philosophy to spiritualism, yoga, astronomy, the occult, and transcendental meditation. Also, a few dealt with physics, medicine, and artificial intelligence.

But he realized his mind was probably too agitated to concentrate on reading tonight. So he checked *TV Guide.* In a minute he tossed it aside. Forget it. There was nothing on worth spending the time to watch. In his mind, reality shows and ones about cooking were about as fascinating as watching paint dry. And the movies he considered decent ones, he'd already seen.

His thoughts turned in another direction. Gloria, his current significant other, was on a flight to Mexico City and back, serving drinks to grumpy passengers. That eliminated another activity that might relax and revivify. So what now?

He sat down on the carpet, crossing his legs in the Lotus Position, making circles with his thumbs and forefingers while resting his hands on his knees, and closing his eyes. "Ohmmmmm," he intoned in a low voice, trying to let his mind go blank. His thoughts dissolved into grayness.

The phone rang. He groaned. It rang again. He jumped up to grab it.

"Hi, Daddy," she said.

"Holly, is that you?"

"How many daughters you got, Daddy?"

Sixteen-year-olds. "Sorry, I was concentrating on something."

"That's nothing new."

Now what was she angry about? Had he really offended her, or was it just teenage angst? "What's up, honey?"

"I wanted to try to get on your busy social calendar, you know, for Saturday night. I've got a piano recital at the school auditorium. Do you think you could come?"

Uh, oh. "That sounds great, I'd love to. I do have some tentative plans, but I'm sure they can be modified."

"Not with the stew with the big chest?"

"Holly, you know her name, and that comment is uncalled for."

"It just seems important to you."

"Now, don't be insolent." Jeez, he sounded like a high school principal.

"Sorry, Daddeee. I just wanted you to be at my recital."

"I know, and I'm sure I can. Hey, maybe we'll both come."

"Sure, that'll be vaporous."

"Enough, already. What else is going on?"

She gave a heavy sigh. "Same old crap. Homework, piano practice, trying to suck up to get on the cheerleader squad."

"So looks and talent aren't enough?

"Not possible."

"I'll bet they take you next year."

"You always say that."

That was true. He'd better change the subject. "So, how's Scott?"

"How should I know?"

Because he's your brother, and you both live under the same roof? he thought. "Is he around?"

She screamed the name over her shoulder. There was no response. "Maybe he went to Chad's house."

"When you see him, tell him I said 'hi.'"

"Sure."

He felt as if he'd just sent an e-mail to the White House. "All right, then, thanks for calling, Holly. And I'll see you Saturday night."

"Okay. 'Bye, Daddy."

The dial tone hummed in his ear. He felt that he'd scored

no points tonight. But was he playing a game?

It had been four months now since he'd moved out of his house. How could anyone be a good father living separate from his kids? He didn't even know what was happening in their lives. He just knew that they were growing up without him. And that gave him a terrible, hollow feeling in his gut.

It also made him think again of the missing baby. It made him wonder how the Baldazars must feel tonight. As Alexander Pope had written, "Is not absence death to those who love?"

How could anyone who didn't have children ever know what the loss of one could mean? Even he, with only a temporary absence from his kids, could feel a layer of ice on his heart. But at least he knew where they were.

And that they were alive.

* * * * *

Kathy tugged open the door to her apartment, relieved to be home. She plodded into the bedroom, shrugged out of her jacket, and hung it in the closet. Then she kicked off her shoes. Sliding the holster and gun and a magazine pouch off her belt, she dropped the whole shebang in a drawer. Then she rotated her shoulders and stretched her neck to each side, feeling some of the day's tension slide away.

She slipped out of her slacks, blouse, and bra, then pulled on an electric blue bodysuit. Catching a glimpse of her figure as she passed the dresser mirror, she stopped, checking her profile. Her abdomen and buttocks were slim and rounded, her legs well-developed and muscular from years of jogging and bicycling. She touched her breasts. They felt tender, almost sore. Maybe she'd strained a muscle when she was working out.

Now she pulled on her jogging shoes. But she felt a nagging weariness from the hectic day's work. Better go easy tonight.

So, she lowered herself to the carpet and did some stretches. Most of them were various yoga positions she'd learned in a class a few years ago. She did the Reverse Posture, with her legs extended straight up in the air, her shoulder blades resting on the carpet, her arms on the floor, holding her body elevated, and her hands supporting her lower back. The reversal of position from standing erect was said to reverse time and make one younger. She was all for that. Then she did a Vakrasana, or Twisting Posture, seated, with her back twisted to one side for several minutes, then the other. It was great for stretching out the spine.

Finally, she fetched a rubber tube exercising device—the old bust-builder. Actually, she wasn't bad in that department; she mostly used the thing to tone her arms when she couldn't get to the gym. She could do some good bicep and tricep movements with it.

She wondered if Steve was at the fitness center tonight. She hadn't missed many workouts since she'd met him there last winter. She first saw him using the lat machine and was impressed. Her gaze wandered back to him during the evening as he'd moved from station to station, and she'd judged he also had great deltoids, pectorals, et cetera.

He must've approved of her bodily apparatus, too, because he'd walked by, stopped, and engaged her in some small talk about working out. She discovered he also had a brain, being a member of the mayor's staff, with his own political aspirations for the future. With his master's degree in political science and some good connections in town, he might have a shot at it. And resembling a farm boy version of John Kennedy, Jr., couldn't hurt his chances.

She dropped the stretching device on the bed and clambered onto her stationary bicycle. She supposed it was his smile that finally did her in. His sense of humor, and that big laugh and silly grin when something tickled him. Oh, shoot, truth be told, the bottle of Lambrusco and her raging hormones had been huge factors, too.

She got off the bike and switched on the CD player. Then she climbed back aboard and pedaled away as Reba McEntire and Faith Hill worked out their vocal chords on some romantic numbers that got her to thinking in ways she shouldn't.

Twenty minutes later, perspiration slicking her forehead, she stopped churning the forever immobile bike and paced into the kitchen. She reached for a cold can of Miller's, but she hesitated. Instead, she snagged a bottle of grape juice, clicked on her small TV, and plopped down in a kitchen chair.

A spate of commercials stretched into infinity. Most of them were the split-second shots of sexy guys or girls performing daring or silly or sensuous acts in revealing outfits. By the time she watched a few of these chopped-up, frantic montages, she was ready to bite nails and spit out staples.

She glanced at the wall clock. Another TV show would be starting soon. Then she studied the calendar beneath the humming timepiece. Pulling down a page, she skimmed the month of March. Uh huh, just as she thought.

* * * * *

Ransom and Kathy stared at the hospital parking lot as the dawning rays of sunlight streaked across the blacktop and gleamed from parked car hoods. There were no clouds this morning, and the warmth of the sun was already establishing itself. Ransom figured it would be a steamy bitch of a day.

"This morning's weather reminds me of New Orleans," Kathy said.

Ransom gave her a look. "Everything reminds you of New Orleans."

"Except the food, music, and men."

"You can't have it all," he said.

"A little piece wouldn't hurt." And she gave him a sultry Cajun leer.

He turned back toward the lot. "I can see where you'd miss the food."

Lieutenant Sanchez stood beside them, scanning the scene. A young detective with a flattop named Gorb or Glorp, or something, yawned as he waited for the interviews to begin.

The night crew was still working in the hospital. There'd been no arrivals yet from the daytime bunch. Then a tiny Toyota rolled onto the lot.

Ransom walked over to it, waited as the woman struggled to extricate herself, then said, "Excuse me, ma'am."

"Yeah, whaddya want?"

So we're surly this morning. Standing five-foot-nothing, she wore a flowered dress the size of a buffalo hide. Her hair resembled a fright wig, she'd applied a heavy layer of pancake makeup, and she sported two wide slashes of lavender lipstick on her thick lips.

Ransom flashed his badge at her. "We're investigating the disappearance of a baby from the hospital yesterday morning. Were you here then?"

She squinted at him. "Are you really with the FBI? I never seen anyone with the FBI, except on TV."

"Yes, really. See?" He pointed to his picture on his

credentials.

Still looking doubtful, she shrugged and said, "Yeah, I was here."

"You arrive about this time every day?"

"More or less."

"Did you see a woman in the lot yesterday morning with a baby?"

"I don't recall nothing like that." She slammed her door.

"Do you remember seeing a woman around here in the last week or so that you don't normally see? Like a brunette in her mid-thirties?"

"Nope, I don't think so. Is that all? I gotta get to work."

"Yes, thanks for your time." And he watched her waddle away. She vaguely resembled a rhino he'd recently seen on *Wild Kingdom.*

The other investigators were talking to more arrivals. An older Mercedes pulled up a couple of spaces away from Ransom. Okay, back to business.

A diminutive codger with a thin white moustache stepped out swinging a miniature umbrella that looked like a Cuban cigar. He wore a suit and tie, and his black shoes gleamed in the sun. Ransom wondered if he was a doctor. But if so, why would he park in the general use lot? And why didn't he have a fancier car?

He stopped the small man and started with his questions. The fellow listened, his mouth scrunched into a pucker, staring into the distance, and then said, "Yes, I may have seen something, Inspector." He spoke with a guttural European accent. "A woman was watching me as I left my car. She stood by that door, smoking a cigarette."

"Did she have a baby with her?"

"She held a large book bag. I don't know about a baby. There could've been anything in there. Hand grenades. Three or four Uzis. Who knows?"

"Did the bag move? Did you hear anything coming from it? Like cries or other sounds?"

"I tried to ignore the woman. I didn't want her to know I was on to her."

"*On* to her? How's that?"

"I was on to the fact that she was watching me."

"Oh, I see." Not really. "Do you work here?"

"Yes, I work days, now. I did work nights, but the bats in the basement got to me."

"The basement, you say?" *Bats?*

"It's the heart of the power plant. Generators, wiring, the whole business. I keep it humming like a Gerschwinn tune." He fiddled with his pygmy parasol.

Zero for two; maybe it's not my day. But here came another car. As Goethe said, "In all things it is better to hope than to despair."

The driver was in her thirties, nice cheekbones, cute nose, figure like an aerobics instructor, large green eyes. Could she please be sane and observant? "Excuse me, Miss." And he went through the routine.

She deliberated in silence. He loved people who did that.

"You know, I *did* see something odd."

"What was that?"

"A woman carrying a bundle that could've been a baby."

"What did she do with the bundle?"

"She put it in the front seat of her car, being very careful with it. Yes, it must've been a baby. Then she got into her car and did something strange."

He looked up from his notepad. "Yes?"

"She tugged at her head, and something came loose, and she dropped it onto the back seat. After that, she fussed with the baby for another minute. Then she drove off, going pretty fast."

"What did she look like?"

"My age, or a little older. She had dark hair, and she was average looking."

"What would you estimate her height and weight to be?"

"I'd say she was about five-foot-four. Maybe 120 pounds."

"What was she wearing?"

"Light blue scrubs. Like a nurse. Maybe she just took off a cap—I couldn't see her that well when she got into the car."

He hadn't seen any of the nurses wear a cap. "What kind of car was she driving?"

"It was sky blue. I'd say about five or six years old. It looked like a Chevy or a Pontiac."

"Which way did she go when she left the lot?"

"I just saw her drive toward the exit, but I didn't watch her leave."

"Do you think you'd recognize her if you saw her again?"

"I'm not sure. She was a ways off. Do you think she took that baby that got kidnapped?"

"It's possible. We're getting a sketch done of a suspect.

Could I show it to you later?"

"Sure. I hope I can help you." She said she was Marnie Phoenix and gave him her address.

"You've been a huge help." He smiled, and then handed her his card.

She glanced at it. "Would you like her license plate?"

His jaw fell. "You got it?"

"Well, not all of it. I noticed it had an M and a P in it—my initials—and the number six, which is supposed to be lucky for me."

Lucky for me, too, he thought. It was only half a plate number, but as Kathy said, a little piece was better than nothing.

* * * * *

Harvey hunched over the table swallowing bitter coffee and watching his wife heat a bottle of milk in a pan. He felt like shit after getting almost no sleep last night. All because of that damn squalling brat. He lit a Pall Mall, coughed until he gurgled, then said, "Do you think that baby's gonna keep howling all the time?"

Lyn turned from the stove, her face hard and stormy.

"Do you think I'm a fortune teller, Harvey? Are you saying I look like a gypsy?"

"No, I don't think—"

"That's right, you *don't* think. I have to do all the thinking around here."

"I meant you don't look like no gypsy. But you suppose the kid's sick or something?" He flicked an ash at a saucer.

"I'm no doctor, neither, and I—"

"That don't matter, but I'll tell you, I need some friggin' sleep. I may have to go on a haul pretty soon."

"I ain't had no sleep, neither, and I'm the one taking care of this baby. You ain't lifted a finger to help."

Now she had her hand on her hip, sassin' him. He didn't like that crap.

"You know I don't know nothing about taking care of no baby." He took a deep drag on his cigarette and exhaled a gray cloud.

"You best learn, then. We got to keep her awhile yet."

He had a knot in his stomach. He clenched his fist, and then relaxed it. It wasn't worth it. "Okay, whatever. I'll tell you what, I'll go to the store and get her some Pampers."

He had to get out of there. Besides, he was about out of smokes. He picked up his ball cap and fiddled with the brim.

She squirted some milk on her wrist, and then set the bottle on the counter. As she turned back to face him, her face softened. "That would be nice. And get her some formula, too. She may not take to regular milk."

"Formula?" he said. He tugged the bill of his cap down over his forehead.

Her eyes narrowed, but she remained calm. "Yes, just ask the girl at the store to help you. It's a kind of artificial milk for babies."

He knew when to just go along. "Sure, I'll do that. See you later." Anyway, he needed those smokes.

* * * * *

Back at the office, Ransom called the Behavioral Science Unit at Quantico. He was directed to Jim Fanning in the National Center for the Analysis of Violent Crime. He gave the man the details of the kidnapping.

"This happened yesterday, you said?"

"Yes, about six in the morning."

"You've got a real stressful situation there," Fanning said, "but the best approach is to handle it like any other case."

"You mean chill out and cover the bases?"

"That's about it."

"We can do that." He hadn't been a psych major for nothing. He knew the more calm he was, the more relaxed the parents would be. And maybe even the kidnappers.

"That's fine. Now the good news is that the odds are in your favor. In the past ten years, in about 90 percent of the cases of infant abduction in the U.S., the baby was located. A high percentage of those cases were solved within a week."

"But there's bad news?"

"It's just that every case is different. And then, of course, no kidnapper's the same."

"Are there any standard indicators as to what makes them do it?"

"Different strokes. It could be sexually motivated, maybe for profit by selling the baby, or to collect ransom from the child's parents. Then, of course, you could always have an emotionally disturbed person, a child killer, or just a miscellaneous criminal."

"Any profile on a Caucasian woman, mid-thirties, wearing nurses' scrubs?"

"Most baby snatchers are female, most often in age

groups of 16 to 21 or 32 to 42. This could well be a neurotic personality disorder type kidnapping."

"Refresh my memory on exactly what that means."

"You're looking for a woman who has low self-esteem and has probably suffered some precipitating stressors that pushed her into snatching the baby."

"What type of stressors?"

"Maybe she lost an infant or a child. She possibly had a miscarriage or just entered menopause. There might have been the breakup of a relationship, or she may have suffered a hysterectomy. Basically, we're talking about filling a void from a loss, or maybe pressure from a mate to bear a child."

"Those sound like tough things to check."

"You'll need co-operation from your local hospitals. Get lists of all women suffering miscarriages, hysterectomies, and loss of an infant, including sudden infant death syndrome cases and stillborn babies. You might even check with gynecologists in your area about women experiencing infertility problems."

"Assuming that the woman is from around here."

"That's right, she may not be. But another thing is to make sure you review requests for birth certificates from people claiming they had home births."

"No problem."

"When you do that, check not only for the date the baby was born, but also for the date of the kidnapping."

"Why's that?"

"The woman may think of the time of birth of the baby as the day she first held it in her arms."

"Thanks, Jim, you've been a big help."

"I hope so. I know it's daunting, but hang in there."

"As Carlyle said, 'Every noble work is at first impossible.'"

"Oh, you're a man of letters."

"More along the lines of *Postcards From The Edge*."

* * * * *

After the call to Quantico, Ransom drummed his fingertips on the desktop, his nerves dancing a jitterbug. Kathy yakked interminably on the phone. He got up and paced down the hall to the break room where he studied a couple of vending machines, deciding on a candy bar and a Diet Coke.

Finally wresting Kathy away from the phone and into the

car, he sped to the hospital. On the way, she tried to squash his enjoyment.

"You know, that candy will make you plump as *un porc.*"

No translation needed on that one. He shot her a withering glance. "You're missing the point."

"Ah, well, enlighten me."

"You see, this has nothing to do with calories or being hungry or gaining weight. It has to do with state of mind."

"My state of mind tells me you're going to get fat."

"With my metabolism, not a chance. Anyway, the idea of the intake of phenylethylamine—or chocolate, to you—is to achieve a mental and emotional lift. Chocolate makes people feel optimistic, peppy, and sociable."

"I thought that was cocaine."

"Different tokes for different folks. Chocolate is the thinking man's way to the sublime elevation of the spirit."

"Now, Jack, I can't say your spirit has seemed all that elevated lately."

He angled off the expressway. "Okay, I've been dealing with some problems at home."

"More like problems away from home."

"I guess I'm looking for something. I'm not even sure what. And, who knows, maybe it's not to be found."

He zipped into the entrance, snatched a parking ticket, and pulled into an empty spot in the hospital lot. As they approached the hulking building, they had to dodge several reporters clutching microphones. An attractive blonde woman stepped into their path, smiled, showing teeth much whiter than new snow, and asked straight out, "Our viewers want to know if there are any suspects in this case, and when you expect to find the baby."

Ransom had no answer for either question. "Sorry, no comment," he said, and he skirted the woman as the cameraman followed him and Kathy. The reporter tried to yell another question to their retreating backs.

"Thank God, Jenkins is handling this mob," Ransom whispered to Kathy.

Once inside the hospital, Kathy said, "Just so you know, we're not through with our discussion about your problems. I'll get back to you on this later."

Great, he thought, I have my own personal watchdog.

Other agents and detectives were still doing interviews. He'd requested the teams not talk to the head nurse. He wanted to handle that one himself, hoping she'd have an answer that would put them on the right track—something he felt they desperately needed.

4

"Winona Blankenship," the head nurse said, giving Ransom and then Kathy firm handshakes. They'd found her in a cubbyhole office near the nurses' station, where she was going over some work schedules. She had gray-streaked hair, glasses, and scrubs as immaculate as a Marine's dress blues.

Ransom and Kathy sat down, then he fixed the administrator with a strong gaze, hoping she could give them information about the workings of the hospital and its employees that would give them some investigative insight. He said, "Mrs. Blankenship—"

"Winnie, just call me Winnie," she said. "Everyone does, even the old poop who runs this place."

Grinning, he said, "All right, Winnie. You know this hospital and the people in it better than anyone else. I need your expertise. I'm sure you realize what we're up against here, and I'm not going to pretend it's going to be easy to solve this kidnapping."

She nodded, but held her tongue.

"We're looking for a dark-haired woman, about 35, medium height and build. She seems to be familiar with the layout of the hospital and the routines of handling the babies. She knows how to look and act like a nurse, and she may be desperate."

"Desperate? What do you mean?"

"Maybe she's frantic for money, we don't know, there's been no ransom demand yet. Maybe it was done for some sort of twisted revenge. It could be she just wanted the child. She wanted it so badly she stole it away from its own parents."

"I see." She played with her ear lobe. She didn't look nervous, just evaluating the information.

"Do the description and the possible motives bring anyone to mind?"

She stared at the desktop for several seconds, and then looked up. "I can't think of anyone right off. But maybe if I puzzle it out some more, I'll come up with an idea about someone."

"We'd appreciate any thoughts you have on it. By the way, are the nurses' scrubs kept where the public could get to them?"

"The hospital no longer supplies them. It's a cost-cutting measure. Everyone has their own."

"Where do they get them?"

"There are several places you can buy or rent them. Ours are not unusual. But I suppose someone could steal one from here, too."

"How could they do that?"

"The nurses have a locker room. Most of them keep their scrubs in there. Some use a padlock, others don't bother. They figure who'd steal a pair of scrubs?"

Ransom shot a look at Kathy. That, indeed, was the question. They'd ask the nurses if any of them had lost a pair recently.

"Does the hospital furnish the name tags?"

"That's right."

Kathy said, "Has a nurse named Mary ever worked here?"

"Not that I recall, but we've had some turnover."

Dover frowned. "How do you get the name tags inscribed?"

"We take them to an engraving place at Ingram Park Mall."

"Where do you keep the blank tags?" asked Kathy.

She opened her desk drawer. "Right in here."

They asked some more questions, and Winnie gave them the expected responses. Nothing unusual had happened on the obstetrics floor the past couple of weeks. No one strange had been seen hanging around. And she couldn't imagine how anyone could slip into a patient's room without one of the nurses or other staff seeing her.

Ransom let that go. "How many babies were in the nursery yesterday?"

She picked up a clipboard, not consulting the computer terminal on her desk. Good, Ransom thought. Too many people let the damn things do their thinking. Thoreau was ahead of his time when he said, "Men have become tools of their tools."

Finishing her count, she said, "Twenty-one at the end of the last shift. Jacobson, Farrell and Hernandez left during the day, then Baldazar . . . . " She blanched at the thought and put aside the clipboard. "There should have been twenty-five yesterday morning."

"Any idea why April may have been picked by the kidnapper? Is there anything unusual about her? Does anything stand out to you?"

She raised her shoulders. "Not that I can think of. She was, rather, *is* a healthy baby. Her dad's a rich attorney and a Senator, as you know. That could be your money motive."

"Yes, it could be. Let's see, who else had a room near that exit?"

She checked her clipboard. "The mother of baby girl Jaimina Jones. Her room was on the other side of the hall across from Mrs. Baldazar's room."

"That would actually be closer to the exit than the room where April was picked up."

"Um hmmm. But . . . ."

She clamped her lips together.

"Go ahead, Winnie. What are you thinking?"

"I was just thinking that the Jones's baby is black."

"All right, maybe that's meaningful. And what babies' mothers are located next to the exit door on the other hallway?"

She skimmed the names. "The mothers of two boys. Allen and Josh. And they're both Caucasian."

Ransom nodded, having no idea if this meant anything. He glanced out the door. Down the hallway he could see a small clutch of people staring straight ahead, looking entranced. Of course, they were admiring the babies!

"Is the nursery down that hallway?" he asked.

"It certainly is."

Kathy lit up like Las Vegas. "Can we take a look?"

The nurse rose from her desk. "I take every excuse to go by there."

Ransom studied the well-lit nursery. A couple of nurses moved from isolette to isolette, closely examining their wards. There were twenty-some babies: thin ones, chubby ones, red-faced and squalling ones, those who slept with the peace of the Lord, and several with thick tufts of dark hair. Different skin colors, different builds, different dispositions. All created equal? Not that important. The overwhelming sensation was the opportunity! To start anew, with no mistakes behind you—would be so wonderful.

"Nothing like them, is there?" said Winnie, her hand against her chin.

"Nothing in the world," said Kathy. Her half-smile reminded Ransom of the painting, *The Mona Lisa.*

Ransom could only nod. He was thinking of the past. It was a very special time for him.

* * * * *

"What do you think?" Beverly had asked as they'd stood together in a similar hallway some sixteen years before.

Ransom put his arm around her, feeling her firm shoulder through the thin robe she wore. But he didn't take his eyes off that tiny face shining from the crib.

"She's beautiful," he whispered. "It's incredible. The whole thing is a miracle."

He hugged Beverly to him, her tangled blonde curls falling across his shoulder. A smile glowed on his face.

"And you did a fantastic job, honey," he added. "Just unbelievable."

"I'd say the doctor helped." Then she laughed, and said, "Plus the miracle of modern pain medicine played a significant role."

"No, you did the hard part."

Then he looked into her eyes and saw the same alert expression that Holly would carry with her all her life.

"So, Jack, was it worth my being fat all those months?"

"I thought you looked terrific. You know you'll always be beautiful to me. And being the mother of my daughter just makes you more so."

She lay her head against his shoulder, feeling spent. "I'm tired. Maybe I'd better shuffle back to my room."

"Shuffle away, I'm right here beside you."

* * * * *

His thoughts snapped back to the present. Winnie had gone off to her duties, and Kathy stood there with her arms folded across her chest, an amused expression on her face.

Ignoring his fadeout, Kathy asked, "What should we do now?"

He glanced around for inspiration. Down the hallway, he could see the "beehive." Which meant the nurses could see the people viewing the babies. "Come on," he told Kathy as he headed for the busy nurses' station, "let's see how observant the gals of mercy are."

They interviewed each of them, with Ransom taking the lead and Kathy throwing in questions to draw them out. He wanted to know if they had seen anyone viewing the babies who weren't members of the family, but they didn't have any helpful answers. Also, none of them knew of anyone that was missing a pair of scrubs.

They drove back to the office, and at his desk he typed the results of his interviews into his notebook. He packaged up the printed copies and threw them in the case assistant's basket. Then he ambled into Jenkins's office to discuss the case.

Jenkins was upbeat. They talked about the leads that had been covered thus far. Then Ransom told him about the suggestions he'd gotten from the agent at Quantico.

"God," Jenkins said, "checking miscarriages and that other stuff could take forever."

"Especially when it's just a theory," Ransom said, agreeing with the sentiment.

"Do you think we should follow up on it?"

Ransom let out a pent-up sigh. "I'm not sure, Sonny. I don't have a handle on that yet."

"What's your gut feeling?"

"That so far we're firing blanks. Sure, there are lots of avenues we can try, but what I'm searching for is the nexus. There's always a link, an interconnectedness of events, people, motives and desires. As Kathy might say, the *raison d'etre* of the crime. That's what I think we're missing so far."

"So, how do you find this nexus?"

"Current thinking seems weighted toward the theory of the random nature of the universe. If that's so, we'll have to—"

"Look everywhere?" asked Jenkins, raising his bushy eyebrows.

"Exactly. But I'm . . . old-fashioned, or more fundamental. I think the circle is the most important symbol of life on earth, maybe in the universe."

Jenkins tented his fingers on the desk. "So we go around in circles looking for clues?"

"No, Sonny," Ransom said, smiling. "Here's how I see it. People and animals may sometimes evolve, but mainly they revolve, going through the same patterns of behavior in recurring cycles. Look at ladies' fashions—every forty years the new fad is what grandma wore when she was young."

"My grandma was never young. She grew up starched and stately."

"Okay, she's an exception. Life itself is a circle—ashes to ashes, dust to dust. And many of these circles link up. When you find a pattern of interconnectedness in a situation, in this instance a criminal act, then you can determine the rationale and motive. You can see the instigators. You can solve the crime."

"Then let's solve it."

Random raised his hands, palms up.

"I've been trying. But it's still too diffuse. I need a focal point, an area of concentration."

"Well, Jack, we always start with the unknown and the general before we narrow it down to the known and the specific."

"But we're not usually on such a tight timetable. We've got a baby missing. There's no time for false starts or wasted maneuvers."

Sonny folded his hands and leaned on his elbows, thinking it over.

"We're not gods," he said in a solemn tone. "We can only do our best."

"'When we know what God is,' Ransom said, "we shall be gods ourselves.'"

"From Hamlet?"

"George Bernard Shaw. A not-so-great humanitarian."

Jenkins shrugged. "What can I say? Hang in there. Keep plugging."

Rather than dodge any more platitudes, Ransom agreed to plug with the best of them, then made a speedy escape.

* * * * *

As Ransom left Sonny's office, Hank and Jester walked into the squad room.

When Ransom spotted them, he jerked his head at Hank, motioning for them to come over to his desk.

"Hey, guys," Ransom said as they approached, "you get anything new?"

They both looked a bit forlorn, but Hank attempted a smile and said, "We've got nothing yet from the patients who were on that floor. There are still a few more of them to interview. But we did get some new info. from the alarm repairman."

"What's that?"

"He tested the alarm three ways from Sunday. It functioned just fine. So, he's still trying to figure out what happened, but it's hard to say."

"I think we've got to operate on the theory that someone knew how to defeat the alarm. I don't think it just failed at the time someone took the baby out, then started working again."

"I know, Jack. I'll keep you posted."

* * * * *

Ransom made his way down the hall to a room where banks of glowing computer screens hummed, as nimble fingers clicked at the keyboards, making entries into various data banks. Cheryl Ginsford had been picked to work on the case. She was bright and aggressive, and Ransom was glad for her assistance.

After he asked her how things were going, she twirled a forefinger in her long brown hair as she looked up at him with bright green eyes.

"I didn't know exactly what you wanted, so I've been messin' around with what the agents have given me."

Her accent was pure Texan, her voice as soft as summer rain.

"What've you got so far?"

"I entered the names and addresses of the parents of all the babies that were in the nursery as of yesterday. I divided them by quadrants of the city."

"And do you see a pattern?"

"Two other families lived in the same quadrant as the kidnapped baby's folks. They both had boys."

"Did you make lists of the babies by sex and race?"

"There were thirteen boys, twelve girls. Of the girls, five were Hispanic, three black, one Vietnamese, and three Caucasian."

"Anything else different about them?"

"There's coloration. One of the Caucasian girls had red hair."

"Did you get the names of the babies' obstetricians and pediatricians?"

"I sure did. There were a few duplications. See?"

Her fingers clacked at the keys, and the lists of doctors flashed onto the screen. Mrs. Baldazar's obstetrician had delivered two of the other babies. He was catching 'em faster than Alex Rodriguez.

"Some of the pediatricians handled two or three of the newborns, too."

"Have you entered the background information of the hospital staff?"

She pointed to a stack of papers as thick as a large dictionary.

"That pile's waitin' for my supple fingers to copy it."

"Great. Are you set up to make cross checks from one list to another?"

"Absolutely. That's one of our biggest assets."

And as she twirled her silky hair again, she broke out a Miss America smile. She was way too young for him, but she was definitely a charmer. He patted her on the shoulder.

"Super job, Cheryl. We'll be bringing you a lot more information as this case goes on. And feel free to experiment if you think of an angle."

Now her smile wattage lit up the room. It wasn't too often in FBI work that anyone was told to use their instincts and run with the ball.

"I'll do it, Mr. Ransom."

God. Mr. Ransom was his father.

He paced back to his desk, just in time to grab his ringing telephone.

"Ransom."

It was Jim Fanning from NCAVC. He sounded agitated.

"I forgot something important when I talked to you before. Damn Alzheimer's set in early."

"Scientists are supposed to be absentminded."

"But not lame-brained. Anyway, check with the hospital to see if they do an HLA sample on newborns."

"Which is?"

"Human leucocyte antigen. It's drawn from the umbilical cord, and they can use it to identify the baby."

"Thanks, I'll check. But we've still got a problem."

"Yeah?"

"We need a baby to compare it with."

* * * * *

The room was muffled and black, with dark mini-blinds clamped shut and heavy drapes yanked tight. The area had a battened feel to it, with its sound-proofed walls and ceiling. There was a wall-to-wall dense wool carpet in sepia tones.

In the center of the room the tall man sat on a chair in a

rigid, upright posture, staring straight ahead, lulled by the quiet and the press of humid air.

After his body loosened to the velvet blackness, he reached out and touched a wooden stool sitting before him. Atop the stool was a candle in a holder, and he traced the pliant wax of the slender spire upward until he touched the curling wick. Pulling a matchbook from his jacket pocket, he twisted a match free, then scraped it alive.

He blinked at the sudden flare. Then he held the match to the wick, which stole the tear-shaped flame. Snapping his wrist, he killed the match.

He sat back, staring at the flame, mesmerized by the changing colors, the shimmering patterns, the dancing energy. How great it would be to absorb that force, to feel it swell inside him and be his own. How wonderful to possess an enormous power that could devour and destroy everything on Earth.

His heart pounded with excitement, and his emotions ran wild, like old racehorses released from their stalls into boundless meadows of grass. He fixed on the flame. Yes, to channel and control such energy, that would be worthy of a high *palero* priest.

He reached inside his shirt and touched the hammered golden Cross of Nero hanging from a chain around his neck. When he worked magick, he always felt a surge of power from the ornament. It seemed a way to summon the spirits, to make a connection, to share their knowledge of both worlds and their dominance of all things living and dead.

The time had come when he needed such power. And much depended on what happened the next few days. He was moving toward a new plateau, he was sure. He could feel the vibrations in the atmosphere. The *orishas* were whirling and dancing and seeking fulfillment.

The celebration of Beltane was near. This would be the most important festival ever to both him and the members of his group. Everything must go off as planned. The ceremony must be perfect. All depended on it.

He stared again at the candle, focusing his will. The plan he'd conceived was working; it would succeed. And he'd achieve untold glory.

* * * * *

Ransom sought some physical release from the tension of the day. Arching his upper body away from the floor, he extended his arms straight beneath him, stretching his neck up and back. He held the stretch for ten seconds, and then lowered his chest back to the floor, turning his face to the side and resting his cheek on the carpet.

Now his body tingled, alive with new energy from performing the yoga move. He spun around and crossed his legs. Sitting in the Lotus position, he let his mind drift.

In a few minutes, with his muscles feeling more relaxed, he rose from the floor and walked barefoot into the kitchen where he unwrapped a candy bar. Chocolate, do your stuff. Bring on the dopamine.

The phone rang. Again? His timing was bad this late in his career.

He answered and was surprised by the caller.

"*Cuñado*, where you been? All the chippies at the Bombay Bicycle Club have been asking about you."

"Rudy, *que pasa?* How you doing, *amigo?*" Rudolfo Martinez was a friend who worked on the white collar crime squad. Since the kidnapping, Ransom had hardly seen him.

"Without, mostly."

"Why don't I believe that?" He heard pounding funky music in the background. "Anyway, what drug you away from the bar to call me?"

"So many *señoritas,* so little time. This one I met here tonight has an *amiga,* man, I kid you not, with *pelo rojo* and a body that's driving guys *loco.* Come down here *pronto, amigo,* and take her off my hands before I ask the two of them to do something pornographic. *Por favor?*"

Okay, he was tempted—a redhead with a great body. But he couldn't be out all night while he was working this case and with the marathon a little over a week away. "*Lo siento,* Rudy," he said, truthfully. "I'll have to beg off tonight. This kidnapping case is running me ragged."

"And all that trotting you do. You should save your energy for something worthwhile. But it's your loss, *amigo.* I just hope you don't have to bail me out of the *cárcel* tonight."

"Try to keep it down to a low roar."

"*Seguro*. Like *el rey* of the jungle." And he hung up.

Yep, that was Rudy, a lion—the king of the jungle—and the prince of single Latina women throughout South Texas. Rudy would be having a hot time tonight. In contrast, he knew his evening would be lukewarm, at best. It would be like Chile peppers versus dill pickles.

He sifted through a stack of books on the table—Ed

McBain, Robert Crais, Michael Connelly—then picked up Elmore Leonard's latest. There was nothing like a good crime novel to entertain him and to put his thoughts in order.

An hour-and-a-half later the suspense was mounting, but he'd had a long day. The book settled into his lap as his eyes fluttered, then closed. And then, slumped in his chair, the movies in his head began.

He dreamed of the days when men wore shining helmets decked with plumes and tilted at each other with lances. The handle of his battle axe bore many notches. And he was popular among the ladies of the king's court. But as he stood next to his armored horse, the sun glinting from the polished metal, he recalled there was trouble in the kingdom. He had to correct it.

People milled about in a frenzied state. There was much wailing and teeth gnashing and boot stomping. And then he felt a chill: a gigantic shadow fell across him, and he turned to view the largest dragon he'd seen in all his days of knighthood. He reached his hand toward his battle sword, which he'd stabbed into the dirt next to a tree. The handle felt good in his hand. But he couldn't pull the blade free. The sword was stuck tight, and though he pulled and twisted it, the weapon stayed captive in the hard soil.

The beast advanced on him, and its eyes shone volcano red as it breathed its fiery breath. The scorching heat seared his face. He smelled the rotted flesh of the dragon's last victim stuck between dagger-like teeth.

And then his eyes flicked open, and he stared at the carpet, his mind foggy and befuddled. His head slumped to the right, and the hot bulb of the gooseneck floor lamp shone in his face. He squinted as he twisted the switch, dissolving the light, as well as the image of the dragon.

But he was puzzled. Dreams usually represented the fulfillment of wishes. So why would the sword, the symbol used to express the latent idea, be unavailable to him to kill the dragon? Did this mean he'd "dropped his dick in the dirt"—screwed up in some way that his subconscious was wrestling with—or did it mean he really didn't want to solve this crime?

Maybe it signaled he wasn't using his strongest innate powers to unravel the enigma. But that didn't seem to be the case. He thought he was giving the kidnapping his all in both mind and body. He simply didn't get what the dream signified.

In the bedroom he shed his clothes, ambled to the bathroom, and splashed water on his face. As he was brushing his teeth, the phone rang. The parents got a call! *flashed* in his mind.

"Jack, it's Kathy. Did I wake you?"

"No, what's up?"

"I'm sorry to bother you, but I had to tell you about Jester."

"Jester?" He thought he heard a worried tone in her voice. "What's wrong?"

"He rushed his wife to the hospital—her water broke, and she's having contractions. She's in the delivery room. It looks like her baby's on the way."

Alarm bells went off in the back of his mind.

"On the way? But it's too soon. She's not due until . . . July, August?"

"August 3rd. She's about 14 weeks early."

"Oh, God. Which hospital is she in?"

"Metro. It has the best neonatal ICU in the city."

"Are you going over there now?"

"Jester said for everyone to stay home, we'd just get in the way. He promised to keep us posted on what was happening."

"I see." But he didn't like this. It felt like a time for action, not for staying home and trying to sleep, which would be impossible anyway.

"Jack? Are you still there?"

"When you hear some news, call me back, no matter what time it is."

She agreed, but as he hung up, he felt an impending wave of doom.

* * * * *

Billy scrunched his motorcycle to a stop beneath the boughs of a stand of hackberries. He climbed off the shiny black hog and peered around in the darkness, seeing nothing and no one. Then he pulled off his black nylon jacket, his T-shirt, and his jeans. Slipping out of his briefs he stood there, rigid in anticipation.

From a saddlebag he removed his black satin robe, shrugged it on, and then stuffed his clothes into the bag. He burped, a result of the two beers he'd swigged just before the ride here. Swaggering, he made his way toward a large clearing.

Soon it would start. Other dark-robed shapes now moved from different parts of the field toward the clearing, and as they gathered in a knot, He felt he was part of something mysterious and powerful. At the center of the clearing several figures gathered together, standing apart from the others. They were the leaders. The others shot glances at them and pawed the ground with bare feet.

Billy didn't see the head priest, a tall man with a voice like thunder, who always wore a black robe with red splotches on the front. Three other men stood there, ready to begin the ceremony. Nearby, a naked young blonde girl lay in the center of the pentagram.

Some neophytes passed through the group with trays loaded with sugar cubes, and Billy popped one in his mouth. In a minute, his muscles loosened, his mind's eye soared outside him to look down on the assembled clutch of robed followers, and dizziness made him feel his body was floating above the ground. A chalice of blood passed from hand to hand, and Billy swigged from it, a red trickle chasing down his chin which he wiped away with the back of his hand.

Someone signaled the beginning of the ceremony, and the followers stood like blocks of stone as one of the leaders called for the members of the group to feed the bloody cauldron simmering beside the girl. Billy was prepared. As he roared there tonight on his Harley, he'd plowed into a yellow cat, knocking it into a ditch. Seeing an opportunity, with his pocket knife, he cut out the animal's heart.

Now he moved to the cauldron, unwrapped the bloody organ from his handkerchief, and dropped it into the pot. The meeting leader nodded his approval, adjusted some sticks protruding from the cauldron, and spoke of the magick and power of the gooey red mixture. Billy ignored the ceremony, watching the blonde, a twenty-year-old babe he'd screwed at the last meeting; she had tits like a topless dancer, with no silicone implants—all real, firm flesh.

Now the leader got Billy's attention, saying, "The nudity of flesh will blush, though tameless. The nudity of bone grins shameless. The unsexed skeleton mocks shroud and pall."

Now wine and more sugar cubes were passed about, and the members of the group drank and danced and pressed against each other and fell to the ground, their robes opening to the rubbing of flesh on flesh, and Billy proceeded to have a hell of a good time.

5

In the glow of daybreak, Ransom ran with abandon, enjoying the exertion, the cleansing of his blood and breath. His muscles warmed to the pounding, and his legs seemed to stretch farther than ever before. Enveloped in the morning coolness, he sprinted through the light breeze, trying to escape the burden of reality.

He thought about his daughter, Holly. And Scott, just twelve years old and losing his father. A boy that age needed a male role model. The whole situation was so unfair, not just to Holly and Scott, but to him, as well.

He'd left of his own free will, but in a larger sense, he'd felt pushed out of his home, his life turned upside down when Beverly strayed after seventeen years of marriage. He found her locked in the arms of a neighbor and friend. The pain of that moment still tore through his heart like an auger.

He settled back to a more moderate pace. The exertion still felt good, but his legs were not as springy as when he started his jog. Still thinking about Beverly, he realized that even though he'd been out of the house since the first of the year, he still felt alone in his apartment. It *was* a temporary comfort when Gloria was snuggled up next to him, but still . . . the fact was, he was on his own, and he felt unprepared to handle it. He'd thought of himself as a family man for many years, and he didn't want to abandon that role. But what could he do?

His legs were tiring, now, and he eased his pace to a slower jog. There was no use killing himself, he had a long day ahead. They'd be looking for the baby again, trying new ideas, hoping to think of a different tack that would put them on the right path. Forty-eight hours, and they'd accomplished nothing. They didn't even know if the child was alive or dead. It was both disconcerting and discouraging.

No ransom demand had been made. In fact, there'd been no contact of any kind. Those were bad signs. And so far he'd thought of no creative way to find April. His lack of progress and initiative made him feel as worthless as a roach. He churned down the road with gray clouds of despair gathering in his mind.

Back in his apartment, he sat on a wicker dining room chair and read the paper as he cooled down. The kidnapping story was on page one. Of course, what could be more dramatic than a baby being snatched? And she was a Senator's child, to boot.

By granting afternoon press conferences, Jenkins had been able to ride herd on the media. So far, anyway. They were keeping speculation out of their reporting at this point, which was unusual. They were printing just the facts, ma'am. Which were grim enough.

Then he realized he hadn't heard from Kathy about Jester. Surely everything had gone well—or had there been another disaster—something too horrible to pass on? No, Kathy knew there was a meeting at the office this morning, so she was probably just waiting until then to give him the details.

He fixed cereal and orange juice. After he finished, he put the dishes in the sink. It was time to go get some results. He thought they should talk to the parents again. It would be uncomfortable, but maybe if he nosed around, he'd think of something that would help jumpstart the investigation.

He chose a sports coat and slacks from his closet. And, of course, comfortable shoes were a must. More cases were solved by burning shoe leather than by any brilliant flashes of intellect.

* * * * *

Harvey turned a page of the newspaper, then finished reading the article about the kidnapping. The damn feds didn't have a clue, he decided. He tossed the paper on the card table, sipped some coffee, and fired up a weed. But, Jesus, he felt tired

It had been another long night of screechin' by that kid. He wondered if you could die from not gettin' no sleep. He felt like he was pretty damn close to it. Now the wife trudged into the kitchen carrying the baby in her arms, rocking it back and forth, talking to it soft.

"She finally quit cryin', did she?"

She frowned at him and mouthed, "Shut up." She fussed with the baby and its blanket. Then she gave him another evil-eye stare. "She might go to sleep, you know, if you'd keep your loud yap shut."

"And maybe I'd get some sleep, if she'd ever shut up." He didn't lower his voice; this was *his* fuckin' house.

"She ain't doing it on purpose, you know. I'm sure she just don't feel good."

"What the fuck's wrong with her, Lyn? You been pickin' her up and givin' her bottles every time she squeals."

"Harvey, I don't know what's wrong with her. I don't know nothing about babies. You never wanted . . . ."

She hesitated. Yeah, he thought, you'd better shut up. You'd better not be plowing that ground again, if you know what's good for you. He gave her a cold glare, letting her know he wasn't in the mood for it.

"I'm no damn kid expert, neither," he said, "but I 'spect they ain't supposed to spit up and screech like a bandsaw all the time."

"So what do you want me to do about it, Harvey?"

He had no idea, but she had that look on her face, and he could tell she was backtalkin' him. He felt the heat rise up his neck and his ears start to burn. He was about at his limit. There was only so much a man could take from a smart-aleck woman. He might just set things straight here and now.

Then, suddenly, he thought of something.

"Let's get your sister to take a look at the kid. I mean, why the hell not? You know, maybe somethin's bad wrong with it. Maybe she could tell what the problem is."

She slumped into an easy chair. The baby had gone to sleep, and she stared down at the tiny white face. She glanced up at him, looking unsure.

"No, the baby's fine. Something's bothering her, but she ain't sick. Besides, we can't—"

"It wouldn't hurt, you know, if your sister—"

"No, we can't risk having her come here. It's not safe."

He hadn't thought of that. But then, his brain was pretty damn muddy right now, what with getting' no fuckin' sleep and all. "I reckon not," he said, his lips tight with frustration.

"Let's try a different kind of formula," she said. "I think this one hurts her tummy."

Yeah, the kid did screw up her face like something was

paining her. And her poop was drizzly and smelled like a country outhouse. Maybe the wife was right this time. Shit, every dog gets lucky sometimes.

"I'll go get some kinda new formula," he said. "We can give it a try."

Besides, he needed some beer. His nerves could stand some soothing.

* * * * *

At his desk, Ransom reviewed his notes about the case. Teams of agents and detectives were assigned to compile lists of hospitals and doctors, finish up interviews of hospital workers and patients, and talk with neighbors and friends of the Baldazars. He and Kathy would hit the places that sold or rented scrubs, and then they'd talk to the Senator and his wife again.

There had been no calls to the parents at home or at the Senator's office. The hot line to the FBI office had received twelve calls. Ransom looked them over.

l. Anonymous caller: Check out whoever is mad at the hospital. They may be doing this to get back at the hospital for letting someone die or for charging too much.

Ransom supposed that was true, but he decided that it would make for a hell of a long list of suspects. He balled up the scribbled note and hooked it overhead into the circular file. The next seven were similarly vague, unhelpful, or indecipherable. Two others mentioned specific names of women who had newborns, but with nothing to indicate why they would be suspected of wrongdoing. He'd ask one of the other agents to investigate further on those.

5. Mary Phillips, 6673 Walzem Road: Ellen Tarmack, a member of the Way of the Lamb church, who lives on Perrin-Beitel Road, has a new baby. She wasn't pregnant, and she won't answer any questions about the child.

Calling the dispatcher, Ransom ran a driver's license check. Computer records showed Tarmack was a white female, age 39, five feet six, 135 pounds, brown eyes. That was close enough to the suspect's description to make him interested. He called the FBI resident agency in Austin, asking an investigative clerk to get a DL photo of Tarmack from DMV and send it to him ASAP.

8. Deputy Al North, Bexar County Sheriff's Office: One of the Metro nurses, Sue Kraff, shacks with a guy who just got out of Huntsville prison on a bank robbery beef. Word on the street is the guy is planning a big score. Call North at

the SO between three and eleven p.m., or at home at 555-1306.

Ransom covered his mouth with his hand. Could it have been a *professional* job? Maybe it was. But, if so, why hadn't a ransom demand been made? And who is the woman who made the snatch on the kid? He checked his watch: eight o'clock. The Deputy had worked the late shift, so he'd better let him get some sleep. He could call the guy in a couple of hours.

Kathy walked in. Her shoulders were slumped, and her mouth was set in a grimace.

"Jester?" he asked. "Is everything—"

"The baby was born about 4:00 a.m. It weighed two pounds, one ounce. It's a little boy. His lungs are underdeveloped, and the heartbeat's irregular. They're keeping him in an incubator, hooked up to monitors and other equipment."

There was fear behind her eyes, and Ransom didn't like the look.

"Damn. That sounds scary. What are his chances?"

"It's going to be touch and go for a while. They'll monitor him and address whatever comes up. The longer he makes it, of course, the better his odds. At least Sharene's doing all right, except for being scared to death."

"What can we do to help, Kathy?"

"Jester said for us to find the missing baby. He'll take care of his little one."

Ransom was silent for a minute, staring at the wall. Then he blew out a breath. "All right, we'll do it the way he wants." He didn't like it, but he'd go with Jester's wishes for now. Besides, he was at a loss as to what he might actually do.

He threw some papers in a briefcase and stuck his automatic into the holster. He caught Kathy's eye. "Are you ready to try our luck at some rental places?"

"Sure, whatever it takes."

He tried to lighten the mood. "Hey, you might see a costume that what's-his-name, the weightlifter, would like you in."

If looks could kill, he'd be a goner.

"If that refers to Steve, my workout partner, that's all he is."

Then why was her face tinted to complement her hair?

"Sorry, I thought you dug muscles."

"In appropriate places, I do. But, mostly, I like sensitivity. Of course, that's as rare among men as intellect."

She seemed to turn even redder.

"You're all a bunch of *fous,* I'm telling you."

He smiled to himself. When she got angry, she slipped into French with her daddy's Cajun rhythm. "Hey, give us a break. You know the saying: 'Forgive many things in others; nothing in yourself.'"

"Ah, well, says who?"

"Ausonius, for one."

"Un autre imbécile. I suspect he's no good old boy from Texas, either."

"No, no," Ransom said, "he's from farther east. But he still makes a point."

"So why not cut ourselves some slack, too?" she said.

He blinked. "That's a good philosophical perspective, Kath. You just blew me away."

"I never thought you'd admit that, *chéri.* There could be hope for you yet." She picked up her purse. "Shall we go?"

"If you're waiting on me, you're backing up."

They had eight uniform sales places and seven rental shops to visit, trying to collect names and addresses of possible suspects. They soon found that most of the rental places required customers to furnish a driver's license or a credit card as identification when they rented an outfit. If the customer paid cash at the sales places, there was usually no record of the purchaser by name. However, it seemed that most customers used their plastic, apparently patterned after the national pastime and probable downfall.

At the sixth place they checked, a woman with a beehive hairdo and a thick Texas accent helped them with the records. "This is our rental record book," she explained. "We keep customers' records by the year. How far back do you want to look?"

"March and April should be good enough," Ransom said. He scanned a page of the book. "You've got the date, name, address, driver's license number, and type of outfit. So, I'd say that your records look good for our purposes."

"I'm glad to help the FBI. My husband was in the military. He was an MP for a while. But he tried to break up a brawl and got his front teeth busted out with a chair. He decided to look for quieter duty after that."

Ransom grimaced. "I don't blame him. We'll be in the

back, if that's okay."

"Sure, there's a desk, if you can find a clear spot."

Ransom sat down, pushed aside a stack of receipts and an overflowing ashtray, and began to review the book. He was looking for women who would have had a set of scrubs rented as of the day of the kidnapping. Kathy moseyed around fingering some of the outfits hung on pipe racks.

"I see you in the tiger stripe one," Ransom said.

"Any more smart remarks and you'll end up in the hospital reading that book, *Tiger's Revenge,*" she said.

His brow furrowed. "I'm not familiar with that one."

"You know, by Claude Balls."

"Ouch. I see where you're going, tough girl."

He made some notes. Two women had rented light blue sets of scrubs during April. Angie Martinez for three weeks, still had them, but she was probably Mexican-American. Not that she couldn't be Anglo and be married to a Latino. Or she could be very light-complexioned. They'd better check her out, just to be sure.

Next, Marilyn Byron—what a great name. He muttered the wonderful line under his breath.

"'Roll on, thou deep and dark blue Ocean—roll!'"

"What's that?" Kathy said, materializing like a ghost right by his shoulder.

He jerked, but he hoped she didn't notice. "I'm just mumbling literary references. It was nothing important."

"*Que ordures.* You bookworms often miss the flavor of the gumbo."

"Garbage? Well, at least I don't suck the heads off crayfish like some people from the Gulf area whom I know."

She smirked. "It's better than licking the other end, *vous comprenez?*"

That one left him speechless.

"So did you find anything?" she asked.

He held up the list. "I see two that I think have potential. Can you run drivers' license checks to get their dates of birth and descriptions?"

"Can do. How many is that all together?"

He pulled the other lists from his jacket.

"Five women so far that either bought scrubs with a credit card or rented them and had to show identification. But we still have another nine places left to hit."

"So we might end up with more than ten?"

"Physical descriptions will lower that number." He shrugged. "It's gotta be done."

"You mean, ours is not to wonder why . . . ."

"Leave no stone unturned."

"Climb every mountain." She smiled.

"Try, try again."

"Never give up."

She was pretty good at this. "Just do it."

"Oh, Jack." Her huge eyes rolled upward. "That's so lame. I thought you had a quote for every occasion."

"Hmm. Okay, Benjamin Disraeli: 'The secret of success is constancy to purpose.'"

She groaned. "Can we cut through the sawgrass?"

"You bet. Roll on, big blue."

* * * * *

Ransom and Kathy visited two more stores, obtaining four additional names of women who'd bought scrubs in the right time frame. As they climbed back into the stifling car, the radio crackled.

"Five alpha to five romeo."

Atherton was calling. Ransom scooped up the mike and answered.

"Five romeo. Go ahead, five alpha."

"We just talked with the last of the parents from the hospital. One mother stayed in a room down the hall from Mrs. Baldazar, and she remembered a candy striper delivered her a message around six that morning."

"Hmmm. Lt. Sanchez is talking with the candy stripers. I'll ask him if any of them took a message to a room on that floor, and if they saw anyone or anything unusual."

"Sounds good," Atherton said. "See you later." And he signed off the air.

"We'd better check in with the office," he said.

There was a message for him to contact Jenkins, and he was transferred over. "What's up, Sonny?"

"Your sketch of the suspect just came in from the Bureau."

"Great, we'll drive by and pick it up."

As soon as he hung up, he called Deputy Al North at home. When the deputy answered, Ransom told him who he was. The deputy gave him a short rundown about his information.

"Okay," Ransom said, "so this guy just got sprung from

Huntsville prison, and you think he could be in on our kidnapping?"

"I'm just saying he's a good possible. He took a hostage when he robbed the bank, so he's no cherry. 'Course there may be no connection, but the fact he's fresh out of the slam and he's porkin' the nursie at Metro Hospital made me snap on him."

"There may be something to it, Al. I'd like to know more details. Could I come see you?"

"Today's my day off. I'll be around."

He scribbled the guy's address in his notepad.

"We'll be by later. It'll probably be a couple of hours."

"No problem. I got nowhere to go."

Sounds like a lonely guy, Ransom thought.

Kathy looked over with pleading eyes. "Isn't it lunch time yet?"

"*Por supuesto.* You bet it is." He stopped at a Mexican restaurant, The Fiesta Café, on Houston Street, which was a plain brown brick building with a small gravel parking lot. It was a Mom and Pop operation, the kind of place where the best and most authentic Mexican fare in the city could usually be found. They slid into a red vinyl booth. The aroma of cooking meat and spices made Ransom's mouth water. He watched a fifty-something Mexican lady in a glass-sided cubicle as she made fresh tortillas using an imposing stainless steel machine.

They ordered from a bouncy young dark-haired girl, then nursed some soft drinks and munched on tortilla chips dipped in *picante* sauce as they chatted about the case and other things in the news. When the waitress came back with their plates piled with steaming goodies, they both smiled, and then commenced to gobble down their tasty tacos, enchiladas and refried beans. Kathy ate every bit as much as Ransom. She and that weightlifting partner must work out a hell of a lot, he thought, for her to be able to chow down like that and still stay slim and fit.

* * * * *

Feeling full and a bit sleepy, Ransom drove to the field office building. Once inside, they went directly to Jenkins's office. As he saw them enter, Jenkins reached over to a pile of papers, picked up a manila envelope, pulled out a sheet of paper, and handed it to Ransom. It was the sketch of their suspect as drawn by an artist at the Bureau based on descriptions given to Ransom by Mrs. Baldazar and Ms. Phoenix.

"I like it," Ransom said. "Now I can put a face with the crime."

"She looks pretty *plaine*," Kathy observed. "She'd never be asked to ride on a float."

"She sort of reminds me of a Bassett hound," said Jenkins.

"Zoomorphic comparisons aside," Ransom said, "we gotta go with what we got. So let's get this safari underway."

As they slid into the car, Kathy said, "Going after these kidnappers is like hunting a 'gator."

Ransom stared at her. "What the heck do you mean by that?"

"Cajuns say you got to get the 'gator 'fore he gets you."

"Now *that* sounds like a good idea. Let me know if you hear any splashes."

She smiled with her gorgeous white choppers. "Peg leg, by then it's too late."

He frowned and shot out of the lot.

"I hope Mrs. Baldazar's doing all right," Kathy said.

Ransom still had visions of a gator's gaping jaws. "It would sure help to get a validation of the sketch."

"Maybe someone at the hospital will recognize who it is," Kathy said.

"And we could run it in the papers. If we get it out to the public, maybe we'd get a tip."

* * * * *

Traffic was sparse, so on the way Ransom busted a couple of yellow lights. They arrived at the area in eight minutes, and they were now facing a roadblock two blocks from the Senator's house. It was designed to keep the press from camping out in front of the Baldazar's home.

Ransom showed his badge to get through the blockade, and then he parked and studied the house. To him, the place seemed shadowy and dismal. "Do you get a feeling about their place?" he asked Kathy.

She studied it for a couple of minutes. "I don't know why, but it sort of gives me the creeps. It looks like a house we kids in my neighborhood would never approach on Halloween night. The place was just *too* scary."

"That's exactly my feeling, too."

He climbed out of the Crown Vic with a sense of

foreboding.

Senator Baldazar answered the door. His complexion was as pallid as a pile of bread dough. The man hadn't shaved that morning, and maybe the morning before. He had hair as frizzy as a wire-haired terrier. That's got to be a perm, Ransom thought.

Baldazar nodded at them in mute recognition, and then he motioned them in.

In a low voice, Ransom said, "How's your wife doing?"

"Not well, I'm afraid." He stroked his whiskery cheeks, and a Rolex gleamed on his wrist as the afternoon sun leaked in through a window of the foyer. "She won't eat, and she just keeps staring at the phone. The doctor gave her some sedatives this morning. He said she should be kept as calm as possible."

"I see," Ransom said. He waited a beat. "Have you gotten any calls?"

"Just a few personal ones. Nothing in relation to April. Is that bad, Mr. Ransom? Don't the parents usually hear from the kidnappers by now?"

"No, not always."

They continued to stand in the hallway, with no one having anything more to say, and none of them wishing to enter the kitchen where Mrs. Baldazar was conducting her vigil.

Ransom broke the strained silence. "There's no typical pattern, Senator. You may not hear from the kidnapper right away, and possibly never."

"But then, you'll never find April!"

"There are many ways to find kidnappers, sir, and we have several approaches going. Just try to be patient and stay calm. It will help Mrs. Baldazar if you remain cool."

Thoughts looked to be spinning in the Senator's head.

"I'm sure you're right," he said. "But can't you be more aggressive? Are there any experts in D.C. that could suggest a plan?"

"We're in touch with Headquarters. We know what we're doing, just give us a chance."

Baldazar looked doubtful, but he seemed unsure whether to challenge them. There was a short standoff of silence. Then he gave a half shrug and a nod.

"Headquarters sent us a sketch they drew of the kidnapper," Ransom said. "We'd like to see if it looks like anyone you know or have seen around the hospital."

"All right," the Senator said. "Let's go into the den, and I'll look at it."

They trekked down a hallway to the left, then turned left into a room that looked more like an office than a cozy den. An oversized desk that appeared to Ransom like it was made of walnut, shined up, with two gold-stemmed desk lamps perched atop it, commanded the far wall. The senator settled himself into a black leather chair behind the desk and motioned toward the two burgundy leather chairs that fronted the desk. Kathy settled into one of them.

Ransom approached the desk, pulled out the sketch, and handed it to the senator. The tall man laid the piece of paper on his desk, adjusted his glasses, and bent over and stared at the drawing for a long time. He pursed his lips, then shook his head. "She doesn't look at all familiar to me."

Ransom said, "That's all right. Maybe you've never seen her. Could we see what your wife thinks of the sketch?"

The senator sighed, then arose from his chair, and they all made the painful trip into the kitchen. Mrs. Baldazar leaned against a counter, a forgotten cup of coffee clutched in her hand as she stared at the telephone. For a moment, they all focused on the silent instrument. If it had rung, they'd likely all have had heart attacks.

She kept staring with vacant green eyes. Ransom felt her emanations of despair snag his breath. He cleared his throat, but she didn't look up.

"Mrs. Baldazar, our lab men finished the sketch of the suspect woman. We have it with us now. If you don't mind, I'd like you to take a look at it."

Her eyes seemed to glaze over, and then she placed the cup on the counter, took a deep breath, and held out her hand.

He handed her the sketch. She took the piece of paper gingerly, as if it might be contaminated, then she examined it with care. For a long while, she made no comment.

When she raised her head Ransom asked, "Does it look like her? Like the woman who took April?"

She tilted her head, her brow crinkling. "It could be her, but I really don't know. I didn't see her for very long." She shook her head.

He wasn't sure if she didn't think the drawing was accurate, or if she didn't recall how the woman looked. Either way, it wasn't much help.

"Would you change anything to make the drawing look more like the woman as you recall her?"

She glanced back at the sketch. "I don't know what to change. It resembles her. That's all I can tell you."

She held out the drawing toward Ransom. Her eyes were downcast, her complexion pallid, and her mouth locked in a permanent frown, making her look like a woman without hope. Ransom studied her for a moment. When she glanced up at him, her gaze seemed like a vortex that might suck him under to his doom.

"We're sorry to bother you, Mrs. Baldazar. Thanks for your time."

She nodded and mumbled something Ransom didn't catch. She'd gone back to focusing on the phone. She probably thought it was her one lifeline to sanity.

Guilty as he felt about it, Ransom felt joyful to walk out of that house into the glaring sun. The rays baked into his head and face and soaked into the fabric of his jacket, erasing the cold sweat he'd felt inside the gloomy house.

"She's not doing well," said Kathy.

"No, and I'm afraid it's only going to get worse."

"But we'll find the baby, Jack. We've got to."

Ransom glanced at her, seeing doubt in her eyes, and a plea for reassurance. He squeezed her arm, saying, "We'll find her."

They slipped into Ransom's car and sat motionless for a minute or two, stewing.

Ransom turned on the ignition, then flipped the A/C to high, enjoying the cool blast of air that hit his face. But he hesitated, not putting the car in gear.

Kathy broke the silence. "You want to try more rental places?"

"First, let's show the sketch to our other witness."

"And we should check in on Jester."

"You're right. Let's do that now."

* * * * *

As they entered the neonatal ICU at Metro, the cop bravado that usually shielded them from fear, doubt, and insecurity slipped away like a shed raincoat, leaving them vulnerable. Their gun, badge, and street savvy on which they depended every day to perform their job and to save their asses were all worth nothing here. This was different territory with distinctive rules of conduct.

A glass wall fronted the hallway, and they gazed in at the gleaming equipment and the thirty or so plastic-sided isolettes, some stationed beside special machines, some nestled like small islands in the relative security of the center of the mesmerizing room.

"Look, he's over there," Kathy said, pointing.

Ransom and Kathy both studied Jester's baby, so small, with tubes sprouting in all directions as he lay squirming in his plastic cubicle. Ransom noted that the little guy was wiry and looked like a fighter. At least, he thought, he had the genes for it.

Minutes passed as they watched in silence.

Then Kathy wiped away a tear and cleared her throat. "Where do you suppose Jester is?"

"He must be in Sharene's room. Let's go take a look."

As they passed a waiting room, Ransom spotted Jester sitting in a chair in the corner, his head buried in his hands. His shoulders were trembling, and his cheeks were wet. Motioning to Kathy to wait for him, Ransom eased into the room.

In a minute, Jester noticed him. He swiped the back of his hand across his eyes. "Jack, I didn't see you there." He pulled out a handkerchief and blew his nose.

"I just now came in." The room felt close, almost suffocating. "Hey, Jester, Kathy and I saw your baby."

Jester looked at him with desperate hope in his eyes.

"He's a beautiful kid, Jester. And you know this is the best damn ICU ward in the state. They'll take good care of him."

"The doc says he's hanging in there, and if nothing else goes wrong, he'll be getting stronger every day."

"That's great. I'm sure he will." Ransom nodded. "And how's Sharene doing?"

"She's a big worrier. She's wearing out that Bible she carries around."

"It never hurts to get outside help."

"That's what we need most, I suppose."

Kathy poked her head in, and Jester waved her into the room. She hugged him, then Jester took a deep breath and told them about the baby. The child had awful problems. Painful, threatening obstacles just to draw breath and keep his heart beating. He might make it, but the odds weren't good.

After a few minutes there was nothing left to say.

Ransom put an arm across Jester's back and squeezed his shoulder. Then Kathy gave him another hug, and they walked out of the room.

Before leaving the hospital, they looked in on the head nurse, Winnie. She informed them that newborn babies were indeed tested for human leukocyte antigen shortly after birth, and the sample from the Baldazar baby had been preserved. It was another small piece of the puzzle that would hopefully lead to a solution to the kidnapping.

6

Ransom and Kathy drove away from the hospital with heavy doubts about Jester's child. But they had to continue their search for the kidnapped baby. So, within fifteen minutes, Ransom pulled up to the apartment complex where Marnie Phoenix lived, and he and Kathy got out. The buildings' natural wood with sturdy lines was calmed by clusters of burgeoning plants and thick stands of flowers. A subtropical breeze kissed the agents as they walked among crimson hibiscus, pink oleanders, and purple pansies on their journey to find the witness.

When they located her apartment door, Ransom rang the bell. A stereo played inside. He heard it being turned down.

Ms. Phoenix opened the door and broke into a smile. "Well, Mr. Ransom. You must have gotten the sketch back." She stepped backwards, swinging the door open.

"Oh," she said, spotting Kathy.

"Ms. Phoenix, this is Agent Devereaux."

She shook Kathy's hand, then said, "Please come in."

"Thanks," Kathy said, looking serious.

Ms. Phoenix wore a T-shirt and snug shorts, sprouting shapely legs. When they'd all settled in, with Ms. Phoenix tucking her legs beneath her on a sofa, Ransom pulled the sketch of the woman kidnapper from his jacket pocket. "This is the drawing the artist made from the descriptions of the kidnapper that you and the baby's mother gave us. Do you think it looks like the woman you saw in the parking lot?"

Kathy stared at Ms. Phoenix. It was often hard to read what lay behind Kathy's big blue peepers. Ms. Phoenix didn't seem to notice the extra attention she was getting.

As Ms. Phoenix reached for the sketch, Ransom noticed that her long fingernails shone a pastel pink. While she studied the face in the drawing, Ransom observed her shiny green eyes hooded in long, brown eyelashes. Her hair lay soft and gentle against the curve of her neck as she stared down at the drawing.

After a bit, she shook her head. "I'm afraid I can't help you."

"You don't think it looks like her?"

"Maybe . . . maybe not. I guess I didn't see her all that well. I thought I might recall her, but now I'm not sure."

"If you saw her in person, do you think you might recognize her?"

"It's possible. Do you know where she is?"

He took the sketch back. The woman's scent wafted his way. Was it a hint of honeysuckle?

"Not yet. We're still looking for her."

She considered that a moment. Then she asked, "Did you get anything from the license plate numbers I saw?"

"Ahhh," he said and shot a glance at Kathy.

"We're still checking them out," Kathy said. "There will be a lot of cars with the numbers you gave us."

"The make and color will narrow it down, won't it?"

"Oh, sure. General Motors. Sky blue."

Ransom rose from his chair. "Thanks, Ms. Phoenix. We'd better be going."

"Call me Marnie, please. I haven't done much, but I wish you luck. That poor mother must be frantic."

Kathy's stolid mask softened. "Yes, she's very distraught," she said. She studied Ms. Phoenix a moment longer, then asked, "Do you have any children?"

She shook her head, frowning. "My sister has two kids, but I've never been married." Then she brightened. "I do love playing auntie, though."

Kathy's glance darted to Ransom.

The poor young woman, he thought.

Kathy said, "We'll be in touch, Ms. Phoenix."

She smiled at Ransom, and he returned it.

"Please feel free to call me any time," she said, still focused on Ransom. "I want to help however I can."

Kathy made a low noise in her throat.

She sounded like a 'gator, Ransom thought.

Outside, they made their way through the flowery courtyard back to their car. Ransom opened his door, and Kathy hers, then they paused, waiting for the overheated air to escape from the cab before climbing in.

Kathy said, "We still need to talk about your family situation."

It seemed like a challenge to him. She had her hands on her hips.

"You bet," he said. "We'll have to do that."

"I mean like now."

"*Now?*"

"Get in," she said.

They pulled away from the curb. "I couldn't help noticing the way you looked at that woman," Kathy said.

Was this for real? "The way I *looked* at her?"

"Looked her over, that is. You can tell me it's none of my business, but I've seen a big change in you lately. I don't think it's for the better."

"I don't know about—"

She held up a hand, and he lost his train of thought.

"Just listen. Sometimes others know you better than you know yourself."

"I'm not even acquainted with Mar—I mean, Ms. Phoenix. We're just covering leads here, Kathy."

"Forget about Phoenix. The issue as I see it is whether you're going to work at your relationship with Beverly."

"I know you mean well, but I can handle—"

"I don't think you can." Her eyes shot a stream of blazing blue particles. "You've been in a deep funk for two months now, and I think it's time you took a hard look at your situation. When it comes down to it, neither Ms. Phoenix nor Gloria the sex kitten is what you need in your life right now."

His jaw tightened, but before he could say anything, she continued. "What I'm trying to get across is that you've got a family to think about. Your happiness is important, but only in terms of the unity and well-being of your family."

His ears were burning, and he wondered if his cheeks were flushed. Mark Twain was right when he said, "Man is the only animal that blushes. Or needs to."

"There are some considerations you don't know about," he finally said.

"I'm sure that's true," she conceded. "If you feel like talking about them, I'm here."

The thought of Beverly's infidelity sent a blast of arctic air through his innards. "Maybe sometime we will. I really can't do it right now."

She maintained a steady look, her lips tight, then took a deep breath and slowly let it out. "Excuse my preaching. If you want, you can tell me to butt out. I know I can be a ring-tailed bitch."

Scotch-Irish-Cajun mix. Feisty and gorgeous. Hell, she could be anything she wanted. "No, I'm not telling you any such thing. I value my health more than my privacy."

She gave him an exasperated grimace. "So getting back to business, Mr. Lothario, what's next on our agenda?"

He gave her a fake leer, saying, "Let's go inspect some more nursie outfits."

After another two hours they'd covered the last of the rental shops. The list of possible female suspects had grown to twelve.

Ransom glanced at his watch: straight up four o'clock.

"Are you ready for some cop talk?"

"You mean we're going to see that deputy?"

"I told him I'd drop by. You can stay in the car if you want."

"You think I'd let you go in an unknown house alone after seeing *Silence of the Lambs?*"

* * * * *

As he slid to a stop in front of the slumping white frame house, Ransom swiveled his head and stared laser beams into Kathy's eyes, giving her his best Hannibal Lecter frozen smile.

"All right, my dear, step right this way."

She gave him a twisted frown, but said nothing.

They approached the small house with its peeling paint, a cracked driveway alongside, and the blank look of curtained windows. A cardboard square covered the glass pane in the front door.

The porch was swaybacked, and Ransom checked it for structural weakness. The flooring sagged under his weight, but he didn't fall through, so he eased toward the front door. Creaking boards announced each step. Kathy followed a couple of paces back, her squeaky steps a syncopated echo.

A spider had fashioned a web beside the door, using the doorbell as a fastening point. Rather than wreck the silky netscape, Ransom rapped his knuckles against the thick wood door. The lace curtain at the front window moved an inch, and then slipped back into place. When the door swung open, it squealed on its hinges.

Ransom held up his badge. "Jack Ransom with the FBI, Deputy North. I called earlier?"

The man had wide-set brown eyes and a primo poker face.

"Come in," he said, backing into the murky room.

They slipped inside. Ransom introduced Kathy, then they followed the deputy into the living room. Wood floors clicked with their footsteps, and Ransom noticed the furniture was from another era. Like before Frank Sinatra.

Resembling an amorphous bear, the deputy dropped into an overstuffed chair and laid his beefy arms on the armrests, crossing his feet at the ankles.

Ransom and Kathy both sank into the sofa, which Ransom thought felt like sitting in a tub of Jello

"Have you been with the Sheriff's Office long?" Ransom asked.

"Ten years. Long enough, I'd say."

"That's a lengthy time, all right."

Now the guy folded his arms across his chest. He didn't utter another peep. He wasn't your typical Oprah guest.

Kathy crossed one knee over the other, tucked her skirt under her legs, and stared at the man of wood. Then she said, "So what's with this suspect you mentioned?"

Ransom blinked. He wondered what had happened to Kathy's southern hospitality.

"I'm surprised you guys didn't snap on him before," said the deputy. "He seems like a hot pick to me."

"We're not on TV anymore," Ransom said. "It takes longer than an hour to solve 'em now."

No laugh. No smile. Tough crowd. The guy recrossed his ankles.

"I ain't tailed the mope or surveilled his place, uh, his dolly's place, but he sure could be good for this job. He's so new out of the joint he shivers when he sees a bar of soap, and I hear he's looking for a score. Besides, the gal he's shacked up with is a nurse at Metro. Go figger taste, huh? Hers, I mean."

He gave them a lopsided smile. Showing gray, crooked teeth. Go figger.

"They would've had to use another woman to make the snatch," Ransom said. "Any idea who that would be?"

"Nah, unless it was Susie's sister."

"Susie?" said Kathy.

"The nurse from Metro he's seeing. Sue Kraff."

Ransom thought about it. At this point anything was possible.

"What's the guy's name and description?" he said. "And where's this Susie live?"

The deputy filled them in. Parker Tipton was forty years old, six feet tall, 190 pounds, black hair, brown eyes, jailhouse tattoos on both arms. He'd been inside for six years. Carried a .45 pistol in his botched bank job. The nurse had been at Metro for a couple of years, having moved to San Antonio from Amarillo. She lived on Blanco Avenue in a small rental house.

After he finished making notes, Ransom struggled out of the whale blubber couch and shook the deputy's hand. "Thanks for the tip. We'll follow up on it, and we'll let you know if it's righteous." He handed the man his card. "And if I can ever help you, give me a call."

The deputy looked surprised. "Sure thing. I hope it helps."

They walked out onto the undulating porch. As Gloria Estefan would say, they were coming out of the dark.

* * * * *

Back in the car, Kathy said, "*Righteous?* If it turns out *righteous?*"

"The deputy and I are of another era."

"The Pleistocene?"

He gave her the hairy eyeball. "The golden Creedence Clearwater age, if you must know."

"Who?"

In frustration he pulled away from the curb. "Never mind. Anyway, what was your take on the deputy's information?"

"*Qui comprends?* I really don't know, Jack. Maybe Tipton was involved, but we need to know more than he'd like to score a job and he's doing the bayou boogie with a Metro nurse."

"You're right there. Maybe we could put a tail on him, just to see if he looks hinky."

"Why not? Let's go for it," she said, brushing back her thick hair. "Anyway, how'd you like his place?"

He chuckled. "Freddy, the guy with the hockey mask, would love it."

"Or the Addams family could use it as a set."

"Who do you suppose was his decorator?"

"His mom," she said.

"You really think so? Why's that?"

"I think she lives there. The furniture was old—it looks like my grandparents' stuff—with carved legs, dark wood and a patterned fabric. And did you catch the afghan on the couch and the copy of *Better Homes and Gardens* on the end table?"

"Maybe he's just expressing his feminine side."

"To the point of wearing lilac body powder?"

"Sherlock, you're amazing." He pulled onto Loop 410.

"Thanks, Watson. Where are we going now?"

"To the other side of town," he said. "That fundamentalist church woman, Tarmack, lives on Perrin-Beitel Road. She's the one we got a tip about on the hot line."

"Oh, right. Do you think she'll let us see her baby?"

"I hope so. We've got no warrant and no probable cause to indicate she was involved. We can't force anything." He passed a slow-moving truck, and then fell in behind a Lincoln.

"But we've got to find that baby, Jack."

He gave her a sly wink. "I didn't just fall off the turnip truck. I've got a few tricks planned."

* * * * *

Ellen Tarmack's house was a brick-and-wood ranch style, landscaped with precision, with a newer model Buick Regal parked in a two-car garage. Ransom scribbled down the license plate number. They approached the bastion of *bourgeoisie*, and Ransom rang the bell. There was no spider at work there.

A thin woman with dark hair and a bleached complexion pulled open the door, surprise skittering behind her eyes when she saw them. She wore a yellow blouse, tan slacks, and a harried expression. "Yes, can I help you?"

"Are you Mrs. Tarmack?"

She blinked. "Why, yes." She looked to Kathy for a feminine connection.

Ransom flashed his credentials and told her they were feds.

Kathy gave the woman a smile, saying, "May we come in?"

"My husband's not home, but if it's urgent . . . ."

"It's important, Mrs. Tarmack," Kathy assured her. "And we don't need to speak with your husband."

She sucked in a small breath, and then backed away. "All

right, come in."

As they did, she said, "Excuse the mess, we're a bit unsettled at the moment."

Harum-scarum was more like it. The room was rampant with baby bottles, pacifiers, disposable diapers, rattles, and a half-assembled crib mobile. Ransom riveted on Mrs. Tarmack's face. She was the right age and had about the same physical description as the subject. And she looked pretty close to the dog-faced sketch. As much as any female Homo sapien could, that is.

She sat upright in a straight-backed chair. Ransom selected a recliner, and Kathy perched on the edge of a sofa. For several moments, an awkward silence seized them.

Then Ransom said, "Mrs. Tarmack, we're trying to find a missing baby." He hesitated, but saw no reaction from her. "You may have seen the case in the newspaper or on television. The child was taken from Metro hospital. She's been gone for two days, and there's grave concern about her welfare."

The woman blinked again, but her gaze remained steady, and she looked more interested in the situation than fearful that something might happen to her. Her hands were folded in her lap, holding steady, not trembling. Her breathing appeared even.

"I don't understand. What does that have to do with me?"

"Mrs. Tarmack," Kathy said, "we sometimes get tips from various sources, and we have information that you have a new baby."

Now she looked concerned. Her brow wrinkled and her hands worked at each other. She gave three quick blinks.

"Yes, we brought Nancy home a couple of days ago, but that has no connection with—"

"We didn't expect it did," said Ransom, "but we need to follow out all possibilities. It's just a routine investigation."

"How would you do that? Follow out what possibility?"

"We'd just eliminate the chance that Nancy could be the missing baby. We could check the baby's birth certificate. And we'd like to take a quick peek at the child, just to be sure there's no physical resemblance to the missing baby. If there's any question, we might take a footprint."

Now her eyes went as large as a doe's sensing danger. Her hands became more agitated. Pink coloration crept into her cheeks.

"Wouldn't you need some kind of warrant to do all that? You can't just come barging in here and—"

"You invited us in, Mrs. Tarmack," Kathy said, "and you can give us consent to do everything Mr. Ransom mentioned. It'll just take a few minutes."

"But the baby's sleeping, and I just don't like the idea. We didn't steal anyone's baby. Nancy is ours."

"What hospital was she born in?" Ransom asked.

"Well, none. She was born at home, with a midwife assisting."

"Now you're confusing me," Ransom said.

"I don't under—"

"A minute ago you told us you brought the baby home two days ago. Now you're saying the baby was born here?"

She twisted her hands, and her pupils grew huge. "I didn't say that." Then she jumped up from the chair. "I'll have to ask you to leave now. There's nothing here that is connected with your case."

Kathy started to say something, and then stifled it. They stood up and stepped toward the door. Then they paused.

"We're sorry to have bothered you, Mrs. Tarmack," Ransom said, taking a last look around, more curious than sorry. He wasn't about to miss this curveball. With her mystery baby, Mrs. Tarmack had just made herself suspect *numero uno.*

Ransom drove away from the Tarmack's house. Two blocks down the street he curled a tight u-turn, drove back a block, then turned right and stopped. They had a good view of the Tarmack's house from here.

He grabbed the mike and transmitted, "Five romeo to control."

"Go ahead, five romeo."

"I need a 10-26 on Texas plate KCJ 57P."

"Stand by."

In a couple of minutes, they learned the plate was registered to Kenneth and Ellen Tarmack for a 2009 Buick Regal. The FBI's computer, NCIC, had no criminal record for either individual. Locally, Ellen had two speeding tickets. Kenneth apparently drove more sanely.

"I guess they're not your big-time hoods," Ransom said.

Kathy shrugged. "They don't need to be. Maybe they just wanted a kid."

Ransom opened his cell phone and got Jenkins.

"Sonny, we've come up with a possible suspect I need eyeballed. Can you get a surveillance team out here?"

"I'll check with SOG. What's your location?"

* * * * *

At six o'clock, a car rolled toward them, slowed, and then pulled alongside their Crown Vic. Two agents wearing knit shirts gazed at them. Bill Howerton sat in the passenger seat; the driver was a new agent in the office whose name Ransom couldn't recall. He wore a Spurs ball cap and an eager expression.

"What'cha got?" Ball Cap asked.

Ransom told him the scenario, and then asked, "Can you babysit them awhile?"

"We just got back from a job in Austin, so we're free." He adjusted his cap. "There's another unit down the street. Consider your suspects covered."

Just then a medium blue Pontiac Sunbird zipped down the street behind them. Ransom spotted the plate over his shoulder. XPM 26J. Could this be the car Marnie Phoenix described? The auto turned into the Tarmack's driveway and pulled into the garage. The brake lights flared, and the garage door slid down.

"Did you see that?" Kathy said, her eyes wide.

"It fits, except Phoenix said the M was before the P."

"That's close enough for government work. *De plus,* maybe she was wrong."

Ransom agreed with her assessment and told the surveillance agents to keep an eyeball on that car, too.

Howerton said something that got lost in the sound of the car engines.

"What?" Ransom said.

Ball Cap relayed, "He says they may be buttoned down for the evening."

"Yeah, they could be. Anyway, where do you want us to set up?"

Ball Cap raised and lowered his bill as Howerton said something to him.

Then Ball Cap turned and said, "You guys go ahead and burn off. The woman has seen your car."

Ransom started to protest, but Ball Cap added, "Hey, we get paid extra to work these crazy hours, and we love it."

Two lies for the price of one. But they were right about the Crown Vic. Mrs. Tarmack might make them if they helped with the tail.

"Thanks, guys. Be sure to call me if anything happens."

* * * * *

After dropping Kathy at her car, Ransom headed across town, where minutes later he wheeled into the police parking lot. He entered the four-story building and talked with the receptionist, who buzzed him into the work space. He found Lieutenant Sanchez in his office.

"We got back the artist's conception of the phony nurse," he said, dropping it on the Lieutenant's desk.

Sanchez studied it. "She looks like *una perra.*"

"Exactly. Jenkins says a basset hound."

Sanchez squinted. "Or I'd say maybe a beagle."

Ransom leaned over to stare at the drawing. "Yeah, I can see where you get that. Mrs. Baldazar and our other witness aren't crazy about the sketch. But maybe it's good for elimination purposes."

"Sure, like no one pretty could be a suspect."

"*Exactamente.*" Ransom stared at a curved sword that hung on the wall. "Did you get anything from your interviews of the Baldazar's neighbors?"

Sanchez turned his palm up. "They say the Baldazars keep to themselves. He's out of town a lot, and she's not too social. Nobody says anything bad about them, they just don't know much, except that he's a lawyer and a big shot Senator." He shook his head. "No one could name any suspects in the kidnapping."

"One other thing. Atherton told me that one of the parents at the hospital said a candy striper delivered them a message around six o'clock. Their room was on the same hallway as the Baldazar mother's room. Maybe she saw someone."

"None of them have mentioned being on that floor around that time. But I've still got two of them left to contact."

"Okay, *amigo,* let me know what they say."

"No *problema*, friend."

Ransom then briefed him on what they'd learned about the ex-con and the Tarmack woman.

"Besides that," Ransom continued, "we're chasing out leads on women who bought or rented scrubs. Probably nothing will develop there."

"*Quién sabe?* I figure everyone can be considered a

suspect."

"*Todo el mundo?*" Ransom asked.

"Absolutely everyone." His coffee eyes blazed with intensity. "Now I'd better get home to *mamacita_*and the *niños* before they think I've got a *novia.*"

"Take it from Emerson: 'All mankind loves a lover.'"

"Maybe so, but womankind doesn't take it too well."

Ransom nodded. "*Eso es.* For sure, *amigo.*"

7

Kathy changed into her electric pink shorts, her "Bad Girls Run Fast" T-shirt, and her best Nike running shoes, then began a slow jog along a lonely road close to her apartment. She usually ran four miles at a brisk pace, and then when she got back to her apartment, would go through a dumbbell routine. But tonight, she realized after a mile or so, her legs felt rubbery. Her shoes pinched; the ones she'd spent a days' pay on. Great.

Maybe it was the long hours they'd been working, the late night calls from Jester at the hospital, and the concerns about his endangered baby. Now that she thought about it, there was good reason for her to be tired. There was no use in punishing her body. She slowed to a walk.

The heat enveloped her as though from an opened oven. But a southerly breeze pushed at her bangs, fluttering the leaves of the trees along the road, and cooling her a bit. She turned onto another narrow path, which was a shortcut back to the complex.

Patches of shade mottled the ground as she plodded along the dirt trail. She mopped her shiny brow with the back of her hand and adjusted her pony tail. As she moved along the trail, her legs seemed to regain strength.

Come to think of it, she'd been carrying on with a busy social calendar, too. Today was no exception. She was up late last night, worked hard all day, and now tonight she had plans for dinner, then a comedy club. It seemed to her that—

Uhhh. She stubbed her toe on a rock in the path, and she stared hard at the chunk of limestone. Then she kicked it into the bristly grass beside the trail.

She supposed that was just like life. You're going along with everything under control, then something unexpected trips you up. It could be a minor bump, something you'd hardly notice, or you could pitch over a cliff.

Just look at the Baldazars. What could be worse than to lose your child? And in such a sudden and strange fashion. She couldn't imagine the pain they must be suffering. Then there was Jester and his wife having to watch their tiny baby struggle for his life.

She resumed walking. She decided that it would be worse for the Baldazars—not knowing what was happening to their baby must be the most awful torture possible. It had to be devastating to have a newborn baby by your side one minute, and then to have her vanish. Just disappear and be gone.

She had to find that baby. Somehow, she and the others had to figure out who had taken the child and where they'd gone. And to determine the reason they'd snatched her.

She reviewed the steps they'd taken in the investigation. It all seemed logical to her, so far. But their progress had been glacial. They weren't doing enough.

Of course, it was early in the investigation to narrow down the leads. There was still a broad spectrum of people to check. Hospital workers, volunteers, visitors. Neighbors, friends, infertile women. Sky blue cars, nursie scrubs.

She spotted her apartment building through the trees ahead. Soon she'd be in the shower. Then she'd have to get dressed to go out with Steve.

She'd told Ransom he was just her workout partner, nothing more. That wasn't really true. But as a rule she never mentioned her social contacts to the guys in the office unless it got serious. Otherwise, she'd be taking a ribbing for every guy she dated that didn't work out because of whatever.

And the reasons for breaking off with someone were legion. Personality conflicts or just different interests. Clashes of tastes in entertainment, social values, and religious beliefs. Varying uses or abuses of alcohol or drugs, opinions concerning sexual behavior and preferences, and attitudes about career, family, and goals.

Not to mention the small stuff like halitosis, snoring, bad table manners, offensive jokes, obnoxious laughter, no sense of humor, insensitivity to others, narcissism, awkward dancing, poor conversational skills, sloppy living habits, fetishism of any type, and clumsy performance in kissing, hugging, petting, and doing the wild thing. Could it be that she was too particular?

She unlocked her door. As she walked into her bedroom, she glanced at the dumbbells. No way, not tonight. She peeled off her shirt and shorts. A warm shower would do just right.

As she stood under the cascading water, with soap suds trailing from her breasts down her torso, she re-examined the lists. Steve scored well in about any category she could devise. And he cared for her. She really believed he did. And she . . . cared for him, too.

So what was bothering her? Why hadn't she told Ransom about him? She was prying into that poor man's private life with both hands. Since everything was coming together fine in hers, she should be happy to share it with others. Maybe it was even time, as her mom would say, to "get serious."

Or maybe it was too soon. They hadn't known each other that long. She ran a soapy hand across her abdomen. She imagined Steve there with her, rubbing her shoulders, then moving his hands over the rest of her body. She felt a warm glow. They might have to skip the comedy routines tonight. After all, there were other pleasures in life besides being amused.

* * * * *

The man waited in the sombrous room, eager for the woman to arrive, but unwilling to capitulate to his desires. She'd be along. He closed his eyes, feeling the texture of the blackness around him and letting his thoughts soar.

His mind ranged the universe, consorting on an astral plane with the powers and spirits that roamed the seen and unseen worlds above and below. He sought to understand the secrets, to attain the knowledge of magick that would make him powerful and wise. He wished above all to be one with all.

There were many paths to the wisdom and spiritualism he sought, he was sure, for brilliant and passionate men had searched for the same truth and power in a myriad of diverse ways over millions of years of human existence. He'd tried any number of methods himself.

He saw strengths in beliefs such as those held by the cabalists, who sought to approach God through knowledge, attaining the sefirot, or ten points of light. He believed that knowledge of the workings of the universe must be a part of becoming one with the system and learning to change and control it. And how could he deny the beauty of the Pythagorean argument that numbers were at the root of all knowledge and understanding? Mathematical integration of the interactions among physical manifestations in nature was clear from any basic study of physics, chemistry, or engineering.

He liked the idea of the universe as an interconnected organism. Humans, animals, plants, all combined as parts of a whole. Of course, the complex interrelationships of the intertwined threads would be almost too enormous to contemplate.

Most appealing to him, he'd decided, was tantric spiritualism, an offshoot of Hinduism. The basic philosophy was simple, and it tended to parallel some of his other beliefs. He sensed the simple truth of the idea that man could achieve his highest purpose through the practice of erotic pleasures.

Tantrists looked to achieve a heightened state of consciousness through sexual union. They sought a transformation of their minds through the use of drugs, meditation, and sex. Best of all, it was thought that the tantrist could achieve divinity, could become a part of the universe through the energy taken from the sex act.

He recognized the kernel of truth in these beliefs. They made sense to him. During coition the union was prolonged, with the man holding back his orgasm as the woman experienced hers. He would thus absorb her energy, adding to his own power. And if the act was repeated often enough for long enough, the practitioner could acquire immortality. These ideas matched his beliefs, and the purported result was exactly what he desired.

His heart thumped stronger and faster as he imagined the sex act itself, repeated several times during an evening with the group. The thought of attaining divine power and of continuing the ecstatic sexual unions forever infused him with rapture. And as he dwelled on the idea, he almost missed the soft rapping at the door.

He didn't move. There was total silence. Then the gentle tapping came again. He stepped quietly to the door and rapped a knuckle on the solid wood in response, striking it five times. Two more raps came from the other side.

He opened the door and ushered her inside. The murkiness of the room enveloped her. She kneeled beside him, and then he lit a candle.

They stared at the flame, not speaking or touching. Then they gazed at each other. She had silken, straw-colored hair that fell past her shoulders, big azure eyes, and an eggshell complexion. Her lips were the hue of fresh blood.

He reached to the throat of her black robe, pulling at the string knotted there. The robe fell open, revealing the half moon circles of her breasts. They were full and firm, shaped like grapefruits bursting with juice.

Still on his knees he swiveled toward her, cupping the back of her head in his hand, pulling her to him, kissing her full lips. Her burning kiss poured forth energy as he tasted the hot dewdrops from her tongue. His hands cupped her breasts, caressing, kneading her nipples. A keening noise arose in her throat—pleasure and pain twisted into a throbbing braid of erotic sensation. He loosed the string of his robe, and it dropped away.

Now he pulled her tighter. Their chests and thighs fused as one. Her hips swayed and bucked in exotic motions.

But he backed away, saying, "Take the energy from the candle."

She hesitated. She wanted him, it was clear. And maybe there was some fear there, too. But he knew she wouldn't question him.

She stepped over to the candle, placed her hands on her hips, and spread her legs, lowering her body like an Egyptian dancer toward the flame. Her eyes squinted closed.

About a foot above the flame, she stopped.

"I can't go any farther." Sweat beaded on her forehead.

"But you must."

"Not without your help, Master. Please."

"Then I shall help you, and you will share with me the power from this flickering candle of life."

He leaned in and blew out the candle. The smell of acrid hot gases filled his nostrils. "May your flame die, but your energy enter this woman."

She didn't move.

"Take the energy. Now, before it diminishes."

He could sense her body lowering toward the candle. She came down closer to where it smoldered. Now she groaned, and her breath came in short, nervous gasps.

Placing his hands on her shoulders, he pushed her downward. Then he stopped, holding her poised just inches above the smoking wick. She shuddered with relief; she could feel the heat from the still warm wax puddled in the top of the candle.

"You've shown your courage and obedience in the display of your willingness of spirit to absorb the energy of the symbolic candle. And as you hold youth and vigor within you, I now remove the spent candle of life." He set it aside, then he grasped her arms, turned her around, and guided her toward the floor.

"Now share with me the spirits of eternal youth," he said.

She went down on her elbows, forehead on the floor, her buttocks arched into the air before him.

"I take your offer of immortal life." He slid himself into her. She squeezed herself tight around him. He moved in and out, banging against her harder each time, touching something deep inside her.

"Take my seed within you," he said, increasing his rhythm. He ached, he hurt, he felt wet and hot and hard, and the twinges became wrenching and throbbing jolts, and he bit his lip, and he sucked in air through his teeth and groaned and gave a cry from somewhere deep in his throat as he felt the painful seizure, then his crotch exploded like a gush of water spewing from a rusty pipe, spurting into the inner sanctum of a darkened basement.

* * * * *

Ransom picked up the phone and called Gloria.

"Jack, I've been trying to reach you. I was getting concerned."

"Not to worry. I just spent the day with a sexy redhead."

"It better have been Kathy, bub."

He laughed. "She's a great alibi." Then his smile dropped away as reality came crashing back. "There was a baby kidnapped from the hospital a couple of days ago. We've been pushing hard on the investigation ever since."

"What a terrible thing. Are you doing any good?""

"Not yet, we need a break. Right now, I'd settle for dumb luck."

After a pause, she asked, "Can you still go out tonight?"

He thought about the surveillance on the Tarmack couple. "We've got something working, but it'll probably stay cool tonight. Let's give it a try."

"That would be wonderful. Where did you get reservations?"

"I didn't make any. Something came up. Holly has this piano recital, and I promised we'd go hear her play."

"But don't we need some time alone together?"

"The recital won't last long. We'll have time later."

She breathed through her nostrils into the phone, and then said, "You're lucky we've been apart for a week and I can't stand another minute without you. When's the torture session start?"

* * * * *

A herd of moms, dads, brothers, sisters, and some grandparents packed the small auditorium for the recital, with the press of body heat making the room feel humid and close. Cameras flashed. Camcorders whined away.

Ransom was enjoying the program. It wasn't that bad. A couple of the kids played well, and Holly did passably. Gloria leaned into his shoulder most of the time. She smelled great. She also had the shortest skirt in the place, and the best legs.

He read the next item on the program, and then checked his phone.

Gloria nudged him in the ribs. He knew she found him too serious, never missing a chance to jab him about it. She leaned closer, her breast pressing into his arm, and her scent enveloping him. He felt a stirring in his groin.

"Get a message?" she whispered, her breath hot and sweet.

Yes, he did, but not on his phone.

Just then, the last number for the evening ended, and he shook his head clear and looked back toward the stage, applauding the gangly, flop-haired boy who had played a Beethoven concerto with teen gusto.

After the recital, he and Gloria made their way backstage to talk with Holly. She looked so grown up in her pretty light blue scoop neck dress. He hugged her and kissed her on the cheek, but he could sense she was staring at Gloria.

"Fine job, Holly," he said. "You played like a real artist."

"Yes, Holly," Gloria agreed, "you were quite good."

"Thanks, Miss Ramirez," Holly said with the verve of a tree sloth.

Gloria gazed at Holly, but could think of nothing else to say.

Holly twisted a blonde curl around her index finger.

Gloria took Ransom's arm, gripping hard. "Well, I guess we'd better be—"

Beverly rushed into the room, saying, "Holly, that was just won—" She paused when she saw them there.

"Oh, hello, Jack . . . Miss Ramirez."

Gloria nodded.

Ransom blushed.

"We were telling Holly how well she played," he said.

She looked a few pounds lighter, he thought; not that she'd ever been too heavy. She'd always been a striking beauty. Especially, he thought, when the light caught her pale blue eyes the way it did now.

"Her musical talent must've come from your side of the family, Jack. My relatives are all tone deaf."

Everyone laughed nervously.

"We were just leaving. 'Bye, Holly. I'll talk to you later."

He felt two sets of eyes skewering him as he skulked away. It wasn't a pleasant feeling.

"I need a drink," he muttered.

"Make mine a double," said Gloria.

* * * * *

They stopped for a blast at Maggie's Restaurant. A herd of humanity was crowded into the fern-swathed restaurant, but they lucked into two empty stools at the gigantic horseshoe-shaped bar and climbed aboard. She ordered a margarita, and he went for a Coors Lite. For a time, they listened to the music, swigged their drinks, and rubbed knees. It was too noisy to talk without yelling. Then Gloria leaned close to his ear and half-shouted the magic words.

"Can you come to my place for a nightcap?"

He quaffed the remainder of his beer and plopped the drained mug on the bar with a *thunk.*

"I thought you'd never ask."

The drive was short; the air crackled with anticipation. She pushed into her apartment, switched on a small lamp by the sofa, and slipped out of her high heels. She walked straight into the bedroom, with Ransom trailing. His intentions were not honorable.

"I need to get out of these tight clothes before I turn into a sausage," she said. "Unzip me?"

He was glad to do the honors.

"Want to find yourself a beer?" she asked, holding onto the top of her dress.

"No, I like the view better in here."

She let the dress slip to the floor. She wore a black lacy bra and bikini panties. The effect was staggering.

"Still like it?"

"Better and better."

She moved to him, putting her hand behind his neck. He leaned against her and kissed her. Her mouth tasted better than chocolate.

She fumbled with his belt, unfastening it. The zipper went smoother. He kicked off his shoes just before his pants hit the floor.

The rest of their clothes slipped away, and their hands explored each other's curves and hollows. Then she took his hand and led him over to the bed. Turning the covers down, she stretched out on the lavender sheets like a model in *Playboy*.

"I really have missed you," she purred, "a lot."

He settled beside her, snuggling close, kissing her and stroking her hair. Then he rolled atop her, pressing down.

"God, I need you," she murmured. "*Dios, mio.*"

He caressed her ear. He ran his fingers along her hip and down the length of her thigh. "I need you, too."

Then he slid inside her, feeling her shudder. She clamped her body against him and her legs tightened around his thighs. Her arms pulled at him, urging him closer. He moved faster, searching for the rhythm that lovers die for. He felt the heat of her inner body, the melding of their desire, and the ache of frantic pleasure. And then—

His cell phone played its blues riff. Shit. Oh, shit. It sounded off again. He hesitated. Where was it? It had to be on his belt, which was somewhere on the floor. But should he try to answer it? Switch it off? Ignore it and go on? And then he realized the wisdom of the old saying . . .

He who hesitates is lost.

"Son of a bitch," said Gloria.

He fumbled among the pile of clothes until he found the electronic nuisance. Calling back, he avoided a death ray glare from Gloria as he talked. It was Slattery, one of the agents stationed at the Baldazar's house.

"This is Ransom. What've you got?"

"We received a call here at the house less than five minutes ago. The caller said he wants $500,000 for the baby."

Gloria had thrown on a short robe and was combing her hair with brisk, abrasive strokes.

"Did the caller sound legitimate?'

"I'd say so. As far as we could tell, anyway. He didn't talk very long. He wants the payoff tomorrow afternoon. And he said he'd call back with details about the time and place."

"Did you do any good with the trap and trace?"

"We've got two cars on the way to the phone location. The call was made from someplace on Hildebrand, near Brackenridge Park . . . hold on a sec."

Ransom heard the crackle of a handi talkie breaking a squelch. Gloria sat down beside him on the bed. Her face was more forgiving now, and she patted him on the shoulder.

"We got a call from the kidnapper," he told Gloria. "Cars are out—"

"Our guys just found the spot where the call came from," said the agent on the telephone. "It's a pay phone outside a gas station. The place is closed, and no one's around. They're going to dust it for prints and do a neighborhood check. Anything else we should do?"

"Alert the SWAT team and everyone assigned to the case, and we'll meet at the office at eight in the morning. Also, call Jenkins and brief him. I'll be there in twenty minutes."

As he hung up and gazed at the wall, Gloria stroked his bare leg. He felt a tingle higher up. Kissing her on the cheek, afraid to get more involved, he said, "Sorry, honey, duty calls."

"What about the call of the wild?"

He clenched his teeth in frustration. "That's a powerful summons, too. But time doesn't permit."

"How about tomorrow?"

"We'll be working all day, but I'll try to come by for . . . for a while, if I can."

She sighed, as though she'd heard that one before, and then said, "If you can fit me in."

"No, if you can fit *me* in."

The line coaxed a smile from tight lips. "At least you haven't lost your prurient sense of humor."

"Hey, if everyone loves a lover, my philosophy is they especially sympathize with a horny soul."

He turned from her and punched the buttons on his phone again. After a couple of rings, Mrs. Sanchez answered. She told him the lieutenant had gone out a half hour earlier to work a double homicide at a west side nightclub.

"So, he'll probably be out all night?" Ransom said.

She sighed. "That's what I expect."

Cops' wives were a special breed. The ones that could

take it, that is. "Have him call me in the morning. We heard from the kidnapper."

As he hung up the phone, he glanced at Gloria, measuring her for a minute against all the frustrations the wife of an FBI agent would encounter. Missed meals, calls in the middle of the night, days with no contact, stresses and strains and depression and disillusionment dragged home along with a bone weary body, sometimes bruised, bleeding, or shot full of holes. All of these sacrifices were being made to keep other people from destroying each other and themselves.

He pulled on his pants and shirt. Then he fastened the leather strap on his watch, gave Gloria a final squeeze, and left her apartment, shaking his head. Sometimes, the personal forfeitures one made were extremely hard to bear.

* * * * *

Sitting in his car, Ransom focused on the case. Covering extortion payoffs was tricky; it was something that had to be done with perfect precision. They'd need a solid plan to pull it off. He gunned the Crown Vic, and it leapt forward. As he drove, he tried not to think about the consequences of screwing up.

As he pulled into the Baldazar's neighborhood, he scanned the area, noting the closely mown lawns, the pricey homes, and the high-dollar vehicles gracing the driveways. Despite the supposed protection and security provided by the roadblock, he watched for any person or vehicle that seemed out-of-place. Criminals sometimes did surveillances, checking to see if the cops had been notified about a payoff. He saw no indications that such was the case tonight.

Senator Baldazar answered the door. "Come in, Mr. Ransom."

"I need to talk with you and your wife about the payoff demand."

"Of course, have a seat. I'll just be a moment." He left for a few minutes, and then returned with his pale wife sheltered under his arm. She clutched a peach-colored silk robe close around her. Hunched over, she looked like a woman many years older.

The Baldazars sank onto the living room sofa, and Ransom perched on the edge of an easy chair, gazing at them with an air of authoritative confidence. He needed them to be calm and rational. He hoped for their full co-operation.

"This demand is a positive sign," he said. "The baby is most likely safe and secure, and the kidnapper is willing to deal. We need to—"

"'Most likely,' you said?" Mrs. Baldazar questioned in a strained voice, her eyes red and dreary. She wrung her hands in nervous desperation.

"Almost certainly. Nothing is ever 100 percent, but the fact that the kidnapper made contact with us is very important. At least we're dealing with a rational mind, if somewhat twisted."

"Oh, God," she said, her voice cracking as she burst into another spate of jagged crying. Senator Baldazar put his arm around her and patted her shoulder.

"I'm sorry," Ransom said, "but we've got to turn this situation to our advantage, and I'll need your help."

The Senator stared at him. "We'll do whatever you say. But listen, Mr. Ransom, five hundred thousand dollars in cash is impossible for me to come up with by tomorrow."

"You don't need it. Have you got any cash on hand?"

Baldazar blinked. "Yes, I'd say maybe twenty thousand. I could get more at the bank tomorrow."

"No, we'll use what you have and make up a dummy package. Then we'll cover the drop."

"The *drop*?" Mrs. Baldazar said.

"The kidnapper will ask for the money to be left somewhere. He'll have to pick it up. Usually, they don't wait long, afraid someone will beat them to it."

"And then what?" she asked.

"We'll watch the drop site. We'll either follow him or nab him there, depending on the circumstances."

"And April? Will she be all right?" Mrs. Baldazar's eye twitched.

"We'll follow the kidnapper to her or force him to tell us where she is. We'll do everything possible to get April back safely. You have my word."

"What else can we do?" asked the Senator, squeezing his wife's hand.

"Tell me what you remember about the person who called."

Baldazar said the caller sounded like a Caucasian male in his late twenties or early thirties who used bad grammar, acted nervous, and had a Texas accent. The Senator heard no sounds in the background and recalled no peculiar phrases used. No specific instructions were given. Nothing was mentioned about the location of the drop site.

"He said he'd call back tomorrow," he concluded.

"Did he mention a time?"

The Senator thought about it. "He just said he'd call in the afternoon."

"All right, when he does, I want you to answer it and try to draw the guy out, get him to talk as much as possible. Tell him you're writing down the instructions, ask him questions as if you don't understand some of what he says, and be sure you ask how April is."

"Of course, but how will all that help?"

"We'll have units on the street in the vicinity of where the last call was made. With luck, he'll use the same phone he used on his last contact, or one nearby, and we may be able to grab him before he even quits talking to you."

"That sounds like a long shot."

Ransom shrugged. "We play all the percentages. And we try to leave nothing to chance."

"And then fate still rules," Baldazar said.

The Senator was right, in a way, but he was surprised by the note of fatality in a self-made and very successful man. "'We make our own fortunes and we call them fate,'" Disraeli once said. But, I suppose," Ransom said, "in the last analysis, I agree with you: the hand of God is always involved. We'll all do our best, but it won't hurt to pray, either."

Mrs. Baldazar fixed him with a tormented expression he'd never forget. "That's all I do."

Ransom rose, moved to them, and gave Mrs. Baldazar a gentle touch on the arm. "We'll all send up a plea for April."

She dropped her head in her hands and began to sob.

Ransom talked to the other agents that were stationed there at the senator's house, listened to the recorded call several times, and then telephoned the office. He asked the dispatcher to radio the agents who were eyeballing the Tarmacks' house. The dispatcher relayed back that the crew there said that no one had stirred since he left.

So they're not involved, he thought, tapping his fingertips on the kitchen counter. The husband didn't make the call from the pay phone. His fingers stopped on the hard surface. Or maybe they have another confederate. So, they couldn't be ruled out yet.

He mentally kicked himself that he hadn't put a surveillance team on the ex-con who was shacking with the nurse. He'd get one going first thing in the morning. That would make a lot of things going on at once. But they had to be done.

"Is there anything else you need? asked the dispatcher.

"Sorry, I was just thinking," he said. "No, that's all. Thanks for your help." He hung up, then looked around the kitchen. There was no food in sight, and no cooking smells lingering in the room. Mrs. Baldazar probably hadn't felt up to preparing meals. It might be a long time before their life was normal again. If ever.

* * * * *

As Ransom walked into his apartment, the phone rang.

"So what's happening on the case?" Sonny Jenkins asked.

He filled Sonny in on what they'd done, and then said, "Can we get SOG to watch that pay phone tomorrow?" Then he realized it was already tomorrow.

Jenkins knew what he meant. "Sure. And I got the SWAT team and the other agents lined up to cover the drop. We'll make specific assignments in the morning. Anything else?"

Ransom suggested they put an eyeball on the ex-con. Sonny agreed with the idea. Then they said they'd see each other in the morning.

But as his head sank into the pillow, Ransom's mind swirled with myriad images: The baby, lying somewhere at the mercy of some criminal; the drop site surveillance, requiring the patience of Job, split-second reflexes, and the wisdom of Solomon to pull off; Gloria, the smooth skin and tantalizing curves he'd missed exploring.

He went to the kitchen for a glass of water. Back in his bedroom, he sank into a chair and picked up Walt Whitman's *Leaves of Grass.* He was seeking a feeling of the proper rhythm of life—a sense of order in this chaotic existence. After a half hour he turned off the lamp. It was late, but he knew it would still be a long night.

8

In the morning, Ransom glanced around the squad room at the twenty-some agents there. They were spread out around the square room, some leaned back in chairs, some standing and chatting in small groups, some drinking coffee or talking on the phone. The members of the surveillance teams wore jeans or casual slacks, tennis shoes or cowboy boots, and short sleeve knit shirts or T-shirts. The SWAT guys swaggered about in black uniforms and combat boots, their weapons bristling about them like quills on a porcupine. The others agents wore slacks and sport coats and more merciful expressions.

Jenkins walked into the room from his attached office and called the meeting to order.

Then he started to discuss the kidnapping situation and the ransom demand that had been made. He told how they'd be making the drop of the money package and the surveillance techniques that would be used to cover the drop site. He discussed the details of the basic surveillance plan and then made specific assignments for the various agents. When they started to discuss the details of the plan, Ransom interjected, "Let's have a motorcycle cover the pay phone. If we don't get the kidnapper there, we'll still need a bike rider at the drop site later."

The SOG leader said, "We'll put Phil there with his Harley."

"That's fine," said Jenkins, then asked Ransom, "Have you got the package ready?"

"We're working on it." Then to the group, "We'll have a dummy package with a transmitter you can pick up on channel four. The plane will be up to track it. All voice communications will be on channel two, private."

Jenkins chimed in. "And everyone make sure your radios are coded."

"Have we gotten a time this is going down yet?" someone asked.

"There have been no calls since last night about eleven," Ransom said. "The guy said the payoff would be this afternoon, but he didn't give any more specifics. We'll break off for a while after we finish this meeting, then everyone should be back here a little before noon, and we'll just wait it out."

"Will we take him down at the drop site?" Atherton said.

Jenkins cleared his throat. "That's the big question. It depends on the location of the drop site, how close in we can get, and whether we think we have a good shot at grabbing the guy there. It might even be affected by what the creep says when he calls the Baldazars."

"Who'll make the decision?" said a SWAT guy.

Ransom studied the guy's firm jawline and bulging arms. SWAT team members liked to have everything planned in advance. Which he knew wasn't always possible. But he understood their concern, as they were often putting themselves in harm's way.

"Ransom and I will make the call," Jenkins said. "Jack will wait at the house for the telephone contact, then he'll follow the Senator to the drop. I'll be with the teams at the drop site. We'll confer on the radio, and then we'll pick a strategy."

Jenkins swiveled his head. "Any other questions?"

No one said anything. A couple of guys shook their heads. The SWAT team members stared at their black matte weapons.

"Then we'll see everyone back here at noon," Jenkins said.

Ransom had eaten some cereal and toast earlier, but it could be a long day, so he asked Kathy and Atherton if they'd like to go out for a burrito. Just before they made it out the door, Ransom got a call.

"Ransom," he barked into the receiver.

"It's Billy, Mr. Ransom." Ah, one of his informants.

"Yeah, Billy. Hey, you sound like shit. What's the matter?"

"Oh, uh, I was out drinkin' with a guy last night."

"And you got wasted?"

"Well, I'm feelin' kinda down."

His voice was as gravelly as a country road. It was whiskey rough, especially for a boy barely out of his teens.

"I suppose that will happen."

"I called you yesterday, but they said you was gone."

"I'm sorry, I've been really busy. So what's up?"

"We had a meetin' in the woods the other night." He coughed into the mouthpiece. "There's another one tonight. It sounds like sumthin' big is gonna happen."

Yeah, thought Ransom, like you're going to get laid eight different ways. Why else tag along with that group of loners, losers, and addicts? "Something big, like what?"

"Like they're talking about a blood sacrifice."

"So some farmer's chicken bites the dust?"

"Umm, I dunno. One of the priests was all strung out, like it's some huge deal. He said the head guy would tell us more about it later."

"Okay, why don't you go see what happens, and then let me know. And try to keep Willie One Eye in your pants."

"Aw, Mr. Ransom, I gotta play along with 'em. I don't want to look suspicious."

"Sure, Billy, I understand completely."

He hung up and headed for the door, smiling.

"What an evil smirk," noted Kathy.

"Would you believe the devil made me do it?"

"*Le diable?* I don't want to hear about it."

"Yes you do, but I'm sworn to secrecy."

* * * * *

The restaurant was nearly full with businessmen and people from the neighborhood. It was one of the many Mexican restaurants in San Antonio that had a medium to smallish eating area with bare tables and red vinyl booths closely packed, boisterous sounds of competing conversations, and the clatter of dishes being bussed by slender, long-haired young men. Ransom spotted an empty booth toward the back and they settled in.

As they devoured their burritos and enchiladas and refried beans, Ransom asked Atherton what his take was on the failed security systems at the hospital.

"The repair guy says the alarm over the exit door was in working condition," Hank said. "So, we've got a mystery as to why the baby's bracelet didn't set it off."

"Does the repairman know any way the bracelet can be defeated?" Ransom asked.

"Could it be cut off or compromised in a way that wouldn't set off the alarm?"

"He says it shouldn't happen. Well, there's something called mu metal that can do it, but it's hard to get, and it costs about $1,000 a square foot."

"Moo metal?" Ransom asked.

"M-U metal. It's pretty rare."

"Could someone around here get some of it?"

"He said he doubted it."

"Anything else that would work?"

Atherton nodded. "He said that some kinds of foil could do it. They interfere with the signal, and it doesn't set off the alarm the way it should."

"Damn. What about the security camera?"

"That's another question mark. I've got some suspicions about the security guys who monitor those cameras."

"Like what?"

"I can't get anyone to admit it, but I think one or both of the men going off duty at 6:00 a.m. may have left a little early."

"And what does that mean?"

"If the two security men coming on duty didn't get there at the same time, or if one of them went for coffee, that would leave one person there alone with the equipment at the crucial time."

"And give him a chance to disable the monitor or the camera?"

"Someone who knows how the system works could have pulled a wire loose or somehow defeated the camera and the alarm."

"Who are the two men who came on duty at six?"

"Rolando Garcia and Ben Jackson."

"Let's check out backgrounds on those two. Talk with Winnie Blankenship about them. Get their work records, see who has been there the shortest time and whether either of them have had any problems at work. Put them under a microscope, then let's interview them again. If they sabotaged the camera or the alarm, they'll know who grabbed the baby."

"That's the way I see it," Atherton agreed, his jaw muscles set in determination.

* * * * *

Two burritos and a glass of milk later, Ransom drove in stupefied silence to the Baldazar's house. Kathy rode along, but her mind seemed elsewhere. He radioed the agents at the house. No calls had been received.

"Do you think the kidnappers will call back?" asked Kathy.

"If they want the five hundred G's."

"That's a good point."

He picked up the mike and radioed the surveillance teams who'd been watching the Tarmack house.

Ball Cap came on the air. "It was dead as Kelsey's nuts last night," he said. "They went lights out about ten o'clock. This morning the wife drove to a convenience store, but she came right back. The guy hasn't budged from the house, and we haven't seen a baby."

"There've been no more calls to the Baldazar's house," Ransom said. "So keep an eyeball out. When's your replacement due?"

"Uhhh, let's see, they should be here . . . within the hour."

"That's good. Thanks for the help."

"No problem."

Next he radioed the team watching the ex-con and his squeeze.

"Six lima. We got on them about nine this morning. The guy stumbled out and grabbed the paper a few minutes after ten. He had a three day beard and shaggy hair, wearing ripped up jeans, no shirt or shoes, lots of jailhouse tattoos. Looked like your regular scumbag. He even checked around like he was watching for a tail."

"No shit?"

"It may have just been a reflex. Anyway, he didn't spot us. We haven't seen the nursie, but her car's parked in the driveway."

"Let me know if the guy even passes gas."

"That's a big roger. We're on him like fleas on a dog."

Ransom pulled to the curb beneath a shade tree several houses down from the Baldazar's. He saw no one watching the street, so he and Kathy got out and strolled down the sidewalk. That's right, anyone who's watching, we're just a couple out for a little afternoon walk.

A shiny midnight blue Mercedes was parked in the driveway. The license plate read: SENATE 1. It must be nice, thought Ransom.

The Senator answered the door. He was unusually pale, Ransom noticed. Maybe it was the strain. But behind the coke bottle lenses, the dark eyes shone with intelligence.

"Nothing has happened," he said. "Shouldn't they have called again by now?" He crossed his arms across his chest.

"I imagine they'll call soon," Ransom said. "Here's the dummy package. The cash should go on the outside of the stacks." He thumbed some piles of paper. "This cut up paper will go on the inside. It'll work for a while, until they have a chance to examine it. And we'll nab them before that happens."

"They?" questioned the Senator.

"There was a female kidnapper and a male caller. There have to be at least two of them."

"Of course, I see what you're saying."

Ransom noted that Mrs. Baldazar was nowhere in sight.

The legislator must have read his mind. "My wife's in the bedroom. She's beat, and the doctor gave her a sedative. I can handle the contact, though."

Baldazar did seem quite calm and in control of himself. But even though he was a Senator used to handling crucial problems, Ransom was surprised he was so cool.

Ransom and Kathy sat at the dining room table and assembled the package: the twenty thousand in cash, the cut paper, and the transmitter. When they'd finished their work, the package sat mutely in the middle of the table, and everyone stared at it.

"We might as well get comfortable," said Ransom, shooting a glance into the living room.

"Yes, make yourself at home," the Senator offered.

They all sank into cushiony chairs and sofas. Ransom fiddled with a throw pillow embroidered with a Greek drawing. It looks very expensive, he thought. None of them spoke much for the next two hours. Then the telephone rang.

The trap and trace was on. The agent on the extension activated the recorder and signaled the Senator to be ready to answer. On the count of three, they both clicked on the phones.

"Hello," said the Senator, his voice cracking.

A low voice said, "Okay, Senator, this is what I want you to do."

Ransom watched as the agent scribbled down the kidnapper's instructions: Put money in a brown paper bag. Go to Olmos Basin Park, four p.m. Drive over bridge, stop where red bandana tied to stake, drop bag over side. Get back into car, drive home, wait. Will get call—baby location.

Both the Senator and the agent hung up.

"What else did he say?" Ransom asked the agent.

The man paused, regarding the Senator.

The Senator said, "He told me . . . ." He hesitated, swallowing hard. "He said for me not to call the police, or the baby was dead."

"There's no choice about that," Ransom said. "We've got to play it out all the way."

The Senator stood there staring at the wall, his eyes going unfocused.

Ransom and the other agent watched him.

Baldazar turned to Ransom and nodded. "I'll get a paper bag."

Ransom took a deep breath and called on his handi talkie to the agents watching the pay phone from which the original ransom call had been made. Nothing had happened there. He looked at Sonny Jenkins, who was monitoring the operation of the trap and trace equipment.

"What was the number that was called from just now?"

Sonny said, "It was a different number from the first call. The phone company equipment shows it as a pay phone outside a convenience store, still on Hildebrande, but farther east, on the other side of the expressway."

Sonny muttered something Ransom didn't hear, and then said, "I'll get a couple of guys to cover it, but I'm sure it's too late." He called on the handi talkie. In a few minutes he found out he was right. No one was hanging around the phone or even close by.

"Shit," said Jenkins after hearing the transmission on the radio.

"That's okay," Ransom said. "We'll grab the guy at the drop site."

"Let's get set up out there," Jenkins said. "SWAT can put some guys in the bushes beneath the bridge. And I'll get the plane up."

"I'll be in the Senator's back seat," Ransom said.

They had an hour to make their plans. But in the end, it was pretty simple. They'd make the run to the bridge with the Senator driving his Mercedes and Ransom crouched on the back seat floorboard. Ransom would carry an MP-5 semi-automatic rifle in case he got the chance to spray some people. Otherwise, they'd make the drop, leave the scene and hope the perp showed up so the SWAT guys could nail him.

Ransom fiddled with the transmitter in the package for the third time, making sure it worked. Kathy tried to make small talk, but it fell flat, so they sat there and stared at the furniture. Then Ransom looked at his watch for the hundredth time. "We need to go." He handed the full brown paper bag to the Senator who regarded it as if it were something vile.

Outside, Ransom pulled the MP-5 from his car trunk, checked it over, then handed Kathy the car keys. "Follow us, but stay back a couple of blocks. Someone might try to tail us or force us off the road. Bring one of the other agents with you."

Baldazar climbed into the Mercedes, dropping the bag on the front seat beside him. The door shut with a solid clunk. Ransom eased into the back seat and settled himself on the floorboard. He shoved a loaded magazine into the short rifle.

Baldazar started up the diesel engine and made the six minute drive to the drop site.

Agents were everywhere. In a gold two-door Camaro, a young male and female agent were ostensibly making out. Another agent wearing a cowboy hat slouched in the seat of a dilapidated pickup, reading a racing form. A third vehicle had its hood up, with what looked like two agitated businessmen in ties staring at the dead engine. A faded blue Ford van huddled under some trees, loaded with Sonny Jenkins, four agents, and photographic equipment which included cameras, lenses, light meters, tripods, and shutter cables for remote photo taking.

"I'm approaching the bridge," Baldazar said.

"Do you see anyone around?" Ransom said from the back seat.

"There's no one there. It's deserted. What should I do?"

"Drive across and make the drop."

"Damn. All right, here we go."

Ransom felt a bump as they pulled onto the bridge. The Mercedes' air conditioner was pumping hard, but it was still hot on the floorboard. From that and the tension, Ransom was sweating like a lumberjack swinging an axe at a giant redwood. His legs had started to cramp, and he tried to stretch them, with no success.

"We're halfway across," said Baldazar, "and I haven't seen a . . . wait, I think it's up ahead." There was a pause as the car rolled on. "Yes, there's a stick with a red bandana tied to it. The wind must have blown it over."

"Do you see anyone around anywhere now?"

"Not a soul."

"All right, go ahead and stop by the bandana and drop the package off the bridge."

The Senator trod the brake a little hard, thumping Ransom into the back of the front seat.

"I'm sorry," he said, "I'm really nervous."

"That's okay. Just make the drop and get back in."

Baldazar opened the door and slid out.

Ransom listened hard. A helicopter whop-whopped overhead. He could hear highway noises. Hot, humid air poured in through the open door, making it hard to breathe. His heart slammed in his chest about a hundred miles an hour. He gripped and re-gripped the rifle.

In a minute, Baldazar climbed back in and shut the door.

"What happened?"

"I dropped the bag off the bridge. It landed in some tall grass. I didn't see anyone anywhere around it. Should we go on?"

"Yeah, let's roll."

Baldazar hit the pedal and pulled away, bumping along the top of the bridge. Once across the span, he continued on, taking a different route back home.

On the way, Ransom radioed Kathy on his handi talkie.

"Did we have any company?"

"Negative. There wasn't anyone anywhere close behind you. I've still got the bridge in sight, and I don't think anyone has made a move on the package, either."

"You'd better go back to the house in case we get a call to pick up the baby."

"Ten-four. I'll see you there." As she stared at the scene, she remembered the Cajun story of the bridge over the bayou that was a giant alligator. At night it would eat farmer's cows. She hoped *le pont* in this case wouldn't take a bite out of anyone's *derriere.*

Ransom eased himself out of the confining space and up onto the back seat. He glanced out at the passing scenery as he rode in the luxury car with a driver. So this was what it was like to be rich and have a chauffeur. Not too shabby.

* * * * *

Hank Atherton stretched his arm out, grabbed the stalk of a long blade of grass that kept tickling his face, and bent it away from him. His fatigues were too heavy for this heat, and lying in the brush and long grass down beneath the bridge made him feel itchy all over. But at this moment, he wouldn't want to be anywhere else.

He was twenty-five feet from the brown paper bag that Baldazar had tossed from the bridge. Other SWAT team members were there, too, dug in and hidden like trapdoor spiders, but he was the closest. He'd likely get first crack at the kidnapper when he came after his payoff.

To him, this was what the job was all about. He hated the paperwork, dressing in a suit every day, and he even tired of interviewing people, writing down their lies and excuses for why they'd pulled their particular crimes. But the action—chasing, confronting and handcuffing bad guys— that was what brought cheer to his soul and kept him slogging through the dull moments of the job.

When you got down to it, he wouldn't mind cranking off a few rounds at someone. He hadn't been in a real shootout yet. It might be a rush.

He scanned the grassy field. There were a few worn paths from people walking or biking, but at the moment, the area was deserted. That is, except for the SWAT guys spread around the site. Jenkins had given them the green light, so once the creep came after the package, there was no way he'd get out of this little valley. They'd wrap him up like a caterpillar in his cocoon. They could use their weapons, if necessary. But they didn't want to kill the suspect. They wanted to be able to squeeze the jerk until he told them where the kid was.

Now that kind of interview he could handle.

He waited for another forty-five minutes. A wire from his handi talkie ran up his back, out his collar, and ended in a plug in his right ear. Every ten minutes or so, the SWAT team leader would check to see if anyone had seen anything, although he knew they hadn't. It just made it seem like they were doing something.

Now Atherton heard the far off buzz of a motorcycle, and the hair on the back of his neck stiffened. He wiped sweat from his forehead before it could leak into his eyes. Sure enough, the sound of the motor got louder and louder. And then he saw a red Suzuki entering the field from the far end of the bridge, following a dirt path, heading toward him.

The rider was a Caucasian male, about twenty-five years old, maybe six feet tall, stocky, long dirty brown hair, moustache, no helmet, wearing a white T-shirt and jeans, with scuffed motorcycle boots—Atherton absorbed it all in seconds as the guy gunned the bike down the trail.

"This might be him," said the team leader.

Atherton was flexed, ready to spring. But he had to wait until the guy grabbed the bag. Come on, punk. Do your thing, so I can do mine.

And now the motorcycle slowed, just at the right time. The rider wore steel-rimmed glasses, and his eyes searched the ground. And it looked as if he'd spotted it. He slowed to a stop, still wrenching the cycle's throttle, racing the motor. There was a blue bandana tied around his forehead, but his neck and cheeks were slick with sweat. He leaned down to the ground and snatched up the bag.

Atherton was up. As he charged, he caught glimpses of other dark shapes in his peripheral vision, all converging on the bike. But he focused on the guy's hands. One held the bag, and the other still revved the throttle. If the hands made a move toward the waist or back, or any part of the cycle, and a dark or shiny shape came into either of those hands, Atherton would point his pistol first at the man's chest, then his head. He'd snap off two shots to each spot.

Now the man saw him, his eyes got wide behind the tinted lenses, and he leaned forward on his bike and let out the clutch. Atherton was ten feet away, his legs pumping. He'd hit the guy with a forearm shiver on the chest or shoulder and knock him off the bike.

Dirt flew from the cycle's rear tire as the man roared forward. Atherton was almost there. His left arm came up to deliver the crunching blow. The target was moving, and Atherton adjusted his attack.

He missed with the forearm, but his elbow hit the man's shoulder, tilting him over. The guy was going down. Atherton got ready to pounce.

But the man jerked himself to an upright position, revved the throttle hard, and managed to roar away, with none of the other agents able to block his escape.

Someone cracked off two shots, with no effect.

"Hold it," the team leader yelled, for the car and the van were in motion, trying to block the guy's exit, putting themselves in the line of fire.

With the tails of his blue bandana streaming straight out behind him, the guy angled to his left, plowing through heavy grass, cutting a new path. He skirted the vehicles that were trying to stop him, then cut back to his right and climbed the ridge, which gave him a clear run onto the road.

As he sped away, the roar of another bike joined in, and an agent who'd been stationed at the far end of the bridge zoomed along the top of it at a speed that made Atherton hold his breath. The hog bounced hard a couple of times, but the agent wrestled the handlebars to keep it upright all the way across the bridge, then he swung onto the highway behind the fleeing figure.

"Come on, man," Atherton yelled. "Stay on his ass!"

9

As they waited for the scene to play out at Olmos Park basin, Ransom, the other agents, and Mr. Baldazar sat in upholstered chairs in the Baldazar's living room, drumming their fingers on the wooden arms or crossing and re-crossing their legs and jiggling their feet. At various times they got up and paced around the room, their footsteps muted to silence by the thick carpeting. Coffee was offered, but no one wanted any. Nervous trips were made to the bathroom. But still, there was no call from the kidnappers.

They all listened to the radio traffic on a handi talkie. For a while, nothing at all happened. Then they heard that the perp had picked up the package and taken off on a motorcycle. On their feet now, they heard that the van and another car were scrambling to block the guy's escape, but somehow he evaded them and made it onto the highway. An agent named Phil Lighthall was riding close behind the guy on his Harley. Other vehicles were joining the chase.

Ransom just managed to avoid swearing. All he could do was grit his teeth and listen to the drama being relayed on the air. He wished he could commandeer an F-16 to swoop down, target the kidnapper, then strafe and destroy him.

In fact, as the transmitter in the package beamed its signal, an FBI plane was up and locked onto it. The spotter in the blue-and-white Cessna Centurion had an eyeball on the subject tearing along the highway, followed by another cycle, and, farther back, two bureau cars, a pickup, and a van. The subject was headed north on the McAlester Freeway, or Highway 281, which meant that soon the plane might have to circumnavigate the crowded air space over the airport. It would likely have to quit the surveillance until the chase entered a less congested area.

Traffic on the freeway was moderate, and the agent on the motorcycle, who roared along a hundred yards behind the subject, radioed that he was glued to the pigeon. He sounded confident that he could stay with the fleeing kidnapper.

* * * * *

Phil Lighthall loved to run his Harley Super Glide on the open road, the wind rushing around his faring, the thunder of the motor vibrating beneath him and falling away behind. Like Atherton, he loved the thrill of the chase. The trouble was, he could chase this guy to Kerrville, but he didn't know how to stop him. Maybe the asshole would run out of gas, he thought. Or he might go down on a curve. But the prick seemed to handle his crotch-rocket Suzuki well, so Phil wasn't too hopeful about those possibilities.

He considered creeping up closer to the man's bike, but he could visualize the guy twisting his upper body just enough to allow him to fire some hunks of lead back at him. Phil was wearing a bulletproof Kevlar vest, but if he got hit while pushing his Harley ninety miles an hour on pavement, there would likely be nothing left of him but a long grease spot to scrape up and bury.

He tried to flow with his own rumbling machine's momentum. He willed himself to relax, to hang loose. But his adrenaline was pumping about a quart a minute, making him quite jittery.

Sonny Jenkins radioed him, but Phil could barely make out the message. Sonny was in the trailing van and wanted to know the situation. Something about the state DPS setting up a roadblock.

"This is two lima, number five," Phil answered. "I'm right behind him, coming up on the Loop 410 exit, and he's . . . okay, he went straight, didn't take the exit. He's still heading north on 281."

"Stay with him. We're right behind you."

Typical position for a supervisor, thought Phil, banking into a curve.

With the DPS radio in the van, Jenkins got through to a couple of state troopers who were working a speed trap north of San Antonio on the freeway. Being jostled as he talked, with the van blazing along at ninety-five, trying to close the gap on the motorcycles, Jenkins explained the situation. The troopers said they'd be glad to set up a roadblock ahead of the approaching motorcycles.

In a few minutes Phil saw the two patrol vehicles, angled nose to nose, blocking the highway lanes. The troopers were crouched behind the vehicles, shotguns extended over the trunks. It looked as if this could be the moment he'd been waiting for.

The FBI Cessna glided low, watching the action. But just then a helicopter swerved in from the right, angling down toward the highway, a camera pointed at the roadblock. It was headed into the Cessna's path.

"Son of a bitch!" the Cessna pilot shouted, veering to the left.

"What's the matter?" Jenkins yelled.

"Some fucking press helicopter almost clipped us. We're out of position, now. I'll have to come back around."

"Can you see the troopers? Are they stopping the guy?" Jenkins asked.

"Just a minute," said the pilot, banking into a turn.

Beneath the din of the hovering helicopter and the circling plane, the biker with the bandana squeezed his handbrakes hard, tires screeching, slowing. Still two hundred yards to the barricade, the biker thought, trying to decide how to play it. Within seconds, he wheeled to his right onto a rutted dirt and gravel road some forty yards in front of the barricade, headed east.

Lighthall also made the turn. Dust flew high, and the road surface scrunched and gave way, causing him to twist like a snake to keep his balance. This was a brand new game.

The kidnapper had nullified the roadblock, and he'd found a potential escape route. Chances were that the trailing cars couldn't keep up with the motorcycles on this barely graveled road. Phil hit a jarring bump, cursed, then roared ahead through the gritty mist being thrown up by the fleeing man's bike. But he'd ridden on a lot of country roads on weekend trips. He might be able to stay with the kidnapper. That is, if the man didn't push his sleek bike even harder.

Within a few minutes, Phil saw in his rear-view mirror that the other vehicles were falling back. Now he knew it was up to him to stop this guy. He took a deep breath, goosed the throttle, and moved up on the kidnapper. If he could only hang on, maybe he could bring the prick down.

Forty yards away, thirty, fifteen. Now the guy seemed to sense his presence and he throttled up the pace. But Phil was committed to the chase, and he revved his Harley to a throaty scream. He closed the gap until his front wheel was even with the rear tire of the Suzuki. The guy looked over at him, but he didn't go for a gun. If he had, Phil would've creamed the bastard.

He signaled the man to stop, but the guy turned his head to the front and tried to push the edge of the envelope. They were about as flat out as they could go on this surface without flipping up to the moon if they hit a bad rut. Now Phil had no choice. He moved up, inches at a time, then angled over, trying to bump the rear tire. The guy flinched away.

Twice more he tried, but the guy kept dodging. They were nearing the left side of the road. If a car came over a hill heading their way . . . .

This is it, Phil thought. He wrenched the throttle open, edged up beside the hurtling Suzuki, gathered himself in, then kicked his left boot into the man's right leg. The guy's front tire wobbled—he was going down.

But no, the son of a bitch was still up and highballing. He'd somehow pulled his bike back on track.

They rumbled ahead, spewing dirt and pieces of gravel from their tires. Phil caught up again, and then stayed even with the guy. He tried to signal him again, but with no luck. He clenched his jaw and moved closer to the Suzuki.

This time he'd kick as hard as he could, praying that he connected with something solid; if he missed, he'd probably go down. He held his breath, launched his leg into space, and his boot crunched into the man's right shoulder. The guy teetered over to the left, tried to straighten up, then he lost it—the Suzuki spun out from under him—and he hurtled along the rough road without benefit of wheels.

The scruffy biker tumbled and skidded every which way. Throttling down his bike, Phil watched the show in awe. Finally, the whirling form came to rest, now totally limp, face down in the dirt at the side of the road.

"Jesus Christ," Phil said as he braked and stopped thirty feet from the downed man. He got off his bike and pulled out his pistol, then approached the motionless lump with cautious steps. He heard the vehicles of the other agents braking and crunching dirt as they pulled up behind him. When he got within a few feet of the body, he heard a moan. Phil held his breath. Another groan, a leg twitch, and then the man moved his right arm.

Phil hustled up to the guy, grabbed his arm and pulled it behind his back, clamping on a cuff. Then he cuffed the other hand. He turned the man's dirt-encrusted face to the side.

"Are you all right, man?"

The guy raised his head a little, his forehead scraped and bloody, then opened his eyes and peered up at Lighthall. "Don't you fuckers ever give up?"

* * * * *

They took Easy Rider to the emergency ward. The doctor could find nothing wrong with him but a plethora of cuts and bruises. "By tomorrow," he said to the bandaged figure, "you'll know a new meaning of the word sore."

"We'll need to keep him a couple of days for observation," the doctor told Sonny Jenkins who was standing by the bedside, his arms crossed, wisps of hair strung crossways, staring at the guy as if he'd like to fillet him.

"We need to talk with him," Jenkins replied.

"It'd probably be better tomorrow," the doctor hedged.

"This is a life-and-death matter. Unless it's extremely threatening to his health, we're going to talk to him *now*."

The physician adjusted his glasses and studied the patient. "Well, he's not in any immediate danger."

"Good. We'll start in five minutes."

Jenkins found Ransom pacing the corridor.

"Did you find out anything?" Ransom asked.

"Not yet, the doc's been checking him out. They can't believe the guy doesn't have internal injuries, so they're watching him close. You want to take a crack at him?"

Ransom grinned. "It'll be my pleasure."

Jenkins briefed him on what he'd learned about Herman Manson's background. Hopefully, he noted, the guy was no kin to Charlie. They'd checked him on all the computer banks. His criminal record showed several drunk and disorderly conduct charges, one assaulting an officer beef, one burglary, two bad check raps, and a rape charge for which he'd spent four years in state prison at Huntsville. Ransom had seen lots worse.

He turned to Kathy, whose complexion looked like bone china under the fluorescent lights. "Would you care to help grill him?"

"You bet. And I'll bring the hot sauce."

* * * * *

Herman was propped up in bed with a bandage on his head that resembled a skullcap. Ransom was glad it wasn't leaking blood like in the war movies. The guy's face wore scrapes, a stubbly beard, and a scowl. It was obvious that he was no happy camper.

Ransom introduced himself and Kathy, then looked the man over. Behind the cold glare he could see two things: pain and fear. The man adjusted his bent spectacles.

"I know you're hurting now, Herman, but the doc says you'll be fine. And you know you're lucky to be alive."

"If I'm so lucky, you wanna trade places?"

"No, you're right, you're in a jam. We could file so many charges on you that your grandkids would never see you."

The guy stared at his hands. "You *could* file charges? Or you could do *what*?"

Good, Herman was no dummy. He'd caught the implication. Ransom shrugged. "You figure it out."

Herman looked at Kathy.

She said, "Smart fox like you should be able to think of an angle."

He studied his bandaged arm. Then he said, "You want to know about the kid?"

Ransom nodded. "That's the only important thing here."

Herman's jaw tightened. Behind his eyes, thoughts whirred like sharp blades. "Here's the deal," he said to Ransom. "You and me go together. Just us two. No one following us."

Ransom waited, knowing more was coming.

"She's fine. I'll take you to her. You get the kid, and I walk."

Ransom pinched his lip, and then said, "I can't promise you any free rides. You know better. You're in too deep. But I'll tell the prosecutor you turned over the baby. You'll be exposing yourself to a lot less time if she's all right."

"Just the two of us go to find her?"

Ransom shrugged. "I'll ask my boss."

In the hallway he told Jenkins what Manson had offered.

"What do you think?" Jenkins asked.

Ransom glanced at Kathy. "What was your take on it?"

"The guy's savvy to the system," she said. "He knows he's sunk. I think he's trying to salvage what he can."

Jenkins crinkled his brow. He turned to Ransom. "Why would he just want you to go?"

Ransom smiled. Jenkins didn't miss much.

"That's what makes me think it's bullshit. This guy does things off the cuff—his record shows it. He's been a burglar, written bad checks, done a couple of rapes. He's involved in crimes of opportunity. He never plans anything out and then does it, like an armed robbery or a kidnapping."

Kathy said, "So you think he's conning us?"

Ransom's head bobbed as he gave a sly smile. "I don't find a gleam of incentive in the guy. I think he read the paper about the baby and saw a chance to make a score. Now he's scrambling for a way out of his troubles."

"You don't want to go with him?" Jenkins asked.

Ransom shook his head. "Sonny, I can't afford to risk a baby's life on my conjectures. Sure, I'll go with him. Maybe he'll take us right to the child."

"But we'll follow you," Jenkins said, now adamant.

"No, we can't take that chance, either. I need to know the guy's true motives." He looked at the wall and sighed. "I'll take a transmitter with me, strap it on my back, and you guys can follow me. Like from a couple of miles away."

"That's not close enough for us to help if you get in a bind," Sonny said. "He may lead you right to some of his cronies."

"That's true. But I've got to take that risk. Anyway, I'm a hell of a runner when I have to be."

Jenkins grimaced, Kathy muttered some Cajun curses, but they had no other ideas. There was no other way to play it.

* * * * *

Atherton went with Ransom to get Herman strapped into the car seat. The man's hands were handcuffed in front where Ransom could see them. As Ransom slid into the driver's seat, he glanced at the silver manacles gleaming in the lights of the parking lot.

Atherton walked around the car to talk to Ransom. He leaned down and peered into the car, but his gaze was on Herman, not Ransom, as he said, "If this asshole gives you any trouble, don't hesitate to shoot him. We can make up a good story later."

Ransom smiled and gave him an Australian accent. "No worries, mate."

Atherton slapped the top of the car, then he stepped aside as Ransom backed out, dropped the Crown Vic into drive, and said to his passenger, "Which way?"

Herman gave him a series of directions: Wurzback Road to Fredericksburg Road, north until it intersected with Highway 10, then continuing on until they took the eastbound exit at Loop 1604. They drove on until they hit a stretch that was dark, wooded, and secluded.

"We're almost there," Herman said.

Ransom would have bet that was coming.

"Who else will be there?"

"Just my girlfriend and the kid. She'll wait there until I come back."

"You've been gone a long time. What if she left?"

He snorted. "She's in a van with a quarter tank of gas and no money. Where do you think she's going?"

"I gotcha. Does she have a gun?"

Herman laughed. "Don't worry, Mr. Fed, we won't hurt you."

Ransom knew he meant the opposite.

"Slow down," said Herman, pointing, "and take that road up there to the left."

Ransom did, and his heartbeat quickened as he looked the area over, seeing nothing but the foreboding outline of a dense cluster of woods caught in the harsh headlights.

"Around this curve," Herman said, leaning forward, "then stop. The van's back in the woods. We'll walk in. You guys never would've spotted it."

Ransom was listening for every shade of meaning in every syllable. The guy was conwise, so he didn't let out much emotion. Still, there was a nervous edge to the way the words clipped out of his mouth.

Ransom stopped the car. The partial moon overhead struggled to penetrate the gloom beneath the live oak, elm, and hackberry trees. He cracked his window, listening to the wind sighing through the leaves. A scampering sound alerted him. He decided it was probably just a rabbit.

There was nothing else to do, so he grabbed a flashlight, opened his door and walked around to let Herman out. His footsteps were muffled in the soft dirt road. Darkness pressed in on him.

He undid Herman's seat belt, gripped his arm and pulled. "Let's go."

Herman came out of the car, stood there swiveling his head, then said, "This way," and started striding toward the trees to the left side of the road.

In a minute, Ransom could make out a clearing ahead of them, but he saw no tracks that a van would make. The grass was half a foot high in the open field which curved around to the right behind the trees. Herman headed that way, so Ransom stayed with him, his eyes straining in the darkness. He held off turning on the flashlight, not wanting to alert anyone that they were coming. A wavering buzz from thousands of cicadas rained down from the trees, shutting out lesser, but more meaningful sounds.

As they rounded the curve, Herman tilted his head toward a dark space behind the trees. "Over there," he said. And Ransom stared at the spot he'd indicated, could make out nothing at all, and flicked on his flashlight, searching for whatever he could see.

Then Herman jerked to his left, pulling his arm loose from Ransom's grasp. Once free, he drew back his foot and threw a sidekick into Ransom's thigh. Ransom cringed as his muscle cramped and his leg bent inward.

Herman swung both hands toward Ransom's head. Ransom figured it was coming, but he reacted too late, and the blow bounced off the side of his head, knocking him off balance. He fell to a knee and dropped the flashlight, which rolled away into the darkness.

The next kick went for Ransom's exposed side, catching him in the ribs with a force that expelled his breath with a whoosh and a grunt. Herman moved behind him and his hands scrabbled at Ransom's pistol. But Ransom clutched the pistol above the trigger guard, and then twisted his torso in a snapping movement that wrenched Herman's hand free of the weapon.

Now Herman shot his hands over Ransom's head and yanked back hard. The links between the handcuffs cut into Ransom's throat. Ransom clutched at the choking steel but couldn't pull it away. He struggled to his feet, the pressure on his windpipe unbearable. Dizziness consumed him, and his legs felt rubbery.

Tensing his neck, holding off the grinding constriction, he raised his right leg, then stomped the top of Herman's foot, smashing small bones. The pressure at his throat eased, and he sucked in a breath, then ducked his shoulder and shot his elbow back into Herman's solar plexus.

It was Herman's turn to deflate. He bent forward, giving Ransom room to grab his wrists, force them upward, and slip out from under the choke hold. He spun around, still holding Herman's hands aloft, and kicked him in the crotch.

Herman let out a terrible moan and went to his knees. Ransom let go of his hands, then grabbed Herman with one hand by the throat, his thumb digging hard into the trachea.

"Now if you really know anything, take me to the baby."

"You're choking me," Herman gurgled.

Ransom loosened his grip a little. "Where's the baby?"

"You goddamn pig!" He held his groin. "My nuts are killing me."

"All's fair in love and fistfights. Now don't make me ask you again." He tightened his hold on Herman's throat.

"No, wait," Herman said, his hands going to his throat as he kept losing his wind, "I'll . . . tell you," he wheezed.

"So talk."

"It was a scam, man. That's all." He cleared his raspy voice and coughed. "I . . . I lost my job," he said. "I'm almost broke, and when I read about the kidnapping, I saw a chance to make some bucks."

"Why'd you bring me to the woods?"

"I made that up as I went along. It was stupid, but I figured I had a chance to book it." He rubbed the front of his throat.

"You're right."

"Huh?"

"It was stupid."

10

Back at the hospital, Ransom told the other agents about the ambush in the woods. Jenkins's face grew red as Ransom related the details of the attack. The others looked pissed off and grim.

"But you don't think he had anything to do with kidnapping the baby?" Jenkins asked. "Does he have any information at all, do you think?"

"It's possible, but I doubt it. We had a heart-to-heart chat about the situation. It'll be awhile before Herman can talk again without squeaking."

"Spare me the details."

Jenkins glanced around at the tired faces of the agents. "We've done all we can do for now. Let's go home."

As the others trudged out of the room, Jenkins turned to Ransom.

"You took a big risk out there, and you handled it great. Everyone is proud of you." He patted Ransom on the back. "Now get home and get some rest."

"I will, but first I've got to tell the Baldazars—"

"No," Jenkins interrupted, "let me handle that."

Ransom was tempted, but he felt a strong obligation.

"They'll be expecting to hear from me."

"They'll be stunned by the news, Jack. Let them blow up at me, if they need to. You have to keep a good rapport with them. It might be important later."

Ransom thought about it, gave a tired half-smile, and ambled out of the room, his fingertips exploring the welt around his neck. On the way down the hall, he stopped by the bank of vending machines to buy a candy bar and a Diet Coke. Even though it was a quarter to ten, he didn't feel hungry enough for a meal. He thought for a few moments about going by Gloria's, but he felt as tired as a plow mule, and he didn't want to chalk up another failure in the bedroom.

Ten minutes after he got home, his phone rang. It must be Gloria, he thought. Maybe she'd felt a yearning for him, too. Besides, she was probably worried out of her mind.

"Hello there." Ransom said in his sultry voice.

"Hi, uh, Dad. It's Scott."

"Oh . . . hi, son. Is everything all right?"

"Sure, why?"

"It's pretty late."

"I've been calling all evening. Mom said I could try one more time."

"Sorry, I was out working on a case. So what's going on?"

"It's about my stupid math test."

"What about it?"

"I messed up on some things and the teacher gave me a bad grade. But I'll do better next time—really. I promise."

"Just how bad was the grade?"

"I got a D. But I still have a C in the class. And it's a really hard one. Nobody's doing so good 'cause the stupid teacher's so tough."

Ransom recalled his own math teachers had been tough, too. To the tune of an occasional F, as he recalled. Could this be an inherited weakness?

"Have you been studying hard, Son?"

"Yeah, you know. Pretty much."

"Hmm. Okay, next weekend, when you come over, we'll look over your test to see what parts you might not understand."

"Can we shoot some baskets Saturday morning?"

"I've got that marathon race then, but how about in the afternoon?"

"Oh, yeah," he said, some of his verve gone, "I forgot about your race."

Was he thinking your *stupid* race?

"And maybe we could see a movie Sunday afternoon." All right, he wasn't above bribing his kid, if needed.

"That'd be good," Scott said. "Oh, Mom says I got to go to bed now."

This hit Ransom with a thud. He realized how much he wanted to kiss his kids goodnight, and to peek in later to see their faces as they slept. Now he barely connected with them, and it felt as though his spirit, his very being was shriveling day by day.

"Sure, Champ. Goodnight. Oh, hey, is your sis there?"

"Nah, she's out with some creep. She's late getting home, and Mom's pissed off."

"Let's watch the language."

"Sorry. Uh, Mom wants to talk to you. See you later."

"See you," he said, as the receiver clattered on the countertop.

In a minute she came on. "How are you, Jack?"

"Fine . . . well, I'm beat."

"Of course you are. Well, I just wanted to say it was nice to see you the other night."

"It seemed awkward to me."

"I guess it was, but still . . . ." She paused, then said, "You looked quite trim, you must be jogging a lot."

"I'm still training for the marathon." He sagged onto a kitchen stool, feeling tiredness seep throughout his body. He probably couldn't jog a mile right now.

"I've been going to an aerobics class myself."

"I thought you looked, I mean, that's good. Good *for* you, that is."

"I feel more energetic. And I need it with these kids . . . oh, hold on."

He could hear muffled voices in the background. Then she said, "That was Holly coming in from her date. She's late, as usual."

"Who's the guy?"

"Don't ask. He's no one you know, or want to. I hope she dumps him soon."

"Don't tell her you don't like him, or she'll be even more attracted."

"I try to hide my contempt."

"That's a good tactic."

"I'm glad you think so. I miss having someone to talk over ideas with. These kids are difficult to handle alone."

"I'm sure it's hard."

"Every day there are a hundred decisions to make."

"Yeah, that must be a hassle." He squirmed on the stool.

"Then there's the cooking, cleaning, and taxi service. It seems like I never catch up with all there is to do."

"That does sound brutal. Maybe you could get a housemaid."

"I don't have the money for that. But I don't mean to complain. Everyone's got problems, right?"

"Uh, huh. Sure."

"What I'm trying to say is that kids need both of their parents. Even with us apart, they still depend on you as their father."

"I try to keep in touch. It's just that I'm busy at work now."

"You've always been that way, Jack."

"I know. You're right." He put his hand to his forehead. "But we're looking for a kidnapped baby."

"I see. I know that's a crucial situation, but, Jack, I think you have to give some of your time and energy to your own kids, too."

"I was just trying to explain why I've been tied up."

"Holly is volatile and suggestive right now. She needs your guidance. I'm scared she'll go in the wrong direction."

"I don't think she listens to me, anyway."

"She's angry, confused, and lost. She may seem like she's ignoring you, but I believe some of it sinks in."

"That's reassuring."

"And Scott needs a male role model, you know that. All I ask is that you be there for these children."

"Bev, I know what you're saying, but I'm exhausted right now. I'm sorry. We'll talk more later, I promise. Okay?"

"Yes, of course. Thanks for listening. I'll talk to you later, then."

"Good-bye," he said, hanging up. He stared at the phone, feeling like a stupid jerk.

Bev was right. Parents and their kids need to be together, day in and day out. Kids need guidelines to help them negotiate the minefields of life.

He rose from his chair, weary from the stress of his work and the hopelessness of his situation with Beverly. Because even though kids need parents, the parents have to love and cherish and trust each other. And he didn't know if he could do that with Bev ever again.

He snapped off the light and flopped onto his bed. But his mind wouldn't rest as he struggled with the awful question as to whether he'd abandoned his kids. And alone in the darkness, with no one to assure him, his doubts rolled over him like a diesel truck.

* * * * *

Just after two-thirty the phone rang. Ransom searched for the receiver, then fumbled it to his ear, mumbling hello. His head still rested on the pillow, and his eyes were closed.

"This is Greg Cunningham, on the surveillance team. The

ex-con, Tipton, has been on the move for about an hour. First, it was just a short drive to a Quik Trip for smokes, then a little cruising around. Nothing special, you know?"

"I see," Ransom said, his thoughts becoming more lucid, waiting for the punch line.

"But now he's up to something strange. He's stopped twice and made calls at pay phones. Then he drove to a bar on West Avenue, near Basse Road. After fifteen minutes, one of our agents went inside. The guy is meeting with Antonio Rojas at a back table, and they're both talking hard and fast."

"Rojas. You mean "Pit Face"? The heavyweight crack dealer?" He sat up and switched on the bedside lamp.

"Yep, the number two source of rock on the north side. And the guy doesn't usually meet face-to-face with his customers."

"So, you think Tipton is planning to make a buy?"

"I don't think his dirt bag looks and goofy personality are any attraction for Pit Face."

"But where would the guy get enough cash? He's fresh out of the joint."

"You tell me."

"Stay on him, I'll be right over." He rolled out of bed and tugged on some clothes.

One of the surveillance cars was parked near the bar, a hangout for scumbags, burglars, and fences appropriately called the Drop Out II, and he pulled in behind it. He radioed the agents he was coming for a visit. Then he strolled up to the older model Chrysler New Yorker.

They unlocked the back door, and Ransom slid inside. He stretched out his legs. They didn't make cars this roomy anymore. "What's going on, fellows?"

Ben Feldman, a young agent, turned his head and smiled. "*Nada*, right now. Typical surveillance, hurry up and wait."

"Is our agent still inside?"

"Nah, he came back out. But we've got their rides eyeballed."

"What's Tipton driving?"

"The two door red Chevy Lumina parked on the side of the building. It actually belongs to his honey."

"Good job, guys. I'll back you up."

"Shit," said Cunningham, "here they come."

Ransom clambered out of the depths of the back seat

and stepped into the tepid night air. He caught a glimpse of Tipton, Pit Face, and some beefy Latino, probably a bodyguard, shouldering their way into the small Lumina.

Ransom slid behind the wheel of his Crown Vic just as the Lumina's backup lights flared. The Chevy pulled onto West Avenue, heading north. Feldman and Ransom followed at a distance. Two other surveillance vehicles proceeded in the same direction on a parallel street.

Ransom was wide awake now, his senses alert, and his mind whirling with possibilities as to what this group of criminal misfits had in their crooked little minds. He wondered if there was any connection with the kidnapping. With Tipton being cozy with the nurse from Metro, they'd have to keep on him until something else looked better, or they became certain it was a washout.

Their caravan rolled on north, clipping along fast, in light traffic. Could it be that this asshole knew where the baby was? Was he headed there now? Maybe, but . . . .

He couldn't figure it. Why had there been no ransom demand? Except for the phony one by Herman Manson, of course. Crooks usually didn't have the patience or the discipline to wait long for payday.

The parade of cars crossed the Jackson Keller intersection, and then went under Loop 410. Where the hell were they going? Then the Lumina turned right without signaling. They were cruising the Castle Hills subdivision, an area with rambling, expensive homes.

This would be getting tricky. They couldn't stay too close to Tipton for fear he'd make them, but there were so many turns and twists in the curving roads of the subdivision that they might easily lose him. Also, there were a lot of dead end streets, and they didn't want to meet the grisly gang doubling back.

The Lumina slowed to creep by a grandiose Spanish style house, and then sped up. Tipton repeated the procedure at a couple of other places. Ransom strained to see the addresses when he drove by, scribbling them on a pad.

In a little while, they exited onto Lockhill Selma Road, turning right. The other surveillance cars pulled up into position, and Ransom and Feldman dropped back. The Chevy rolled onto Loop 410, heading east. One of the other agents gunned it, passed the Lumina, and kept ahead of him as the trailing car continued to relay Tipton's location.

Tipton stayed within the speed limit for a few miles, then

exited at Broadway, heading back south. The procession continued straight into Alamo Heights, an older, but plush neighborhood where the Baldazars had purchased their home and stationed their Mercedes in the driveway.

The Lumina did a thorough sweep of the swanky area. Some of San Antonio's wealthiest people liked to have the 09 at the end of their zip code. Tipton and company seemed quite interested in the scenery, even though it was after three in the morning.

They drove through the intersection with the Baldazar's street. Tipton slowed, and the Lumina's occupants all peered down the street. The Baldazar's stucco house with its red tile roof lit up by outside lights was plainly visible in the distance.

Soon the Chevy turned south on Devine Road, passing near the Olmos Dam, scene of the earlier debacle with Herman the motorcycle freak. Tipton took a right, heading west on Hildebrand Avenue. Ransom figured that this was a return route. He radioed for another unit to drop back, and he moved up again.

Tipton turned north on West Avenue, returning to the Drop Out II, to drop out his two seedy passengers. They yakked in the car a minute, then Pit Face and his henchman climbed out. Ransom drove by, taking a quick peek.

As he did, Pit Face glanced over. The creep was the type who could feel a cop's stare the moment it touched his skin. The yellow glow of the street lights accented his limestone complexion and greasy black hair.

Ransom drove on. He'd seen enough of these mopes for one night. He radioed to thank the other agents for calling him, and then he gunned it for home, hoping to get a few hours' sleep.

* * * * *

Kathy wasn't getting her seven hours' snooze, either. The other night there'd been the late call about the ransom demand. She'd reconsidered her earlier thoughts about fun and games with Steve, and she tried to drop him a broad hint about being beat, with more work coming up the next day, but he was too aroused at that point to be dissuaded by anything like reason.

So, after an active and late evening that night, she'd struggled out of bed early the next morning, while Steve slept like a panda bear lolling on her queen size bed. She could've conked him with a dumbbell.

When she dragged home late last night, she ate some leftover Chinese takeout for dinner, slipped into her pajamas and collapsed into bed. But now, at two a.m., even though she was exhausted, she thrashed about under the covers, plumped her pillow a dozen times, turned from one side to the other, then flipped the light back on to do some reading. The problem was that her brain was spinning a thousand miles an hour, with no way to shut it down.

In a while, she closed the book on her lap, thinking. She'd meant to tell Steve during their date. But the scenario hadn't gone as she'd intended. Not at all.

"Here we are," Steve had said, entering her apartment.

She sensed resentment. Steve was crazy about those comedy clubs, so maybe she'd made a mistake asking him to bring her home early. But she had something important to discuss.

She sat on the sofa and turned to face him, but he wandered away.

"I'm getting a beer—you want something?"

"No, thanks, I'm fine." She took a deep breath and let out a sigh, drumming her fingers on the cushion beside her. He came back into the room and she gave him a tired smile.

He took a swig of Bud. "So you worked hard today, huh?"

"We were busier than crayfish in a boiling pot."

He dropped into the recliner across the room from her. She disliked the distance between them, seeing it as a gulf that might swallow the intimacy of her words. But she didn't want to make an issue of it.

"Anything in your case look promising?" he asked, then gulped some more brew.

She'd always refused to discuss active cases with anyone, even a boyfriend. She wondered if she'd feel differently if they were married. Maybe she'd be a little more chatty with him.

"We're running out the usual stuff. There are a couple of possible suspects. But there's nothing really hot going on at the moment."

"Hmm." He studied her eyes, and then took another drink. She had the feeling he thought she was keeping something from him.

"We just hope—" she began.

"So, do you think—" he said at the same time.

"Excuse me," she said.

"No, go ahead. What were you going to say?"

"We hope the baby's okay. That's the main consideration."

"Sure, I know." He drained his beer, then stood up and stretched, flexing his back muscles and tensing his arms. He had super arms, and he always wore short sleeve shirts, even in cold weather, so they'd be noticed.

He shrugged. "I think I'll get another beer. Are you sure you don't want one?"

She shook her head. "No, thanks, but I'd like a glass of water."

"You got it."

As he walked into the kitchen, she noticed that his legs were a bit short for the rest of his body. And he had that weight-lifters' swagger that she spotted right away on most guys, but she'd never noticed him do before.

When he came back into the room, she got him to sit by her, but she could never seem to steer the conversation in the right direction or find the right opening or get up the nerve to just blurt it out. And then after he'd finished his second beer, he got distracted by playing with her hair, and kissing her cheek, and rubbing her shoulders, and kissing her lips, and caressing her arms, and rubbing her tender breasts, and she was about to say something about that—

But with Steve's mounting passion, she never got to bring up the big subject.

Not that they would have reached any decision right away. But at least she would have gotten it out in the open. Then someone else could share the burden, the joy, the confusion . . . the whatever the hell she was going through.

Now she laid aside her book, swung her legs off the bed, and ambled into the kitchen. Pouring herself a glass of milk, she plopped down on a dining room chair and switched on the radio. Shania Twain was warbling one of her favorite country songs. At least that helped relax her. She finished the milk, and then poured herself another half glass. Her stomach still felt empty.

Maybe she should call her mom; she could always talk to her. She was sort of like the sister she'd never had. And even though she loved her younger brother, she'd never had the kind of relationship with him where she talked about serious things, the kind of things in life that really mattered.

Back in her bedroom, she thought about Mrs. Baldazar. The woman must be going through a special hell so painful it could not be imagined. Who or what could comfort her?

Though she'd never had a child herself, Kathy thought she knew what it might feel like to have that precious part of yourself that was more valuable than the whole suddenly ripped away, stolen, taken from your arms. She wondered how Steve or any man would feel if their baby was robbed from them? Could it cause as much pain to a man as it did to the newborn's mother? She slipped into bed, and thoughts whirled in her mind like a kaleidoscope.

The clock read three-twenty, with the alarm set for six. She'd have to read the rest of Jenny Cain's exploits later. She switched off the lamp. Tiredness settled over her, and the fog descended. Then visions of smiling and crying and sleeping babies drifted through her dreams.

11

When his alarm went off, Ransom could barely answer the bell. Worse yet, he had to run eight miles. Maybe he could skip it. Some extra rest would be great. But, no, that would really screw up his schedule. He decided he'd do the miles somehow, but after this marathon was over, he'd take it a lot easier with his running in the future.

The air was cool enough for a summer morning, although the humidity made it feel thick and moist. Worst of all, his legs never loosened up during the run. They felt heavy and lifeless. That wasn't good. He'd need more spring in them if he was going to run twenty-six miles next weekend. Right now, that mileage sounded like a thousand. When he finished his run, he was glad to pull off his gear and hit the shower.

He had another important and probably long day ahead of him. But he didn't mind giving the job his all when the stakes were so high. And often enough, more so than most people probably realized, the work involved life-threatening situations, recovering people's life savings, or preventing crimes that could cost citizens their dignity, money, and physical well-being. He didn't become an agent to get rich; that would never happen. The idea was to give an important and worthwhile service to the American people. He truly had compassion for others and cared about his country. There were few ways to so directly help people and still do a job he enjoyed.

* * * * *

At the office, Ransom made notes about what needed to be done on the case:
>   1. interview uniform renters
>   2. get license plate results (Kathy handling)
>   3. return money to Baldazars
>   4. check out Tarmack baby
>   5. interview candy stripers (Sanchez)

He could handle some of the leads with Kathy's help, but

there was a lot to do. He'd better parcel out the rest of the work to other agents. He knew of too many cases where kidnappers had panicked and abandoned babies in the woods; in rivers, ponds, or lakes; or in dumpsters. Time was crucial in this kind of case. And too much time had already passed. It was making him very edgy.

Kathy came in, her eyes downcast. She arrowed for her workspace and dropped into her chair. She sat there stone still, her hands entwined on her desk, a faraway gaze in her eyes.

Ransom didn't like the shadow on her face. He stepped over to her desk and said, "Is something wrong?"

She motioned to a chair. "I'm afraid so, Jack, sit down."

He perched on the edge of the chair. "Did something happen to Jester's baby?"

She nodded, her lips pressed together, creases along her cheekbones. "I woke up at five-thirty thinking about that frail child lying there hooked up to all those machines, and I had to go see him." She stared at the desktop. "The situation looked grim. I was so upset I probably wasn't any help to Jester."

"What's going on?" he said, trying to capture her gaze.

She looked into his eyes. "The baby had a setback. He's got cranial bleeding. It could cause neurological damage."

"Oh, Jesus. Can they do anything to stop it?"

"No, they just watch him and hope it subsides." She banged her fist on the desk, and then ran a hand through her hair. "The poor kid was just born too early. Even a couple of weeks later would have helped his chances a lot."

"But he can still pull through, can't he?"

"The doctor said not to give up hope. But . . . ."

"So we won't. I'm going by to see Jester. Maybe there's something I can do to help."

Sonny Jenkins walked in, saw they were involved in a discussion, and said to Ransom, "When you get a minute, could you round up the others and come into my office?"

"Sure, Sonny. We'll be right there."

Then Kathy said, "I'm sure Jester would want to see you."

"At least it will give him someone to talk to. Maybe it will help."

Kathy sighed. "I'm as composed as I'll get. Let's go see Sonny."

As he stood up, Ransom considered Kathy in a way he

rarely did, noting what a beauty she was. He wondered if it was her compassion for others that made her so angelic this morning. He decided that the guy she picked as her life partner would be a lucky man.

"Before we go in," he said, "do you know when DMV will have those registrations from the partial license number?"

"They've got someone working on it full-time. The woman I contacted said to call back first thing this morning." She snatched up the phone. "Wait a minute, and I'll check on it."

After a long pause, Ransom said, "They're probably still having coffee."

"It's pretty early, so . . . ." She held up a hand. "Yes, this is Kathy Devereaux with the FBI. Right. Were you able to get those registrations on that partial plate number?"

Kathy hung up. She looked stunned. "There are over a thousand registrations with combinations of the letters and the number we gave them."

"Damn. That's a daunting figure." He thought a few moments, and then he waggled a hand. "But we can probably cross out most of them by vehicle description."

"That's true. But do you really think Miss Phoenix was that positive about the tag number for us to spend so much time checking all those possibilities?"

"She seemed observant enough. And we don't have many other real specific leads going for us right now."

Kathy shook her head. "I suppose not."

"So, let's go see Sonny." As they walked, they told the various other agents in the room about the meeting. They all responded right away.

Jenkins smiled as the troops filed into his office and dropped into chairs or leaned against the walls. But his expression was too mechanical, Ransom thought. He figured that Sonny's mind was probably far removed from politeness.

When Jenkins asked for an assessment of the situation, Ransom summarized what had happened on the Tipton surveillance and where they stood with the Tarmack couple. He discussed the lists of people they'd gathered from searching purchases or rentals of scrubs, as well as the hospital volunteers, all needing to be interviewed. He mentioned the hospital and doctors' records to be handled and the thousand vehicles that matched from the check of the partial license plate number.

"That's a lot of work," said Jenkins, folding his hands on top of the desk. "Plus there's the polygraph to be done on Manson. But nothing's really moving on this case at the moment, and we need to shake something loose." He picked up a notepad. "How many detectives are working today?"

"Lieutenant Sanchez and three others," Ransom said.

Jenkins took a head count. "We've got eight agents working now. I'll request another eight from other squads. We'll put out ten teams of two guys—"

Kathy cleared her throat and stared at him.

"That is, two *investigators* to a team. How do you see splitting up the leads, Ransom?"

"How about four teams work the hospitals, doctors, and infertility clinics, four teams follow up on the license registrations, and one team can interview the candy stripers? Kathy and I will talk to scrubs purchasers and renters, and I've also got an idea of something to try concerning the Tarmack baby."

"That sounds fine to me. I'll divvy up the leads so we'll know who's doing what. Ransom, you and Kathy might as well get going."

"Speaking of lists," Ransom said to the assembled agents, "remember to use the computer entry forms on that table against the wall. Whatever information you get, type it up so that Cheryl can enter it into the computer. These facts we're gathering are no good if they stay in your notes."

Back in the squad room, Kathy pulled her pistol from the drawer, while Ransom picked up the phone and dialed the Baldazars. A zombie's voice said 'hello,' and for an instant, Ransom froze. It was Mrs. Baldazar. He told her he was sorry to bother her, but that he needed to return the money that had been used in the ransom drop.

"Oh." There was a pause. Then she said, "Could you talk with Senator Baldazar about that? He handles our money."

"Of course, that's fine. Uh . . . is he available?"

"I'm sorry, I didn't make it clear. He's not here right now. He just left for his office."

"For his *office*?"

"Yes, he hated to leave, but he had some urgent business to handle."

"All right, I'll just contact him there."

Ransom checked his watch. The Senator should be there by around nine o'clock.

Kathy arched her eyebrows. "Baldazar has gone to work at his office?"

"That's what Mrs. Baldazar said. He told her he had to handle some urgent business."

"Like he's going to get income taxes repealed?"

"I hope it's something that critical."

"Christ, let's get some air." She turned and walked toward the door, her cheeks glowing crimson to match her hair.

Ransom followed, but just then Jenkins stuck his head into the squad room. "Got a second?" he asked.

"Sure, no problem. Hey, Kathy, give me a couple of minutes."

"Okay, I'll meet you at the car."

He trailed Jenkins into his office and took a seat. As Jenkins sank into his padded swivel chair, Ransom noted his disturbed expression.

"What's up, Sonny? Is there a problem?"

"There's something you need to know."

"All right, let's have it."

"I talked with the Baldazars last night. I'm afraid that Senator Baldazar is furious about our handling of the case."

Ransom considered that for a moment. "A fake ransom call shakes up everyone, especially the parents."

"I know. But he was trying to fix blame—unfairly, of course." Jenkins shifted in his chair, his brow wrinkled, clearly uncomfortable.

"Fix blame? On *me,* you mean?"

Jenkins gave a half-shrug and looked down. "I told him that was unreasonable, that we were just following out logical and necessary leads, but he was being stubborn about it."

"So what did he say? Does he want you to take me off the case?"

Jenkins hesitated, and then said, "That was mentioned. I said it would be foolish. I told him that you're experienced and smart, and you never give up on a case. I said that I definitely wanted you to run the investigation."

"I see." Ransom realized his face was hot. "So what's the verdict?"

"He said he'd think it over. And I think he meant it. But there's more to it."

He hated to ask. "What's that, Sonny?"

"Baldazar knows the Director. They went to law school

together."

"Oh, of course he does. Perfect." He wondered if steam was escaping from his ears.

"The Senator told me I wasn't the final authority in this matter."

"That son-of-a-bitch."

"Exactly. Anyway, he agreed to give us a couple more days before he picks up the phone."

"What a damn generous guy."

"Listen, Jack. Don't say anything to him about this. What I said was for your info. only."

"Don't worry, I'm cool." But he realized that his face and neck had probably gone crimson.

"That's good. Let's just play it straight for a couple of days. I'm sure everything will work out all right. Anyway, where are you and Kathy headed now?"

"To the good Senator's office for a little confab."

* * * * *

As Ransom screeched off toward Baldazar's office, Harvey limped into a discount store a few miles away, lifted his hat in a nervous gesture, and plunked down some more hard-earned bucks for another brand of formula—the most expensive kind in the whole damn place, naturally. He was really sick of this deal with the kid. It was friggin' unbelievable what it was costing him.

The spoiled brat wouldn't eat anything. She kept spitting up all the time. And man, did she have the runs. The old lady was even making *him* change some shitty diapers. What a crock that was. Christ.

Also, the kid didn't look so good. She was pale, and she didn't move around too much. She just sort of laid there and made faces. Except when she decided to howl.

The clerk with the big knockers handed him a little change from his double sawbuck. Jesus, the cost was unreal. He took a final glance at those jugs, smiled at the honey, then tugged his hat down and hobbled out the door.

He rubbed the side of his thigh as he limped toward the truck. The lost sleep had wasted him, and now his bum leg ached. Five years since his hog had gone down on a curve in the rain. At least, they hadn't cut the leg off like they wanted to. He'd of died before he let 'em do that.

He hoisted himself into his rusted Ford pickup. It might look like shit, but it got him where he was going and back.

Most of the time, anyway. He tossed the package onto the seat, fished his keys out of his jeans pocket, and cranked the ignition. He pumped the gas pedal a few seconds, the motor finally caught, and he revved it until it smoothed out. The transmission clunked as he dropped her into reverse. He backed out, threw it in low, and left a little rubber as he roared down the street.

He glanced back at the package on the seat, still pissed about what this deal was costing them. This better do the trick with that brat, was all he knew. He couldn't take much more of this crying and pooping stuff.

He stopped at a red light. A young girl in a convertible pulled up beside him, the top down. Whoa, her short red skirt was riding high on her thighs. She was just a teenager, but it still made him hot. The old lady had been in such a snit over this kid she hadn't come across all week. And with them spending all that money and the rent due soon, he'd prob'ly have to make another run right away. Which was not a good situation with him feelin' as horny as a goat and his leg hurtin' like hell. It really pissed him off. The convertible pulled away, and he tromped the pedal.

* * * * *

Ransom and Kathy strode through the door at Baldazar's office shortly after nine. Two agents sat in the reception room, one leafing through a dog-eared magazine, the other tapping a pen against a chair arm. When Ransom asked what was happening, the agent reading the magazine said that Baldazar didn't want them in his office unless he was there and a call came from the kidnappers. He claimed that he conducted too much sensitive business for anyone to be with him. And besides, the Senator had yet to show up for work.

Ransom stepped over to speak with the receptionist. Young, with shimmering blonde hair, she was pretty in a vacant-eyed cover girl way. She sat talking on the phone while gnashing a humongous wad of gum. It gave bilingual a whole new meaning.

He wanted to find out when Baldazar might arrive, but the phone kept ringing, and her jaws kept chomping, so he gave up and sat down to wait for His Eminence. He and Kathy chatted with the other agents, who seemed glad for the company. Minutes later, Baldazar showed up. When he walked in, he appeared startled to see them. From the way the Senator's jaw clenched, Ransom judged it was not a pleasant surprise. Ransom fought to keep his own face from turning to concrete.

The Senator chatted with his receptionist a minute or so, then glanced at Ransom. "Come in," he ordered, and turned his back. So much for pleasantries. They trooped into his office. Kathy seemed insubordinately out-of-step.

Ransom said, "We'll just take a minute of your time. We came to return your money."

Baldazar hung up the jacket of his expensive-looking suit on a gold-colored coat tree, eased into his leather chair and adjusted his glasses. Now he looked more resigned to the interruption. But then, money talks.

"That's fine. I hope I didn't keep you waiting long. I decided to have the Mercedes washed. Driving around San Antonio it gets dusty, you know."

Yesterday afternoon the damn thing was spotless, Ransom thought, but he smiled in pleasant agreement with the man. Then, rustling in his coat pocket, he came out with a thick envelope. "Here's your cash. Please count it, then sign the receipt that's with it."

The Senator riffled the bills. "I'm sure it's all here. I know I can trust the FBI."

Oh, sure, he thought. That's true, but you probably don't really believe it.

The Senator signed the receipt and thrust it back. "But I hope that will be the last payment to the wrong people. We can't afford such a stupid waste of time." His eyes were as hard as flint.

What a prick, Ransom thought. "I know you realize," he said, "that we have to check out any possibilities. There's too much at stake—"

"I know what's at stake, Ransom. My daughter's life is at stake. That's why I'm upset over any wild goose chases."

Kathy leaned closer, "Senator, there was no way of knowing it wasn't the kidnapper who called. We had to play it out. That's our job."

Baldazar glowered at her. "It's your job to avoid going down blind alleys. You should know enough to catch the right people." He glanced at Ransom. "Maybe you should use more experienced agents on this case."

Kathy reddened, and her eyes narrowed. She took a deep breath, ready to unload on the judgmental politico. Ransom had heard her unleash a string of French curses, and it wasn't pretty, even if you couldn't understand her. He knew he had to act fast.

"Senator," Ransom said, "we're all experienced in these types of cases. But every crime has a different twist. You're dealing with quirky personalities. There's no standard situation and no guidelines criminals follow. We have to go with the flow the best we can."

Baldazar picked up an ink pen, twisting the cap off and on. He took a breath which he let out through his nose. "All right, we'll drop that for now. But I want to know what you're going to do next." He stared at Ransom.

"We've got people checking out many different leads. We're down to bedrock investigation. And we're good at it. We'll find April, Senator, it will just take time."

Baldazar still looked agitated, but he leaned back in his chair and laced his fingers over his stomach. "Time . . . ." he said, staring at a spot over their heads. "And as we know, 'Time and tide wait for no man.'"

"True," Ransom said, "but 'Time is the wisest of all counselors.'"

Baldazar's eyes widened behind thick lenses. "That could be," he said with scant conviction. Then he consulted his Rolex. "Now if there's nothing further, I really must take care of some business."

Ransom stood up and turned to leave.

But Kathy hesitated. "Senator, I know you have important work to do, but this is a grave situation, and Mrs. Baldazar needs your support at home. I hope you'll be able to return soon and be with her."

"Oh, of course, I won't be long. And in spite of what you think, my wife will be fine. She's a very strong woman."

As they went out the front door they exchanged a look, and then they both shook their heads. Agitated, they paced in silence toward the Bureau Ford, passing by the Senator's shiny Mercedes which glistened in the morning sun. Nice wash job, thought Ransom. Beautiful finish on the thing, too. It sort of resembled a modern day royal chariot.

Then Kathy said, "Jack, where do you get all those quotations you spout off all the time?" Her head was tilted, a suspicious look on her face.

He paused beside the Mercedes. A few drops of water had beaded up on the right rear fender. "I don't know. I read a lot, and phrases that strike me as meaningful stick with me. It's nothing I consciously study."

Her mouth puckered. "So how do you recall who said what?"

"That's the easy part. The words always fit the man. Or the woman."

"Hmmph," she said. They climbed into the Ford.

"Let's drive by the hospital and visit Jester for a minute," he said.

She stared straight ahead. *"Avance, tout de suite."*

And so he took off in a hurry.

* * * * *

When they pulled up to the hospital, Kathy urged Ransom to go in by himself since she'd visited Jester earlier. She sat in the car with the windows down. As he crossed the lot, Ransom glanced back and saw that she was crying.

When he neared the double doors, once again his legs felt leaden. He took the elevator to the second floor, and then walked to the ward. Some of the isolettes were mercifully empty.

After searching for a minute, he spotted a tiny dark form splayed naked in the middle of his small enclosed world. The baby seemed to struggle for each breath he sucked through a large tube, his pencil-thin arms and legs twitching in spasmodic movements. His brow and face were scrunched in mute protest to the pain and discomfort he'd known in life so far.

Ransom was surprised to see Nurse Pettijohn in the room. Her fire engine red lipstick contrasted with her milky white skin. Her voluptuous body strained at the molded scrubs as she checked the assortment of tubes, monitors, and instruments, and then just studied the little guy.

Then Jester came in wearing a yellow sterile gown and a matching cap. He, too, appeared shrunken and diminished. It seemed that even his life forces were not fully developed.

Jester asked Nurse Pettijohn something, listened intently to what she told him, then stared at the small child who seemed to shudder with each labored breath. The nurse padded off, and Ransom wondered what they'd discussed. He didn't think it was anything good.

Ransom looked away, thinking about the situation, but soon his gaze went back to Jester. Then Jester must have felt his presence, for his head turned, and he stared into Ransom's eyes and lifted his chin in acknowledgment. Jester continued to watch the minuscule child for several more minutes, reaching his hand through a porthole in the incubator and placing his index finger against the baby's fist. The child opened its hand and clamped onto the finger.

Pain squeezed Ransom's throat.

Finally Jester's chest lifted and fell, and he gently disengaged his finger from the baby's grip. He bowed his head and closed his eyes for several seconds, then turned away from the incubator and raised his index finger to Ransom before walking out a door down the hallway. The slim man pulled off the yellow cap as he approached.

"Thanks for coming, Jack," he said.

"What does the doctor say, Jester? Will he be—"

Jester shook his head. "It's the not knowing what will happen that's the worst. He's just struggling so hard . . . ." He looked at the floor, with tears filling his eyes. "His odds are about even right now," he said, then cleared his throat.

Ransom didn't like the idea of the baby's life being decided by a coin toss. "But he'll get stronger all the time, won't he?"

"They work to keep him alive from day to day, hoping he can grow and develop. In theory, each day his odds get a little better." He shook his head, his eyes glazing. "But he was born way too soon. With his borderline development, he's fighting so many problems."

Ransom got a sinking feeling. "I don't know what to say. Is there anything I can do?"

"Just remember Michael in your prayers."

"I'll be sure to do that."

They both glanced toward the incubator.

"Michael. That's a good name," Ransom said.

"We named him after my grandpa. We love our girls, but I'd always hoped to have a little boy to . . . ." He shrugged. "We really need a miracle at this point." Now the tears trailed down his cheeks, and he clamped his eyes closed.

Ransom stretched an arm around Jester's back, feeling him crumple. They stood there together in the hallway for a long minute. Then Jester straightened, sniffed, and wiped his nose with the back of his hand.

"You've got another baby to save," he said.

"Sure, Jester, but if you need anything, please telephone us, any time."

"I will. If I've learned anything out of this, it's that it's damn tough trying to shoulder this kind of load alone."

"Don't do it, you've got your FBI family ready to help."

"I know, and thanks. Now go on, get out of here."
"Lord, I always wear out my welcome."

12

Back in the car, Ransom found Kathy had composed herself, but she looked emotionally spent, with red streaks shooting through her bright blue eyes. He hated to tell her the situation with Jester's baby. When he did, Kathy's eyes clouded as though a hurricane had edged into the Gulf.

"They've just got to save him," she said. She pushed her fingers into her thick hair, clenching it in her fist. "This really sucks. I can't stand it."

He, too, felt rage and helplessness—conflicting emotions that were wearing on him. "We're used to reacting when the shit hits the fan. But in this case . . . ."

She released her hair and blew out an exasperated breath. "We can only wait and let the experts handle it."

Ransom nodded, but he sensed the irony. "That's just what we ask crime victims to do."

"My God," she said, her eyes open wide, "that's exactly what we say."

They sat in silence for a time. But a giant storm brewed inside each of them. Ransom could only hope for the rampaging winds to blow themselves out.

He switched the subject to their case. "We'd better start interviewing those women who bought or rented scrubs just prior to the kidnapping." Then he added, "And I've got an idea for getting a fix on the Tarmack woman."

"Oh, right, you mentioned that in the conference. What's on your mind?"

"You'll see, Red. It's a wrinkle that I thought of last night."

* * * * *

The first name on the uniform list was Angie Martinez, who turned out to be Mexican-American. But when she answered the door, they realized she was so light-skinned that anyone not concerned with nationality might not have noticed she wasn't pure Anglo. Besides, she fit the rest of

143

the description of the woman who'd walked out of the hospital with a tiny baby that wasn't hers.

She stared at Ransom's credentials, and then with some hesitation, invited them in. Ransom noted that her forehead wrinkled in dismay. The house was small, but neat and clean, with the smell of breakfast tortillas in the air. Bright red, yellow, and orange upholstery gave the furniture a vivid presence. Crucifixes hung on the walls, and statues and paintings of the Virgin Mary and Jesus surrounded them. Ransom sat down, noting pictures on the mantle of four children ranging from about six to fourteen.

"I don't understand why the FBI wants to see me," she said. Her gaze shifted from Ransom to Kathy and back.

"We're interested in people who've bought or rented hospital scrubs recently," Ransom said. "Your name came up, and we wondered if you could tell us about it."

"You mean, why I—"

"Bought two new sets of scrubs, yes. Are you a nurse?"

"I'm a certified nurse, not an RN."

Kathy said, "And you're working as a nurse now?"

"Yes, in the afternoons. I watch an elderly lady from noon to six, helping her bathe and dress and so on. She needs some medications, and she needs help while her daughter-in-law works and runs errands."

Ransom said, "How long have you been—"

"About three weeks now. They like me, and they want to keep me on. I can use the money, what with the *hijos,*" she gestured at the pictures on the mantle, "and with my husband not able to find a job in this terrible economy." She crossed herself.

"Mrs. Martinez," Kathy queried, "do you have a baby?"

"Why, yes, Ramon." Once again, she pointed at the mantle. "The little boy with the dark eyes of his father is my *nino.*" The boy in the photo who looked about six was the one she apparently meant.

"Would you mind if we took a look around your place?" Ransom asked. "We won't touch anything."

"All right, if it will satisfy your curiosity."

They peeked into each room, finding no baby or any signs of paraphernalia, and then said their goodbyes. Back in the car, Kathy asked, "Your curiosity satisfied, Mr. Gestapo?"

"*Ja vold.* Let's give her a pass. If nothing else pans out, we can always come back to her. But she's got no baby, no crib, not even a package of diapers."

"Unlike the Tarmack woman."

"Bingo. She has a baby she won't explain, and there's been no ransom demand. She could be our neurotic personality disorder woman keeping that baby right under our noses."

"So, what can we do to find out?" asked Kathy.

"We need more information in order to get a search warrant. And I've conjured up a scheme to help us get it."

"You trust a swamp girl with it, *mon ami*?"

"*Certainement,* chère. But on the way there, think pure thoughts."

* * * * *

The weathered limestone exterior of the Church of the Way of the Lamb reminded Ransom of a small version of a European cathedral. Offshoot religions had to use every tactic, he supposed, in this staunchly Catholic area. The Spanish got a head start by building their missions in the area four centuries earlier.

He'd been a Methodist all his life, although he'd fallen away from church attendance the past few years. Something about organized religion didn't sit well with him. He believed in God, no question. But he disliked the tiresome drills—lengthy prayers, dull announcements, boring sermons. Ritualism ground him down and sapped his energy. And recently, he'd realized how crucial it was to have enough vigor to get through the long and vitally important days he sometimes faced in his job.

As he pulled into the church parking lot, Kathy yanked his chain. "So, now we're going to pray for guidance?"

"Don't think I haven't. But what I've got in mind is more secular."

"And this is the way we're going to check on the Tarmack woman?"

"Exactly. Our original tip mentioned she belonged to this church. I thought that maybe the minister might have christened her baby or know something about where it came from."

"But will he tell us?"

"How can he resist this cherubic face?"

"The same way hundreds of American women have."

"You babes are so shallow." He shook his head in mock sadness. "You're always looking for the beefcake."

"Hey, you male chauvinists invented strippers, then howl

when women like them, too."

"And you bodybuilders are the worst," he persisted.

"If you'd put some of that jogger's energy into pumping iron," she shot back, "you'd have an outside shot at hunkdom."

"I didn't know you cared, my dear."

"You're not my fantasy date, but I could see Bev thinking you're hot."

"Spare me. Let's go have our talk with His Reverence."

She shrugged, and they climbed out of the car. As they approached the building, Ransom thought of the Bible verse about the lamb lying down with the lion.

He pushed open the front door to the church. They slipped into the darkened vestibule, shuffled across the tile floor, and then entered the sanctuary. The air in the barn-like room hung sultry and still. Row after row of dark wooden pews stretched before them until the forest stopped short of the draped alter, over which dangled an enormous light-hued wooden cross. Jesus was absent from the structure.

In fact, they saw no one at all in the dim house of God. They heard nothing. But in the far corner, a patch of light seeped from under a door. Ransom inclined his head in that direction, and they proceeded together down the center aisle as though they were father and daughter in a wedding procession.

They paused as they neared the entryway. Everything remained quiet. Ransom rapped the door with his knuckles, and then stuck his head into the room. It was a cube of an office, your standard fare desk, computer and filing cabinets. A small table was covered with gold-colored collection plates lined with deep maroon velvet.

In an adjoining room with the door ajar, they noticed a figure hunched over a huge desk strewn with books and stacks of paper. As they approached, the man looked up, his mouth open in surprise. "Can I help you?" he said.

"Are you the pastor here?" Ransom asked. He noted a family photograph of the man, his wife, and two girls, about ten and twelve years old. A gooseneck desk lamp with a dark green shade dropped light on the man's hands.

"I'm the Exalted Shepherd of the congregation. My secretary should have greeted you in the front office, but she probably went to the printer's."

"No problem. Do you have a minute?"

He beckoned them with a weathered hand. "Of course, come in, sit down."

When they had settled into chairs, he continued, "How can I be of service?" His pointing finger swung from one to the other. "Are we considering matrimony?"

"Oh, no," Ransom spit out.

"No, no," Kathy echoed. "We just . . . ." And for the first time Ransom had ever known, Kathy seemed at a loss for words.

Ransom showed the man his credentials. "We're with the FBI, and we're here on business."

The man stared at the large blue letters, and a smile spread across his face, showing crowded teeth. "I'm always glad to help the feds. What are you investigating?"

"You may have read in the papers about the baby being kidnapped from the hospital. We're doing some work in that case."

The Exalted Shepherd acknowledged his understanding, his hands together in a prayerful position, index fingers pressed against his lips. "Where does our little church fit into your investigation?"

Ransom studied the man's face. His features were coarse, like those of a hobo that had been hacked at and blunted by life's hardships. Two broken veins on his cheek formed an upside-down letter T.

"Maybe there's no connection at all, but . . . ." Ransom hesitated. Something about the man's hands bothered him, but he couldn't come to grips with what it was.

"We're just tying up loose ends," Kathy said, filling in the silence.

"Yes, and one thread concerns Ellen Tarmack," Ransom continued. "Do you know her? I believe she's a member of your congregation." He watched the man's eyes.

The Shepherd blinked, but his expression remained chiseled. "I certainly do. She's a fine woman. And she's a very devout member of our fold."

"Are you aware she has a new baby?" Kathy asked.

"I know about the child. The Tarmacks adopted her a few days ago."

"Do you know the circumstances of the adoption?" Ransom asked.

Shepherd Barry's hands dropped to some papers on his desk, pushing at them, arranging them, his eyes averted, following the movements of his own knobby knuckles.

Now Ransom noticed a small blue tattoo of a cross in the web of the man's left hand, between his thumb and forefinger.

"Yes, I'm familiar with their adoption." He paused, took a breath, and then let it out in a low sigh. "In fact, I helped arrange it. It's a private situation, and I'm afraid that I can't reveal any details."

Kathy jumped on that pronouncement. "What baby was it, then? Surely you can tell us that. It's not the child we're looking for, I take it?"

The man's mouth puckered around his misshapen teeth. "No, there's no connection with your case. This was an adoption that had been arranged for some time."

He held his hands palm up and shrugged. "And that's all I'm privileged to tell you about it, so unless there's something else . . . ."

Ransom's eyes narrowed. "Do you have any documents concerning the adoption?"

Shepherd Barry glared at Ransom, his face florid. "The papers are being processed by the state. As with all bureaucracies, the simple is made arduous and the difficult becomes next to impossible." He paused, but he was holding another thought. "Since I'm a man of God, I would think my word on the matter would be sufficient for your purposes."

"What would be sufficient," Ransom said, "is for you to tell us the truth as to what happened." He stared at the Shepherd, who blinked again, and then said, "I've felt my leg being pulled the whole time we've been here. Now, I'd like some straight answers to our questions."

"Meaning what, Mr. Ransom?"

"Like, how long have you been out of the joint?"

"You mean *prison*? What an incredible accusation. What do you base that on?" His face went crimson. His eyes glowed like the flaming coals of hell.

"So far, I only have a hunch. If I'm wrong, I owe you an apology. But I'll tell you what I might do." Ransom pointed to his left. "I saw a big old boat of a Chrysler outside with the personalized tag 'PAX' on it, which I'm betting is your vehicle. From the registration on that car, I can get your personal identifiers and run a computer check for your criminal history. I'd guess you've got DUI charges and at least one stretch behind the wall."

The Exalted Shepherd trembled; he seemed unable to

speak.

Kathy's face went as pale as a porcelain doll.

"I'm not threatening to expose you, Shepherd Barry, I'm just telling you I want to know the full story about Mrs. Tarmack and her mystery baby, with no bullshit. This is a life-and-death situation. I'm not playing any more games with you."

Shepherd Barry pointed his index finger at Ransom, but when he started to talk, he only sputtered. Then his face seemed to collapse, and his shoulders slumped. He closed his eyes and began to cry into his beat-up hands. His body shuddered with the effort.

Ransom glanced at Kathy, whose look of shock slowly changed to a sly smile.

In a few minutes the man quit crying, and Ransom stood up and patted him on the shoulder.

"We can still work this out. Just take your time and tell me all about the adoption."

The Exalted Shepherd nodded, his lower lip quivering as he gathered himself, then blew his nose on a wrinkled handkerchief.

"I'm a recovering alcoholic, Mr. Ransom, and you're right, I've had my brushes with the law. Then I saw the light, and this is no bullshit, when I was in the Huntsville pen about eight years ago. When I got out, I joined this congregation, working my way up until I became the leader. You don't have to be ordained—after all Jesus wasn't—you just have to know the true way. I've reformed, and I can only ask that you believe that."

"I've got no quarrel with someone reforming. But I still need the truth. We're looking for a kidnapped baby."

"I understand." He inhaled deeply. "The truth is, Mrs. Tarmack is legally adopting the child, and it's not the baby you're seeking."

He picked up the picture of him and his family, and he pointed to the taller of the two girls. "Jessica is sixteen now. She got involved with a boy. I told her to stay away from him, but she didn't, and she got pregnant."

He wiped away a tear. "Our church is against abortion, so I was in a box. When Jessica delivered the baby, I arranged for the Tarmacks to adopt her. The baby is my granddaughter, Mr. Ransom."

"Oh, God," said Kathy.

Ransom shrugged. "That's no problem. Your secret is

safe with us. We're only doing our job here. Besides, you'll have to admit, you brought it on yourself."

The wrung out man stared at his hands. "I know I did. Just like I've done all my life."

They drove away from the church, which, as Ransom glanced back at it, seemed to waver under the broiling sun.

"I never would have believed it," Kathy said. "The guy was no major babe, but how did you guess he had such a checkered past?"

"Tigers and alcoholics have a hell of a time changing their stripes. And that dumb jailhouse tattoo just added to my conviction. Man, oh, man. Be sure you never have a boyfriend's name tattooed on your butt, unless you don't mind having a battleship drawn over it when the players change."

"You're so full of philosophy, or something, I must admit I'm quite often baffled by your bullshit."

"Join the club, dear girl." He picked up his cell phone and called Sonny Jenkins to tell him about the interview. He suggested Sonny pull the surveillance teams off the Tarmacks. After all, they had a baby to care for.

And he still had one to find.

13

As Ransom shut off his cell phone, Kathy said, "Where to now, *Lapin?*"

He remembered she'd mentioned it before. *Lapin* was a rabbit used in Cajun stories to symbolize someone clever. The rabbit's foil, the foolish hyena, was called something that sounded like the English word "book." Ah, yes, he had it now. "Where do you suggest, *Bouki?*"

Her expression said she'd forgotten having told him before. "You are just as smart as *Lapin,* like I was telling you. So then, you see, you should decide. Whatever you say, that's going to be it, am I right?"

He shook his head in wonder. A drop dead gorgeous redhead rapping with the rhythm of a backwater swamp rat. As Norman Mailer might say, it was spooky, *mon ami.*

"Whatever you say, Jambalaya breath." He grinned. "Let's go round up some more scrubs *aficionados.*"

Her eyes glazed over, but she dutifully consulted the list. "Joyce Akerman and Marilyn Byron are both close by. I'd suggest we try Byron."

"So you do have poetry in your soul."

"No, I just knew that's who you'd pick." *Touché.* She was on top of that like a fox on *Lapin.*

Soon they pulled into the apartment complex with its battered brown buildings showing years of tenant abuse. They knocked at apartment 20, but got no answer. Printed on the mailbox was the name Granges, not Byron. They exchanged a look, and then headed for the apartment office.

A tall woman with shaggy brown hair and huge horn rim glasses sat at her desk blowing billows of smoke from a cigarette as long as a pencil. Her desk plate said "Emma Greenberg, Apartment Manager." When she saw them enter, she placed the cigarette in a half full ashtray, gave them a commercial smile, and asked, "Can I help you?"

Ransom figured she wanted to rent them a two bedroom with a fireplace. "Yes," he said, "we're with the FBI, and we need to talk with a tenant of yours, Marilyn Byron. We've got her address as being apartment 20."

"She's a former tenant," she said.

"Oh?"

"She moved out. A couple of years ago, I'd say it was."

Kathy asked, "Do you have a forwarding address for her?" She and Ransom jockeyed for position to avoid the slipstream of the smoldering ciggie.

"I don't think so," she said, then spun in her swivel chair and yanked open the bottom drawer of a metal filing cabinet, "but I'll check." She flipped through some dog-eared manila folders. "Yes," she said, pulling one out, "here she is." She opened the folder on her desk and studied the contents.

"We never received a forwarding address. It didn't much matter, she never got anything but junk mail, and then that stopped." She looked up at them. "Since she left, you two are the only ones who ever asked about her."

"You didn't forward her security deposit?" Ransom said.

"No, I didn't have to."

"Why's that?"

"According to this notation and my slipping memory," she said, retrieving her cigarette and taking a drag, "it had something to do with burn marks on the carpet in her closet. They had to reweave a section."

Kathy asked, "Do you know if she worked as a nurse?"

The woman regarded them over the tops of her horn rims as though she were wondering if she should reveal all this.

"It's important to an urgent case," Ransom said.

"If you say so. I don't recall her being a nurse. Her application says she was a cocktail waitress at Barney's Blue Light lounge."

"What does she look like?" Kathy asked.

"Hard-looking blonde, thirty-five, shorter than me, probably five-foot-four, maybe five."

"Could we take a look at the application?" Ransom said.

"I suppose it's easier than me reading it to you."

He jotted down Byron's credit references, the type of automobile she drove, and her date of birth.

Then he handed the folder back with his thanks.

"She wanted for something? You're not going to arrest

her, are you?"

"We just need to talk to her." Ransom smiled in a way to verify his words. Then the two of them turned and left.

In the car, Kathy asked, "Do you want to keep chasing her down?"

"Why don't we finish with the others first? We might find the right one and save ourselves some legwork."

"There you go with your male chauvinist patter about body parts."

"Sweetie, if I were a leg man, you'd have to chase me off your front porch every night like a crazed tomcat."

"Cats can be neutered."

"Ouch," he said, pressing his thighs together. He fired up the Ford. Then a message crackled over the radio.

"Station to five romeo."

Ransom picked up the mike and responded.

"Five romeo, please call your supervisor, ASAP."

Ransom pulled his cell phone from its holster on his belt.

Jenkins said, "I'm just checking. Do you have anything breaking on the case?"

"Nothing since I talked to you. Is something up there?"

"Just two things. First, our motorcycle bandit passed the polygraph. He's clean. He's got no knowledge of the kidnapping or the whereabouts of the baby."

"That's not a surprise," said Ransom.

"Right. Second, you got a call a half hour ago from Billy. He insisted on talking with you right away about some cult meeting. Since you were out of the office and not on the air or answering your cell, they switched him in to me. Do you know who I mean?"

Billy. What information could he have that was so urgent? "Yeah, I'm with you, Sonny. Exactly what did he say?"

"He wouldn't tell me a damn thing specific. He just said he had to talk to you, and that it was real important. The boy's no Einstein, is he?"

"No, but who is? Thanks, I'll call him."

He hung up, and then he rang Billy's number.

"H'lo," Billy mumbled.

"Billy, it's Ransom. They told me you called."

"Oh, Mr. Ransom. Listen, can we meet somewheres, like right away?"

"We're working an important case right now, Billy, could it wait awhile?"

"Uh, well, shit. No . . . it'll be over soon."

"What will?"

"I can't say on the phone. But it's something you should know."

Ransom grimaced. He hated to leave the kidnapping case, but Billy sounded agitated. He could tell that the kid thought he had something vital to say. "I'll meet you at Rosedale Park in thirty minutes."

Ransom filled Kathy in. "Manson passed the polygraph. We're back to square one."

"*Damne!*" Kathy said, banging her thigh. "*Le imbécile!*"

"Right. Also, I've got to meet an informant right away, but I'm starved. Can I buy you a sandwich at the Circle K?"

"A carton of milk is plenty for me," she said, recovering from her fit of anger.

No, he thought, it's plenty for a kitten, not a fully grown person. But with Kathy's usual appetite, he'd believe it when he saw it.

In the palace of fine cuisine Kathy cruised the aisles, looking as if she were on full alert, and glommed onto a sandwich, potato chips, and a package of donuts, as well as the carton of milk. Ransom got a hot dog and a Diet Coke. They munched while they drove toward the park. Between bites, Ransom told her he had no idea what his source thought was so important.

* * * * *

The ambience in the small, ragged park resembled the steam bath at the YMCA, leaving it deserted of any life except for squirrels and birds. Outside the car, under the blazing sun, Ransom opened the trunk and then took off his coat, tie, and handgun, placing them inside. He unbuttoned his collar. Then he took off his shoes, grabbed a pair of jogging sneakers from the trunk, and slipped them on.

Standing beside him, Kathy made a snide remark about the smell. He ignored her. As the finishing touch to his garb for meeting a source, he jammed a baseball cap on his head which read, "Born to fish."

"How do I look?" he asked.

"What are you supposed to be?" she replied.

"Never mind," he said, frowning. "You wait in the car, I'll just be a few minutes."

So Kathy stayed in the car as backup, watching the place where Ransom would meet his source. Ransom mosied toward the bench where he'd previously met Billy a couple of times. Thank God, the bench looked to be in some partial shade from a live oak tree. He'd already spotted Billy ambling along from the other direction, dressed in his standard ripped-up, faded blue jeans and black Metallica T-shirt.

Billy's brow was cable knitted, which was odd. The young man was not one to anticipate much beyond the next hour or two, and he never worried about his past mistakes, as Ransom was prone to do. In fact, Ransom had never seen Billy look upset, except when he first met the kid a couple of years before, the night the FBI and DEA raided a meth lab on the outskirts of town.

Billy was a minor figure in the operation, and Ransom convinced DEA and the police not to charge him in exchange for Billy's co-operation in jamming the others. Ransom was also interested that Billy belonged to a *palo Mayombre* cult. Since that law school student had been murdered in Matamoros some years before, Ransom had been intrigued by the group's weird practices. He wanted a good source in case the local bunch got crazier than usual.

They met on the pathway, as if by coincidence, stood talking for a minute, and Ransom laughed and swatted his ball cap against his leg. It was just part of the act, in case someone was watching them. It wasn't good for an informant's health when certain people learned he was talking to the feds. Then they settled on the bench next to each other.

Ransom took a last look around and said, "Okay, what's so hot, Billy?"

Billy fidgeted with his grease-stained hands. The kid had probably been working on his Harley, the pride of his scattered life. His fingernails were short, but still showed black crud beneath them. Even the 666 tattoo in the palm of his hand was smeared with a brownish stain.

"The group I'm in has talked about funny stuff before. And once we gutted some cows and drank their blood, which is awful shit, man. But this is . . . I dunno, I'm really freaked about it."

"About what, Billy?"

"They're talking about making a human sacrifice."

"Say again?"

"The head guy said we're gonna do a sacrifice."

"A *human* sacrifice?"

"That's what he said."

Ransom swallowed. His throat felt like sandpaper. "Did they say when?"

"Yeah, tomorrow night." He picked at a fingernail.

"And where's this supposed to happen?"

"The same place we've been having our meetings. You know, in that clearing about ten miles south of town."

"Right. But, Billy, do you believe them? Would they actually do something like that?"

Billy shrugged. "It sounded for real."

"Listen, have you found out who the head man is yet?"

He shook his head. "Like I told you, everyone wears hoods. And no one uses their real name. The priest goes by some name like a mummy."

"You mean an Egyptian pharaoh?"

"I guess so."

Ransom squeezed his chin, thinking. "Do you know who's supposed to be killed?"

"Nah, he never said that."

"What time is it supposed to happen?"

"We always get there about ten, and we start up a little later. We'll probably do some other rituals first. I think it'll be around eleven or so."

Ransom stared at a tree, studying the detail of the bark, trying to concentrate. "You did good calling me, Billy. I'll make it worth your while."

Billy beamed.

"You know what?" Ransom said. "I'd like to take a quick run out to that spot, look it over again so that I'm sure that I know it well."

Billy nodded like a toy dog in the back window of a car. "That's cool by me. Sure, we can do that."

"Will they have anyone watching it?"

"Shit, I don't think so. It's just a clearing on some land out there. They say it belongs to some guy from out-of-town."

"Then let's do it."

The ride was uneventful until the last mile when they pulled onto a rough gravel road that caused them to pitch and slide. The surrounding land was as flat as a breadboard, bordered with groves of scrub oak and hackberry. In spite of the recent rain, patches of plow-scarred ground looked as dry as gunpowder.

From the back seat Billy told Ransom to turn at a narrow road that led into a heavy thicket of trees and overgrown brush. The road soon deteriorated into a couple of ruts that meandered through the trees. That's a good way to hide all the headlights, Ransom thought.

"Around that curve," Billy said.

Sure enough, as he recalled from seeing it more than a year before, there was a cleared area among the trees. It was probably part natural meadow and part fashioned by chain saw and mower. A hundred or so people could gather there, no sweat.

They scrunched to a stop, got out, then poked around in the field. Ransom plucked a piece of tall grass and stuck the stalk in his mouth. He wiped his wet forehead.

"Where do they have the altar?"

The pallid youth pointed a dirty finger and said, "She's right there, where the grass is tromped down."

Ransom peered at the flattened area; sure enough, there was the pattern of a pentagram.

"She?" said Kathy.

Billy's complexion got rosy. "Uh, yes, ma'am. They use a woman as the altar."

"They *what?*" she said.

"It's part of the ritual," Ransom said. "The altar is female, naked, lying on her back, spread-eagled before the congregation, usually holding a couple of black candles. It's purely symbolic—just for show. The real action starts later, right, Billy?"

Billy was now as red as a freshly-painted barn. "Ah, Mr. Ransom, I can't say about that."

"That's okay," Kathy said. "He's just goading both of us, Billy. And payback's a bitch."

They spoke little on the way back into town, each lost in private thoughts. When Ransom let Billy out at the park, he said, "If you hear any more details, call me anytime. You understand?"

"Sure, Mr. Ransom. We got another meeting tonight, gettin' ready for the blood ritual, they say. Anything else happens, I'll call, don't worry none."

"Okay, thanks. I'll see you later."

As they drove away, Billy stuffed several bills in his pocket and gave a little wave.

* * * * *

When they arrived downtown, they stopped at the Bexar County Sheriff's Office where Ransom outlined to a Captain

Marquez what they'd learned about a planned homicide. Ransom drew a map of the location, and the heavy-jowled man thanked them for the information and promised he'd have some deputies follow up on it.

Settled in the car, the air conditioner blasting on max, they discussed what to do next. Then Ransom said, "I'm worried. Let's drop by the hospital and check on Jester's baby."

Kathy said, "You're reading my mind."

* * * * *

As Ransom and Kathy drove toward Metro, a woman shuffled along a hallway cuddling a child against her breasts. It looked like a fragile doll. Catching her image in a mirror, she paused to study her face. She looked drab, her complexion washed out, and she had bags under her eyes. Swiping at her bangs, she noticed lines on her forehead. That wasn't good. Wrinkles could murder what looks she still had. Why couldn't she have been a beauty like her sister? Life was so much easier for the pretty ones.

Sighing, she stepped into the living room in time to see Harvey pop open his fourth beer of the day and take a hefty swig. She knew he wouldn't be in the mood for this conversation, but she didn't care. She stared at him and took a deep breath.

"The rent's due tomorrow, Harvey. Do we have the money to pay it?"

"Hell, I don't know. All the dough we spent on formula and diapers and shit, I doubt it."

That meant no. "Then what are we gonna do?"

He rubbed the back of his neck as though it were stiff. "I'll make another run, I guess. I'll go when this deal's over."

Her stomach churned, like it always did when they were short of money. And that was most of the time. "You know what the landlord said: 'Don't be late again.' He might boot us out this time."

"I said I'd go on a run, and—"

"But that will take a week," she interrupted. "The rent's due tomorrow, and that old man will be—"

"He can wait a couple of days. It won't kill him."

The baby was squirming now, probably about to start bawling. She was so exhausted and strung out, she felt as if she'd go out of her mind.

"All right, then you answer the phone when he calls. You

talk to him when he rolls up in that big silver Bronco."

"No sweat." He took a heavy slug of his brew. "I can handle the old fart."

Suddenly it struck her that Harvey's hairline had receded. Was it from wearing that dumb ball cap all the time? Just then, the baby sucked in some air and let go with a wail. She took two quick steps toward Harvey. His mouth dropped open and his eyes opened wide.

"And take care of this brat, too," she said, plopping the yowling baby into his arms and knocking the beer out of his hand. The fallen can lay on its side, gurgling foam. From the storm that passed behind his eyes, she thought for a moment that he was going to throw the kid across the room.

"Now look what you done," he said with a stare like a cluster of steel knives. His face was florid, and his ears looked pinched. He shoved the baby back at her, and she grabbed it.

"*You* take the damn kid. You just spilled my last beer, you bitch!"

So that was it. "Oh, sorry. Like you really needed another beer, you prick. When you ain't off in that stupid truck, you don't do a damn thing around here but loaf and suck down beer."

"Just bring home the bacon," he said. His jawline was hard. "More'n you do, layin' around here watchin' soap operas all day."

"Yeah, the great provider. Mr. Trump himself. So how come we ain't got rent money?"

"Because . . . I told you, it's . . . ." he sputtered. Then his mouth clamped shut. He looked like a cornered rat.

She stepped back. "Anyway, Harvey, let's not fight about it."

But it was too late. He took a step closer and swung. His bony fist thudded against her cheekbone, just beneath her eye. The cheek felt deadened, as though it were stunned, followed within seconds by a throbbing ache.

The baby screeched. She wanted to scream herself. She wanted to fling the child aside and scratch Harvey's eyes out. But she hesitated long enough for the primal urge to pass, for the adrenaline surge to backwash. Then she felt exhausted, and she collapsed into a chair and sobbed.

Harvey stood there a minute, and then said, "You oughta watch what you say. A man can only take so much." He picked up his cap, and said, "I'm goin' to get some beer."

After the porch screen door slammed, and Harvey's truck coughed, fired up, then pulled out, she wondered about their spat. Had she been too mean? Harvey did have a job, and he hadn't taken off and left her for another woman, like had happened to some of her friends.

She rocked the baby and talked to it. Finally, it stopped crying and started gnawing its tiny fist. She'd better warm up a bottle. She touched her throbbing cheek. It'd hurt for a couple of days, but then it would heal.

And wasn't it natural for men and women to fight sometimes? Of course it was. It was just a way to let off steam and to clear built-up tension. Then things could settle down and get back to normal.

Besides, why get upset? They'd pay the damn rent. A day or two late didn't matter. Like Harvey said, let the old fart wait.

As she walked toward the kitchen, she smiled and hummed to herself. Maybe she'd fix some T-bone steaks tonight. It was Harvey's favorite meal.

14

Ransom and Kathy approached the hospital with dread. He pulled into the side lot, found a visitor's spot open, and killed the engine. He struggled to project a sense of hopefulness, but he felt as if he wasn't quite pulling it off.

Jester's face said it all as he stood like a bronze statue next to his son's isolette, gazing down at the wiry infant who looked so invaded by tubes, electrodes, and monitors.

Suddenly, Jester's head snapped up, and he gestured at the nurse. Nurse Pettijohn moved to the incubator and peered at the monitor as Jester pointed, his eyes wide and frantic. Reaching inside the portholes, she grabbed the baby under the arms and shook it.

Ransom clenched his fists and grimaced.

Pettijohn and Jester stared at some red numbers dancing on the monitor. After a couple of moments, Jester's shoulders slumped in what Ransom took to be relief. Nurse Pettijohn stood there for a couple of minutes, then looked at her watch, said something to Jester, and moved away.

Shortly, Nurse Pettijohn came striding down the hall, minus her sterile gown and cap.

Ransom said, "Excuse me," taking a half step into her pathway.

"Yes?" She stiffened as she was forced to stop.

"We were just watching, and we wondered if there's some sort of trouble with Mr. Holmes's baby."

"We're not allowed to comment on the babies, their condition, or their treatment. Only family members are privy to that information."

"I understand. But there did seem to be some distress, and from your actions and concern with the monitor, I felt there was a problem."

"Yes, there was," she admitted.

"And was it corrected? I mean, shouldn't you watch the baby awhile to make sure it doesn't recur?"

She bristled, her torso straining at her tight scrubs, giving Ransom the feeling he'd offended an Amazon.

"Any of dozens of problems can and do arise with these preemies at any hour of the night or day. My shift is over, the baby was fine when I left, and there are other nurses on duty trained to do the same things I do." She checked her watch, then skirted them, saying, "Now if you'll excuse me."

Ransom started to speak, but Kathy grabbed his arm. "Let her go," she whispered. "She's as tight as an oyster."

"You're right," he said. And they stood there, uninformed and worried, watching Jester brood over his son.

A few minutes later, Jester walked away from the incubator, stripped off his sterile gown, and entered the hallway. He appeared glad to see them, like a drowning man clutching at a floating log.

"We just had a bad scare," he said.

"What happened?" Kathy asked.

"Bradycardia. Michael's pulse dropped under a hundred. When it slows that much, he doesn't pump enough blood and get enough oxygen to his body. It can be very serious."

"But he's all right, now?" Ransom asked.

"The nurse gave him a shake and a couple of curses, and the little guy's ticker kicked back in. He may be small, but he's a fighter. He might make a good bantamweight someday."

Ransom realized Jester's bravado was the brittle facade of a terrified man. They talked a minute, and then Ransom and Kathy sought each other's eyes.

"We'd better go," Ransom said. "Call the office if there's any change or if you need anything at all."

Jester nodded, attempting a smile. "Thanks, guys. I appreciate you coming by."

They all looked back into the intensive care ward and saw Jester's wife approach the incubator to stare at her tiny baby. Ransom thought she appeared just as frightened as Jester had earlier. What a horrible situation to have to face; he didn't know if he could handle it.

"I'd better get back in there," Jester said.

He paced away, and they made their way down the hallway, past harried nurses and slow-moving women in their bathrobes, shepherding IV stands on wheels. The floor held a microcosm of new life, pain, and death.

As they stepped off the elevator, Ransom spotted Nurse Pettijohn sitting on a bench by the side door, just finishing a phone call. She had changed into some flashy street clothes. She put her cell phone into her small red purse, got up and pushed open the door, then hurried away without noticing them. As they followed her outside, Ransom watched her swaying bottom, now encased in a tight red skirt with a deep split up the back. Red high-heeled shoes clattered on the sidewalk as she strode toward the employee's parking slots.

Ransom was parked not far from where Pettijohn stopped and opened her car door, and he glanced over as she slid into a low-slung red sports Pontiac. Was she wearing red panties, too? He dismissed the idea with a shake of his head.

Her car pealed out. She seemed in a big hurry to get somewhere.

"Do you want to contact some more scrubs renters?" Kathy asked.

"We need to interview them, but after seeing Jester, I feel bad about Mrs. Baldazar sitting there worried sick about her baby. In spite of what the Senator said, I don't think she's a strong woman." He shrugged. "Maybe we should take a few minutes to tell her the investigation's moving along. It might give her a little hope."

"Do you still have any?"

"That's about all I've got, and I'm not giving it up." He dropped the Ford into drive and pulled out of the lot, hesitating to let a Dodge Ram van roll by. He looked for other traffic, but none was coming, so he pressed the pedal. Unlike Nurse Pettijohn, he realized he was in no great hurry to get where he was going.

* * * * *

"Why are you going this way?" Kathy asked.

"I want to see if the Senator is still at his office."

As they approached the small tan building, they spotted the Mercedes scintillating in its parking spot. Ransom felt hot blood surge up the sides of his neck, burning his ear lobes. The bastard should be home with his wife.

As he drove past the Senator's office, the traffic light flicked red. Braking to a stop, Ransom glanced at Kathy and said, "Can you believe this guy?"

"No way," she said, glancing back over her shoulder, "but speak of the devil, here he comes."

Ransom peered at his outside mirror and saw Baldazar open his car door, toss his briefcase into the front seat of the high dollar ride, and slide behind the wheel.

The light changed, and Ransom eased forward, then pulled to the right, angling into the parking lot of an interior design shop.

"Have you got a sudden urge to redecorate?" Kathy jibed.

"I don't want to get to his house before Baldazar does. I'll just tag along behind and give him a few minutes with his wife before we barge in."

"Good idea. She might be upset with him for being gone so long."

Baldazar whipped by, and after two more cars passed, Ransom pulled into the street. The Mercedes was wasting no time, but Ransom mashed the accelerator and kept it in view.

Minutes later Kathy said, "Now why did he turn there?"

Who was she, the Pathfinder? "Who knows? Maybe he has to pick up something at the store," Ransom offered. He made the turn.

"He doesn't seem like the helpful type."

"Everyone has to eat."

"And that from his nibs of Seven Eleven dining."

"That was Circle K's finest. And don't cloud the issue."

But what the hell? Now it was Ransom's turn to wonder what was up as Baldazar slowed and turned into the lot of the Rancho Rio, a watering hole for blue collar workers.

"I told you," Kathy crowed. "The guy's getting a blast before he goes home."

The Mercedes eased into an empty space beside a faded pickup with a large tool box in the bed.

"That makes no sense. He's got that big, well-stocked bar in his house." He shook his head. "But you're right. To hell with it! We're going ahead to see Mrs. Baldazar while he's—"

His jaw dropped. "Wait a minute, that sports car parked two spots over . . . ."

And a freight car load of suspicion rolled over him.

"That's Nurse Pettijohn's red Pontiac," he said.

"Oh, my God, it sure is," she said. "But . . . do you think they'd—"

"You tell me," he said.

He stopped a block away and slipped off his coat, tie, and holster, and from the trunk he pulled out a pair of coveralls he kept for dirty work. He struggled into them, slammed the trunk lid, then reached back into the car and snatched his fishing cap from under the seat.

"I'm going in for a looksee."

"No wig and false beard?" she asked, fighting a smirk.

"This is low intensity work."

She pulled the door latch to get out, but he said, "You stay here."

"No way, I'm going with you."

"Nah, a classy dame like you could cause a riot in there."

She started to protest, but then grinned. "Bogie, you sure got a way with us dolls."

"Right, Sweetheart. See you later." He realized that he needed a cigarette to flick away.

Tugging open the door to the bawdy joint, he stepped into a cloud of smoke and a cacophony of juke box twang. In a minute his eyes adjusted to the weird glow from a bevy of neon beer signs. Fifteen or so laborer types in dirty jeans and ragged T-shirts drank beer in rowdy bunches. Two guys sitting at the bar wearing sports coats, their ties at half mast, caressed highballs.

A bedraggled barmaid set down four pitchers of beer on a large round table, while deftly dodging pinches of her curvy backside. The bartender, who was built like an overweight linebacker, stood stolidly behind the fortress-like bar. He surveyed the place like he was looking for someone to blindside with a killer tackle.

Baldazar sat ensconced in a green padded booth at the far end of the place, in the darkest corner. He ignored the other patrons. From that angle Ransom couldn't see anyone else in the booth, but the Senator yakked away like a typical politician, and Nurse Pettijohn was nowhere in sight.

Moving to the bar Ransom climbed aboard a red bar stool and leaned his forearms on the bar. It was wet. The bartender stared at him, maybe sizing him up for a hit.

"Gimmee a Bud," said Ransom.

"Can?"

"Bottle's good."

The guy grunted, shuffled his big frame a couple of steps to the cooler, caged a longneck from the depths of the crushed ice, snapped the cap off, then lumbered over and slammed it down on the bar. It foamed over. The reluctant server didn't reach for a bar rag.

Ransom tossed a five beside the icy bottle, took a swig while the bartender worried awhile making change, then swiveled on the stool enough to verify the short red skirt, chorus girl legs, and red high heels of Baldazar's companion. The pair leaned toward each other, their eyes locked, and the good Senator snuck a hand under the table, caressing Pettijohn's knee.

Ransom took a few more gulps of beer, the cold liquid constricting his throat. Then he folded a dollar bill, left it in the beer puddle on the bar, and slid off the stool. The pall of smoke in this dive was clogging his sinuses, and he'd seen enough. He tugged his cap down as he left, not giving the Senator or his cocktail chippie a peek at his face.

When he climbed back into the car, Kathy was wound tight. "What'd you see?" Her eyes shone like two Hope diamonds.

"Sure enough, they were having a drink together."

"*Sacre bleu.* Was it . . . intimate?"

He stuck the ball cap back under the seat. "They looked damn cozy to me."

"That son-of-a-bitch!" Kathy spit out.

On the way to see Mrs. Baldazar, Ransom and Kathy discussed whether the tryst between Nurse Pettijohn and the Senator was serious, and whether there might be any connection with the kidnapping.

"That's a very strange dalliance," Ransom said.

"They're the odd couple, all right. I can see the attraction, but considering the situation, it's so damn bizarre."

"Strange as hell, I'd say."

"You think we should put them under a microscope?"

"If we do," Ransom said, "we might see something crawly. But let's run it by Sonny."

* * * * *

At the Senator's house, they spoke with Mrs. Baldazar, and though some of the fire had gone out of Ransom's belly in respect to this mission, the fragile woman seemed to appreciate their assurances and to brighten a little before they left. She apologized that her husband had been forced to work late and wasn't there to see them. They said not to worry about it.

* * * * *

Back at the office, agents milled about the crowded squad room prior to the conference. A few minutes later Jenkins walked in and got the meeting rolling. He called on the leaders of the different investigative teams to tell what they'd found.

The teams working the hospitals, doctors, and infertility clinics had found a lot of names connected with stillbirths, hysterectomies, and miscarriages. It was all being put into the computer for crosschecking and evaluation with other information already entered in connection with the case.

License plate registrants had been sifted for ones fitting the make and model seen by Ms. Phoenix. They'd decided to first contact women who fit the kidnapper's description, of which there were sixty-four. If those washed out, they'd try the other owners, since the car could be registered in a man's name but have been driven by the woman.

Lt. Sanchez told about interviewing the last of the candy stripers. One young lady did recall seeing a nurse in the hallway with an isolette on the morning of the kidnapping.

Ransom asked, "Did she give the same physical description as Mrs. Baldazar and Ms. Phoenix?"

"It was a general description," Sanchez said, "but *bastante similar.* Close enough to the others." Sanchez added that the girl thought she'd recognize the woman if she saw her again. "She helps out regularly and knows the staff. Which brings up something odd she said."

"What's that?" Jenkins asked.

"That morning in the hallway, the candy striper thought she recognized the nurse, and she started to wave to her. When she realized she didn't know her, she just went on into the patient's room to deliver a message."

Ransom squinted. "You mean the woman looked like someone she knew? Someone on the hospital staff?"

"That's about as close as she could describe it," said Sanchez. "But she couldn't think who the nurse reminded her of. She just got that impression. *Quien sabe?*" he added, shrugging.

Yeah, who knows? thought Ransom. "Can she give us information for a composite sketch?"

"We had her provide us the data for one, if you want to try it. Then we showed her the other sketch, which she said was a bit off. So, maybe the new sketch will give us a different look."

Jenkins said, "Put a rush on it. We need a break in this case. Real bad."

"Wait a minute," Atherton said, a puzzled look on his face.

"What?" asked Jenkins.

"When I reviewed the security tapes for the morning of the kidnapping, there not only wasn't a shot of the kidnapper with the isolette, there wasn't one of a candy striper, either."

"I don't get it," Jenkins said.

"And both people should have been on the tape," Ransom said.

"How could that happen?" Jenkins asked.

"Maybe someone put in a phony shot somehow," said Ransom. "Hank, can you go over the tape again, and have the security camera repairman watch it, too? Maybe he'll have an idea of what happened."

"You got it," said Atherton.

The room buzzed with conversations about the tape. Jenkins asked for quiet, and in a minute Ransom told the group about the uniform renters, the Exalted Shepherd's fallen daughter, and the meeting between the horny Senator and the scarlet nurse.

Jenkins was mystified, but amused, maybe from the stress of working the kidnapping and from being dead tired. He chortled, "Once again, sex rears its ugly head."

The others laughed, but no one could offer an angle on how this relationship affected their investigation. The general consensus was to keep on working and see what developed. Many times just hoofing out leads brought them to the clue that would put the whole thing together.

* * * * *

The meeting broke up, and Ransom and Kathy decided to try a couple more uniform renters. But after checking out the young women, they felt once again that there was no connection to their case. *Quelle malchance.*

Shadows were getting long, and they were both exhausted. Ransom had been in this situation enough times to realize adrenaline was a great short term boost, but day long squirts into the nervous system could deep fry the entire neural network.

"Let's call it a day," he said.

For once, Kathy didn't argue.

When he got to his apartment, Ransom ate a chicken pot pie and a chocolate bar and drank a cold can of Diet Coke.

He rinsed his plate and fork and left them in the sink. After dropping into his recliner, he picked up the phone and called Sharene's room at the hospital. Jester answered.

"Michael's been stable since you were last here," he said. "But the doctor was afraid he still had cranial bleeding, so he ordered a sonogram. We're waiting for him to tell us the results."

"Do you want me to come and wait with you?" Ransom offered.

"Thanks, but I'm sure you're beat. Whatever the test says, your being here won't change it. Get some rest. You've got more of the same coming up tomorrow."

"As Don Herold said, 'Work is the greatest thing in the world, so we should always save some of it for tomorrow.'"

"Well, unless crime took a holiday since I came into this hospital, you'll always have plenty to do."

"Jester, some things never change."

"Who said that?"

"Probably about a billion people before I just did."

After Jester hung up, Dover punched in another number.

Holly picked it up on the second ring with an enthusiastic greeting.

"Hi, it's Daddy."

"Oh, hi." He thought he sensed a thud of disappointment.

"What's going on, honey?"

"Nothing. Janie's supposed to call me about this cool cheerleader camp this summer. Mom said she'd talk with you about sending me."

"Why, is there a problem?"

"Well, you know, it's kinda expensive."

"Oh, sure. I see."

"So did you want something? Janie is supposed to call me like now."

"I'm sorry to interrupt. I just wanted to ask if you could come to the race next Saturday."

"The race?"

"The marathon race I'm going to run in."

"Next Saturday?"

"Yes, can you make it? We could have lunch afterwards, and then I could drop you off and pick up Scott."

"I sorta have plans to go to a party at a friend's house. An end of school blast, you know?"

"Tell you what, maybe you can make both." He told Holly where she could meet him.

"Maybe, let me see."

She seemed more morose than usual. "Is something

bothering you?" he asked.

"Oh, it's nothing."

"I'd like to know if there is."

"No you wouldn't."

"Sure I would, let's hear it."

"Okay, it's Mom. She won't tell me whether I can get the pill or not."

"The pills, uh, pill. Oh, you mean . . . ."

"Right, Daddy. Are you sorry you asked?"

Yes, in fact he was. "No, I was just considering my position on the matter."

"It's not up for a vote. If Mom says yes, I'll get them."

He was shocked by her defiance. "I'm still your father, Holly, and I—"

"Yeah, but you're not here. We handle things by ourselves now."

"It's an important decision. I'll discuss it with your mom later."

"I guess I can't stop you."

"No, you can't." He took a deep breath. "Anyway, good luck on your exams next week."

"I'll need it," she said, and quickly hung up.

He thought about calling back, discussing the matter with Beverly, and then having a serious talk with Holly. But then he thought about Jester and Mrs. Baldazar and their situations. This was not such a terrible problem. Sometimes, even if you felt like smacking them, it was great to know your children were still breathing.

15

Though it was one of her regular workout nights, Kathy didn't go to the gym. She didn't seem to have the energy. At her apartment she doffed her clothes and slipped into a cotton robe. It felt great to get comfortable and just relax. She drank a glass of milk, and then lay down on the bed. Fatigue slid over her like a creeping fog bank, and her mind went dark.

Forty minutes later, her eyes fluttered open. She hadn't meant to fall asleep. She glanced at the clock, groaned as she hauled herself to a sitting position, then picked up her cell phone.

At the gym, Sherri of the forty-inch bust answered the phone. She agreed to page Steve. Then a minute later, his deep voice came on the line.

"This's Steve."

He sounded breathless, and she could imagine his bicep peaking as he held the receiver to his ear.

"Hi, it's Kathy."

"Oh, hi, babe. I wondered where you were. Are you coming to the gym?"

"No, I'm really tired. I thought I'd skip my workout tonight."

"Yeah, okay. That's cool."

There was a pause.

She said, "Could we maybe get a salad when you finish your workout?"

"Uh, sure. But I thought you were tired."

"I am. But I'm hungry, too. And I wanted to talk to you about something."

"Oh, well, that's fine."

Another pause.

"Well, I'm in the middle of a superset," he informed her. "I'd better get back to work."

They agreed on a place to eat, she hung up, and then

she went into the bathroom and turned on the shower. Her robe dropped to the floor, and she stepped into the shelter of the warm, soothing spray.

Ten minutes later she shut off the water and toweled herself dry. Catching her reflection in the mirror, she paused to examine her body. Still shapely, though her breasts were somewhat swollen and streaked with thin bluish veins.

She wrapped the towel around her head and applied lotion and perfume. She tugged the robe back on, and she paused to stare into her eyes in the mirror, trying to see if the wisdom resided within to address this situation. She decided that it was a close call.

She drove her Honda Accord to the restaurant. In the parking lot, she watched couples entering and departing. Suddenly, they seemed so young. As they laughed and flirted with each other, they looked so carefree and uninvolved and undisciplined.

She didn't see Steve's Corvette, so she sat there, her window rolled down, the evening breeze pushing at her hair. She thought about her condition and wondered how she'd explain it to her mom. She pondered how to begin her conversation with Steve.

Now she heard the rumble of a throaty engine behind her. Sure enough, she spotted Steve's bright red Corvette gliding past in the rear view mirror. She checked her lipstick in the vanity mirror, closed her purse, and swung her legs out of the car. Steve strode toward her. His arms showed a great pump.

"Hey, doll, you look nice."

She didn't feel that way. "Thanks, dear. Did you have a good workout?"

"Not bad. I had to cut back on my curl sets to get here on time."

She noted some ruefulness. "I'm sorry, but I really think we need to talk."

"No problem. Let's go in. Unless you want to stay out here and suck up exhaust fumes."

She chuckled, and then held out her arm. He took it and steered her toward the front door. She liked being a couple. It made her feel comfortable and mature. And it gave her a sensation of being cared for and supported.

They waited in line for a while, and her legs began to feel weary. Finally, the girl called their name and whisked them to a table. It felt great to sit down.

"Can I getcha something to drink?" the waitress asked. She was a close rival for Sherri in the bust department. Her body put a strain on the café's T-shirt front, for sure. And Steve took it all in.

When he finally glanced over at her, Kathy said, "Just water for me."

Steve looked surprised. They usually knocked back a few cold ones before eating. I'll have a Coors draft," he said.

"Coming right up," she said, smiling with about a hundred teeth and turning in a tight pirouette.

The waitress wasn't too shabby in the caboose department, either, judging by Steve's appraising look as she swiveled away.

When his gaze came back in her direction, Kathy stared at him with a stern look. She saw on his face a look of surprise and fear, like her brother's expression when mom caught him smoking a joint. Men were often so transparent.

"Boy, it's pretty busy in here tonight," he said, trying to act as though he'd been assessing the patrons gathering at the entrance.

She was too tired to mention his wandering eyes and get into a hassle, so she said, "Yes, I didn't expect such a crowd this early."

They talked about some non-issues, then Miss Goodbody brought the beer in a big frosty mug, together with a small glass of water. When she set down the brewsky, the lass gave Steve another big smile. He gave her one back. The water got far less fanfare.

Steve took a hearty swallow of the icy suds.

She took a small sip of the tepid water. That bitch.

"So what did you want to talk about?" Steve asked.

"Maybe we'd better order first," she said.

They asked for the salad bar, then piled their plates with lettuce, veggies, eggs, meats, and cheeses. Steve doused his creation with generous dollops of Ranch dressing. She opted for a light sprinkling of oil and vinegar.

After a few bites, she screwed up her courage, swallowed, and caught Steve's eye.

"I've been thinking that we haven't talked about what we want for the future."

He stared for a minute as if he didn't understand, then he gave a slight shrug. "You know I'm interested in politics, and I know you like working for the FBI."

"I meant on a more personal level."

"Like hobbies and stuff?"

"Like marriage and children and growing old together."

Now he gave her an appraising look. "I don't get it. This isn't like you. What's up?"

She took another sip of water, and then sighed. "You're right. I just didn't know how to tell you. I . . . don't know exactly how to say it."

"So, what's on your mind? Just say it."

"All right, I'm pregnant."

Now he seemed to pale, and he took a big swallow of beer. He placed his mug carefully back on the table, staring at the contents as though they were of profound interest. Then he looked up at her, his face tight with concern.

Then came the questions: Wasn't she always protected? How far along was she? How was she feeling?

And then he asked the part about: What do we do now? Answering his own query, he first sighed, and then said, "I don't think either of us is ready to accept the responsibility of a child right now."

She studied his demeanor. He was acting authoritarian, righteous, and self-serving. Those were the attributes she least admired in a man.

He must have read her silence as acquiescence, because he forged ahead. "In fact, I know a doctor who's an expert—"

"I'm going to have the baby."

He was stunned, but the politician in him dredged up a glib response. "But just think about it. Abortions are cheap and safe. And we can always have another child later, when we're both prepared for it. You know, when the time is right."

She wasn't buying it, and she thought he could read it in her face.

"I'm going home," she said. "You can stay and have another beer."

* * * * *

The man purred along the highway, the whirring of the air conditioner blocking any noise from the traffic. His headlights picked out the turn onto the gravel road, and he cranked the steering wheel, felt the tires bite into the shifting layers of small rocks, and slowed his pace to better handle the uncertain surface. Soon, it would change to a road more earth than gravel, then a plain dirt lane, then tracks into a field.

On automatic pilot now, he let his thoughts wander. His left hand went between the buttons on his shirt front, fumbling until his fingers clutched the gold Cross of Nero that lay against his chest. He felt a surge of power from the talisman, his charm of black magick.

Success was within his grasp, he knew it. The ceremony tonight, in celebration of Walpurgisnacht, would be but a prelude to the greatness of the event tomorrow. Come nightfall on *Walpurgis* Day, a blood sacrifice would be made. The ultimate human sacrifice: that of a newborn baby.

And with that sacrifice would come power and glory. Eternal life would be his. He'd receive an extension of the meager allotment of years given a person at birth. He'd have time to live, to enjoy, to learn and understand the true significance of mortal existence.

He might even become *el padrino,* known to his followers across the nation, a true leader of the cult. And that would give him untold power. Because soon the dark spirits of the *orishas* would rise up to establish their reign on earth. And the high priests of *palo Mayombre* would become mightier than presidents, kings, or even dictators.

The car dipped as the road became bumpier. Dust filtered through the car vents. In spite of the chill air flowing around him, his wet shirt clung to his back.

He touched the wooden box in the seat beside him. Inside were his robe, a dozen candles, and an athame, which he kept on his belt in a scabbard during the ceremonies. He'd used the twisted knife to draw sacrificial blood many times since he first obtained it.

Also in the box were sticks, a human finger bone, and a man's rib. All had steeped in a cauldron of blood and body parts. They were powerful instruments for magick.

He spotted the two ruts leading into the field. He turned, killing his headlights as he drove. As the car slid over the matted grass, bucking when it struck various bumps or depressions, he laid his hand atop the walnut box. Each time he touched the rough container, he felt an electrifying sense of power emanating from within it.

He pulled behind a stand of trees. Several vehicles were parked there, so he drove on farther, found a private spot, and killed the engine. He stared a moment at the box, then opened it and pulled out his robe. Tonight would be the beginning of his new destiny.

* * * * *

The call came around midnight. A surveillance team agent told Ransom that Parker Tipton was on the move. These crooks kept the worst hours, he thought. The only thing for sure was that the mope was up to no good. Ransom shook his head clear, shrugged into some work pants and a dark-colored shirt, and combed his hair with his fingers. There, all set.

By the time Ransom got on the air, Tipton had already drug Castle Hills and was headed east on Loop 410. Ransom dropped down to Loop 410 and Broadway and waited. Tipton exited there a few minutes later, southbound. Ransom figured that the guy had to be going back to Alamo Heights. One of the SOG team members was tailing Tipton in a tan Corvette. Ransom fell in behind, keeping a loose tail.

Tipton had not met with Pit Face or his pit bull bodyguard. Tonight, he was doing a solo act. Ransom radioed the agents at the Baldazar's residence.

"Go ahead, five romeo."

"We've got a package coming toward your location. Have there been any calls?"

"Negative. It's been quiet as a church."

Maybe like the Exalted Shepherd's sanctuary? "Okay, but keep your eyes open. If we get close to you, I'll radio back. If you get a call, let me know right away."

Now Tipton drove past the roadblock, then turned down the next street leading into Alamo Heights. Ransom hoped the meathead had the balls to do something this time. Especially since they had him scoped.

It didn't take long. Tipton cruised through several streets, then a couple of blocks from the Baldazar's house, he parked beside a vacant lot and killed his headlights and engine. Ransom stopped his Crown Vic and watched.

The houses along the street were dark, but several security lights threw white splashes on the bushes beneath the eaves. Neighborhood dogs gave out scattered yelps. Ransom heard a car door open. No overhead light came on in the Lumina, but he knew Tipton was out on foot.

"This's five romeo. I'll be out of my vehicle shadowing the package."

"Need any help?" came over the radio.

"Negative, you'd better stay in your ride in case I lose him." He was out of the car before the response came back.

Pale moonlight shone down through sultry air. He followed Tipton from a block away, trying to stay out of the line of sight by skirting around trees and bushes. He also tried to keep away from the houses, not wanting to excite any dogs.

Tipton glanced around, but he sauntered along as if he were out for a midnight stroll. Ransom found it easy to tail the man. Until he all of a sudden disappeared into the blackness.

Tipton's shirt was dark, and at first Ransom didn't realize it had vanished from view. Then it hit him that all he was seeing was black on black, and no movement. Damn.

What he'd give right now for some night vision goggles. He tried to pinpoint where he'd last seen Tipton. The guy must've slipped between the white two story house and the smaller stucco one with the van parked in the driveway. Ransom snuck along, struggling to see some movement or a shape. He strained to hear a footfall or a scrape against something.

Now he heard the scuff of footsteps on the driveway. They were coming toward him. Tipton must be retracing his steps. Ransom paused, his brain whirring, and then he dropped to the ground and rolled beneath the van. The pungent smell of gasoline hit his nostrils.

Tipton paced up beside the van and stopped. Several seconds ticked away as Ransom's heart banged like a kettledrum. The heavy night air clotted his lungs, and he broke out in a sweat. Had the guy heard him scoot under the van? Was he looking for him? Would he duck down and take a look, maybe with a gun in his hand?

In a moment, Tipton walked away.

Ransom stuck his head out. Tipton passed under a street lamp down the street, headed in the direction of the Baldazar's home. Ransom slid out from under the van.

As Ransom followed, he avoided the puddle of light beneath the lamp pole. Tipton turned a corner, still a block from the Baldazar's, slinking along the street like a murky ghost. Then the black figure turned and eased alongside another house.

Ransom took in a deep breath, walking toe to heel like an Indian scout as he trailed this phantom. He knew the longer he was behind Tipton, the more chance there was he'd be made. And the goof might double back again anytime.

Pausing at the back corner of the house, Ransom at first

heard nothing. Then there was an audible scrape. He poked his head around the corner, and then jerked it back. But he saw nothing. Then he looked again. When his eyes adjusted to the faint glow from a patio light two houses down, he could make out Tipton jimmying a window. Using a regulation pry bar, like a pro. This was just great.

As wood splintered, Ransom eased away and made his way back to the sidewalk, cursing under his breath. When he was thirty yards away, he pulled out his handi talkie. He advised the surveillance units about the break-in, asking them to post lookouts on the periphery.

Then he told dispatch to notify the Alamo Heights police. Two squad cars arrived in six minutes. Not bad.

As Tipton walked out the back door, two young beefy cops grabbed him, spun him around, and slapped on the cuffs. Even the hard ex-con, a graduate cum laude of Slammer Tech, couldn't hide his surprise and disappointment at the instant bust. As they hauled him away, he muttered phrases no one wanted their mother to hear.

The house Tipton had ripped off belonged to a Daddy Warbucks type businessman with lots of candy lying around. The guy must've got off on buying his wife trinkets like ten thousand dollar diamond bracelets and large carat rings, many of which items were stashed in Tipton's deep pants pockets. The guy could've fenced the haul for twenty grand or so. Enough to entice Pit Face out of a kilo of coke or a big sack full of rock.

It was a good bust for the Alamo Heights cops. Tipton would draw a nickel on the rap. But in relation to the kidnapping, the scene was worth less than zero, leaving the perps at large. And the list of suspects was being whittled away like strips off a branch.

Worst of all, Ransom realized with a sinking feeling, the baby remained in limbo.

16

Flames leaped and licked. Fire engulfed bundles of branches on the ground. Red tongues flickered from straw torches carried aloft by a throng of eerie shapes in the dark field. And within the chaos dwelt a force straining to be released, eager to whirl like a tornado among the group, intent on wreaking havoc upon their fragile bodies and rendering their spirits into bits of coal and soot.

As the mass of twitching shapes waited for deliverance from their pitiable selves and their wretched conditions, a tall, shrouded figure stood apart. He clutched a human skull under one arm and held aloft a gleaming sword. With a swish, he swung the weapon in an arc toward the ground, and all at once, the group fell silent.

A naked blonde woman lay on a pallet near the man. She held a black candle in each hand. A silver chalice sat beside her, as well as a candelabrum holding five lit tapers which illuminated her body for the anxious throng.

The tall figure peered at the altar, and then turned to the group as he exhorted the spirits, speaking in unintelligible words while the crowd chanted approval. When the man paused and motioned, two burly, robed men exited the woods, dragging toward the altar a naked man with greasy hair and a scraggly beard. The scrawny man struggled, but it seemed clear he'd been drugged, and his efforts were puny. Even so, his eyes were wide with terror.

The shrouded man spoke some more mysterious words and pointed the sword at the crowd, which seemed to vibrate as though they might fly into the sky like bats. Then he whirled around to face the horrified man. With a primal cry, he raised his arm aloft, and plunged the steel shaft into the man's heart.

Like a charge of dynamite, an explosion emitted from the man's chest, and suddenly a garish red cloud appeared above the people's heads. The crowd shrank away from it, but too late. The pulsing cloud blazed, like a chunk torn from the sun, and the flesh of the celebrants softened, then melted off like candle wax. Tortured screams pierced the air.

Ransom shuddered awake. Hot, humid air pushed in through his bedroom window. The red numerals on the clock announced it was 4:05 a.m. He liked fresh air, but it was stifling tonight. He closed the window, turned down the thermostat, and got a drink of cold water. He was sweating like a draft horse in July.

A couple of hours later, dawn peeked in through the blinds, and Ransom's body came alive a bit at a time. He felt drugged by the continual stress and long hours of the past days. Not to mention his bizarre dreams.

After a shower, he felt more alert. And thoughts of what needed to be done in the kidnapping case swirled through his mind. But he had a feeling of panic that he'd never sensed on any case he'd ever worked before.

* * * * *

At the office he talked with Jenkins, reviewing what their near-term goals should be. The conference would start soon. And they had to get some sort of momentum going in the case.

Then Kathy came in, her body taut and her face rigid. Her eyes seemed glacial. She was fixated on something, not acting her usual impish self.

Ransom went to her desk and sat down in a chair beside it. "You look like something's bothering you."

She looked up at him. "My daddy taught me to use a better poker face than that." She gave a long sigh. "Maybe nothing's the matter, but I'm nervous. Jester usually phones me in the morning to tell me things are all right with Michael." She shook her head. "This morning, he didn't call."

"You think something's wrong?"

"I've got a bad premonition, and I can't shake it."

Ransom felt a tug in his gut. "Things are probably all right, but after the conference, we'll go check on Jester."

Kathy nodded, her lips compressed. "I'd feel a lot better if we did."

Atherton called to Ransom. "Line two for you, Jack."

Ransom walked back to his desk and dropped into his chair. The voice on the phone surprised him; not yet eight-thirty, and Billy was awake. That was very odd. Plus, the boy sounded scared.

"Mr. Ransom, I had to call you. It's important."

"That's fine, Billy. What is it?"

"Well, uh . . . could we meet somewhere?"

"I've got a conference in a few minutes. Could you tell me on the phone?"

"I . . . I guess. I thought you should know right away. Last night . . . at the meeting I told you about?"

"Yes? Did something happen? What was it?"

"They were talking about . . . they said about the sacrifice . . . they said it's gonna be a baby!"

Silence thickened the air. Ransom felt his heart pounding. "Wait a minute, Billy. You're sure you understood them? You weren't high on something, were you?"

"No, I swear. I had a coupla pops and a toke or two, but I know what they said. They were real excited, too."

"And it's still set for tonight?"

"Yeah, like I said, late at night."

"All right. Did they say anything else? Did they say who the baby is or anything about where they're keeping it?"

"Nah, nothin' like that. They started talking about dying and rebirth. And like how we'd all be getting new blood and energy from the kid."

Ransom felt cold all over. "Listen, Billy. You did good telling me this. And don't worry, we'll stop it. No baby is going to die tonight."

"I hope you can, I sure do. I didn't mean to get into nothin' like this. Really, I didn't."

"I believe you. And if you hear anything else, let me know right away. Call me on my cell." He gave him the number. This was too important not to take a chance on giving it out.

"What should I do about tonight, Mr. Ransom?

He thought a moment. "Go ahead and go to the meeting. Just try to act normal. Don't get excited. We'll take care of everything. You've done your part, man. And thanks."

After Billy hung up, the dial tone sounded as hollow as death.

Ransom headed for Jenkins' office, perplexed by Billy's story. A baby sacrifice? That was outrageous stuff. It was the type of abomination a group of psychotic crankheads might hallucinate as they got stoned in the woods, but not actually carry out. Still . . . .

He'd always been able to count on the information Billy had given him. And like a warning about a presidential assassination or the bombing of a federal building, this was too horrible to ignore. If there was the slightest chance that it would happen . . . .

Ransom motioned at Jenkins and then took him aside to tell him the situation. Jenkins thought about it for a minute, and then reluctantly agreed to Ransom's take on Billy's information. Then he asked, "Have you considered that this could be the baby we're looking for?"

"Sure," Ransom said. "It's a real long shot, but it's possible."

They delayed the conference, and Ransom called the Sheriff's Office to talk again with Captain Marquez. He quickly filled him in on his recent information from Billy. The captain seemed to take the news seriously, too. He said he'd be right over with some deputies to talk about a plan of response.

"Just in case, start getting ready for war," Ransom said.

"We intend to," said the captain.

* * * * *

To Ransom, the regular conference seemed mundane, though it was still crucial to the case. Progress was discussed, as well as the leads yet to be covered. Hank Atherton did have a startling revelation about the hospital's security camera tape. He'd reviewed it with the repairman who noticed it had been doctored.

"How could he tell that?" Ransom asked.

"When we focused on the details again, we could see that about fifteen minutes of the tape were bogus. We realized that during that time period it showed the other maternity ward hallway instead of the correct one. We were able to match it with the tape from the camera covering the other hallway."

There were quite a few murmured comments from the assembled group. When the noise settled down, Ransom asked. "Did you figure out how they did it?"

"We think so," Atherton said. "The repair guy thought it over, and he decided it could be done in the monitoring room, because the control panel is in there. He said if someone had used a cable splitter, then the camera in the wrong hallway would show its video for both monitors. And since there wasn't much going on that early in the morning, the guy must have figured it would pass."

"He was right about that," said Sonny.

"Damn," said Ransom. "So, we have to turn up some heat on the two security guards?"

"Looks like it," said Atherton. "I've got my barbecue fork, and I'll put those boys over a very hot fire. They're going to learn the true meaning of being grilled."

"Sounds good," said Ransom. "That could be our break in the case."

Sonny cleared his throat. "All right, we have another matter to discuss. A contingent from the Bexar County Sherriff's office should be here shortly. We'll take a break, then we'll talk about a new development. Let's start again in fifteen minutes."

* * * * *

They reconvened as suggested, their numbers swollen by the Captain and nine deputies. Sonny and Ransom greeted the new group, got them settled into some chairs, then Sonny got everyone's attention. "We have something else to address. Basically, one of Ransom's snitches called this morning with some disturbing news. Jack, can you fill us in?"

Ransom took the floor and told the group about the cult's evil intentions.

There was a stunned silence. Then came a wave of muffled comments, mostly swearing. Jenkins then explained what they'd developed as a general plan to handle the situation. Captain Marquez agreed that both his officers and the FBI should cover the meeting in the woods. The FBI would have a plane up, with agents with starlight scopes. The FBI SWAT team and the sheriff's deputies, all outfitted with night vision goggles, illumination flares, and riot shotguns or MP-5s, would be mustered and ready to move in. Two FBI snipers would also be on the scene.

They broke up the conference, agreeing to meet again at seven that evening. They'd deploy as it got dark. Any disciples of evil spirits coming to those woods tonight would encounter some very deadly force. It could get bloody, but Ransom didn't care, as long as no baby was killed.

Recalling his dream about the devil worshippers, he thought of a quote by Leonardo da Vinci: "Why does the eye see a thing more clearly in dreams than the imagination when awake?"

Why, indeed? Was his mind's floor show last night

derived from some premonition? Maybe it was another example of the subconscious mind being miles ahead of the conscious. Or was it just being hot, feeling exhausted, or getting a suggestion from Billy's tips?

There was no real way to know. There were so many things up in the air. And all of them seemed to be getting out-of-control.

There was Jester's baby, in grave condition; the kidnapped baby still missing; and now the threat of a baby sacrifice by a crazy cult. Plus there was the wild card of Senator Baldazar's illicit affair with Nurse Pettijohn, which he couldn't really assess the meaning of right now. He had a queasy stomach from his lack of knowledge or control over all those situations. And when he had that feeling, he always did some checking.

* * * * *

As he and Kathy approached the parking lot, Ransom noticed a fine film of dust coating his Crown Vic. Those country roads yesterday had done it in; he'd need to get it washed. But first they'd visit Jester.

Ransom didn't see Jester in the ICU. Worse yet, though he craned his neck and moved around to check every isolette, he couldn't spot little Michael. Ice water trickled down his spine. His worried gaze met Kathy's.

She said, "I don't understand. Maybe he's having a test of some kind?"

But her voice was doubtful and haunting. Ransom's stomach turned over. He didn't like this at all. Not one bit.

He paced to the nurses' station and caught one of the women he'd noticed before in the ICU. "Could you tell me where Mr. Holmes and his child are?"

The nurse averted her eyes, saying only, "Mr. Holmes is with his wife in room 326."

They headed that way, a feeling of gloom settling over them. As they approached the room, the door opened and Jester stepped into the hall. He looked surprised to see them, but he barely reacted, as though he were drained. Grief was etched into his face.

"*Mon Dieu,*" Kathy said in a low whisper.

"Jester?" Ransom said to get his attention. "Are you . . . I mean, is the baby . . . ." But he couldn't finish the sentence, and it hung there like a half-inflated balloon.

"Thanks for coming, guys. I'm afraid that . . . . Michael's gone. He slipped away this morning." Jester continued to look at them, but it appeared that his mind was in the ICU, beside the isolette, watching his son.

"He gave a little gasp," Jester continued, tears pooling in his eyes, "shuddered, and then quit breathing. And that was it. The poor little guy just couldn't fight any more."

Ransom felt the slice of a razor across his heart, and his throat clamped shut as though squeezed by a noose.

"Oh, no, Jester. I'm so sorry." Kathy touched his arm.

He looked at them as if he owed some explanation. "Last night the doc said the sonograms showed too much cranial bleeding. Unless a miracle intervened, it was only a matter of time. We prayed, but we got no miracle."

There was nothing else to say. Ransom put his arms around the slender man and held him. Jester started to cry. Kathy rested her head on Jester's shoulder. In a couple of minutes, Jester sniffed and gently disengaged himself, pulled out a wrinkled handkerchief, and blew his nose.

"Sharene just fell asleep a minute ago. She's exhausted from the trauma of the delivery and from worry." He stuffed the handkerchief back in his pocket.

"We're so very sorry, Jester," Ransom said.

"Can we help you with anything at all?" Kathy asked.

"You've already done all you can do. I couldn't have hung in there without you guys. But I've got to help Sharene now, and then I'll see you at the office in a few days."

"Sure, Jester," Ransom said, "you just take good care of her, and yourself."

He nodded, gazing at the door to Sharene's room.

* * * * *

Back in the car, Ransom and Kathy sat in silence for several minutes, composing themselves. They realized nothing more could be done here. And time was getting short for solving the kidnapping.

"You know how I hate monkey wrenches," Ransom said. "Let's confront Baldazar about his liaison with Nurse Pettijohn."

"There may be no connection to the kidnapping," Kathy said, "and it's really none of our business."

"I know, but I've got to ask."

"It's your case," Kathy said, with an inflection that meant she was thinking: It's your ass.

"Then, according to Emerson, we'd better get there quick."

She screwed up her mouth. "I know I'll regret asking, but why's that?"

"He once said, 'In skating over thin ice our safety is in our speed.'"

* * * * *

Sure enough, Baldazar's Mercedes reposed in its usual spot in front of his office. Ransom went in alone. If this thing exploded in his face, he didn't want Kathy getting shredded by the shrapnel. He'd take the heat alone and not look back.

He greeted the two agents sitting in Baldazar's waiting room. Their eyes had the hollow look of the terminally bored. After Ransom sat waiting a few minutes, the blonde receptionist said, "Senator Baldazar will see you now."

"Thanks," Ransom said, "I know the way." He paced toward the man's office.

Baldazar swiveled back and forth in his immense black leather chair. He seemed to look down his nose at Ransom. He was giving a "What now?" look.

But Ransom had a strange feeling. There was something wrong with the usually meticulous man. His tie hung askew, his cheeks displayed dark shadows, and his hair frizzed out like tiny corkscrews. Against his tan face, dusky patches showed beneath his eyes.

The Senator indicated a chair for Ransom, and then leaned back, stroking his chin. As he sat there, Ransom noticed a blemish on Baldazar's normally perfect hands. A bit of something black clung under a fingernail. On his badfinger, as Ransom's son would say.

A bit of . . . what? Ransom couldn't tell. He didn't picture the Senator chewing licorice whips or digging around in a car engine. It was just another damn enigma.

"Senator, there's something I need to ask you."

No emotion showed in those dark eyes. "What is it?" The words were spoken in a flat tone, with the Senator's mind seeming to roam elsewhere.

"First of all, I want to assure you we're doing everything possible to find your baby. That's the uppermost item on our agenda."

"I appreciate the sentiment. But it seems that all the good intentions aren't producing any results." He picked up a leather-handled letter opener and drummed it on his desk top. "Is there anything else that can be done? Our baby could be dead by now, you realize."

"Everything feasible is being done at this time, sir."

Now Baldazar noticed the dirty fingernail, and using the letter opener, he dug out the black bit. He inspected it briefly, and then flung it into a wastebasket. Now the usual perfection had been re-attained.

Ransom added, "But in the interest of being completely informed in this matter, I need to ask you something of a personal nature."

Baldazar's head jerked up as though he'd been jolted with a cattle prod. "And what might that be?" His murky eyes narrowed behind thick lenses.

"One of our agents saw you yesterday with a nurse from Metro Hospital. Since your baby was kidnapped from there, I need to know your connection with her. Don't worry about any disclosure. This is just for our information and understanding."

Baldazar didn't move. Not even his eyes flickered. "Where did your man see us?"

Ransom considered a moment. "In a bar."

"I see." He studied his nails again. Then he glared at Ransom, his eyes as hard as coal. "I hope you don't suspect me of philandering, Mr. Ransom. Especially at this time, it would be most untoward of me, I'm sure you'll agree."

"I'm not here to judge anyone," Ransom answered. "I just need to know the score and the players if I'm going to be effective in playing the game."

"Since we're into sports metaphors, let me put it this way: Miss Pettijohn and I are old teammates. I knew her in college, before I met my wife. After we graduated, we were both struggling to get toeholds in our professions, and we drifted apart."

Ransom nodded, but kept quiet. He knew from long experience that it was a good way to learn things.

"Then I got married," Baldazar continued, "and we maintained our separate ways. But because of the current situation, Miss Pettijohn called me yesterday to ask if we could meet. She wanted to console me. And it did help, I'll admit."

"As I said, I don't mean to pry, but I did need to know the nature of the relationship."

"That's what you do, isn't it? Pry and spy?"

"That, and seek what people hide." Ransom stood up. "Thanks for your time and the information, Senator."

"Certainly." He picked up some papers on his desk and studied them as Ransom left.

* * * * *

Back outside, walking toward his Bureau ride, Ransom appraised the Senator's Mercedes. It embodied understated elegance. It was luxurious, classy, pure glamour embodied in a fine driving machine. Midnight blue, glistening in the morning sun. Nice wash and wax job. Ransom peered at his dirty Crown Vic. Maybe he should ask Baldazar where he took his high dollar ride to be cleaned.

As he passed the vehicle, he touched the front fender, paused, and glanced back toward the office. Then he hunkered down, grabbed the bumper, and dipped down to look underneath. In the undercarriage were clumps of caked dirt. The underbody wash costs extra, and it doesn't show.

He started to get up, and then stopped dead still. Ducking down farther, he spotted something stuck in the suspension. He reached under the car and pulled out a long stalk of a weed.

For several moments he stared at the brown stem with its tiny leaves. Then he stood up, his knees popping, and strode to his Ford. Smiling, he opened the back door and laid the dead stalk in his briefcase.

"What's going on, *Lapin?*" Kathy asked.

"I think I've discovered why the Senator needs so many wash jobs just driving around San Antonio."

* * * * *

"Wait a minute," Jenkins said, forehead furrowed, eyes squinting until they looked like coin slots, "let me be sure I've got this." He cradled his head in one hand as though he had a cluster headache. "You're saying Senator Baldazar is a wrongo here, that he's involved in the kidnapping?"

Ransom shook off the bald statement. "I can't say that. What I'm questioning at this point is his involvement with Nurse Pettijohn. The extension of that is whether it has anything to do with our case."

"Do you think it's connected?" He looked at Ransom, then at Kathy.

She held her hands spread apart. "Who knows? At this point, everything is conjecture. Like whether a 'gator ate your missing dog."

Ransom gave her a look, and then said, "It's something we need to investigate. Maybe it's meaningful, maybe not.

But we can't let it slide."

"I don't know . . . ." Jenkins shook his head from side-to-side, as though it were a large watermelon. "The guy is such a heavyweight." He stared at his desk a few seconds, then his head came up, and his gaze speared Ransom. "Suppose the press got wind that we were investigating the Senator instead of finding his baby. We'd all be collecting unemployment."

Should he tell Sonny, Ransom wondered, that the Senator might also be a cultist? No, he decided he'd better hold back on that. Trying to lighten the mood, he said, "No one will even notice if we take a little look at the Senator. We'll just be a fly on the wall. Besides, it's not something we'd be doing instead, just in addition to the regular investigation. We'll put in some extra effort to help solve the puzzle."

Sonny frowned, and then sucked in a deep breath. "All right, here's the way we'll play it. If you have time in your workday, without disrupting your regular schedule, cover a few logical leads on Baldazar. Just don't overdo it, and don't let anyone know what you're doing."

Right, thought Ransom. I'll be just like The Shadow. "Okay," he told Sonny, "I'd like to have surveillance teams on Baldazar and Nurse Pettijohn. Kathy and I will handle the rest."

"Where do you think those two might lead us?"

"I don't know," Ransom admitted, "but if they hook up again, I want to know what they're doing."

Jenkins shrugged. "No crystal ball or surveillance team needed there. Probably what couples always do in the heat of an affair."

"Very likely," Ransom conceded, "but in case there's more to it . . . ." He let the implication hang. Sonny was no one's fool.

"All right. You can have surveillance teams on both of them for two days, maximum. After that," he pointed a finger toward Ransom, "you're on your own."

Outside Jenkins's office, Ransom lifted his shoulders and rotated them backwards and forwards, easing the tension in his neck and back. Then he gazed at Kathy.

She blew out a breath. "It feels like we're in a broke down swamp buggy without a paddle."

"And the 'gators are circling," Ransom said with a wry grin.

"For sure, *mon ami.* And for all we know, Baldazar may be telling it true."

"No, there's something funky with the whole setup. I can feel it in my gut. But we've got to find it to get our heads straight."

"So where do we look?" She stood with her hands on her hips, challenging him.

He shrugged. "I'm not sure what we're looking for, but as our mentor Emerson said, 'Concentration is the secret of strength.'"

"If we knew what to concentrate on."

"Hold on." Ransom sat down behind his desk and reached for the phone. "I need to make a call, then I'll tell you."

He dialed the Baldazar's residence and talked to one of the agents stationed there.

"Eduardo, did the Senator go out anytime last night, like late at night?"

"He was out when I got here a few minutes to midnight. Sam said he'd left about two hours before that."

"When did he come back?"

"An hour or so later. I was reading and didn't notice exactly."

"Did Mrs. Baldazar go, too?"

"No way, man. She was conked out, asleep like a zombie all night."

"How about Sunday night, did the Senator go out then?"

"*Sí, por seguro.* Same deal."

"Is Mrs. Baldazar there now?"

"*Por supuesto.* Hang on."

In a minute, she came on the line. "Yes, Mr. Ransom. Did you find—"

"No, no," he interjected, "I just need to ask you something."

"All right." She sounded unsure about his intentions.

"The agents tell me your husband went out last night. Did he say where he was going?"

"No, I don't know. Dr. Matthews told me to take a sedative in the evening to help me sleep. By nine or so, I'm dead to the world."

"I see," Ransom said. "Do you have any idea where he might have gone?"

"Maybe he went for a walk or something, just to get out of the house. Being cooped up here drives him crazy. That's why he goes to his office, he's a very active man."

More than you know, he thought. "I'm sure that's all it was."

"Do you think he's in danger?"

"Not really. We just need to know where to contact him if he goes out, in case a call comes in. I'll mention it to him. It's nothing to worry about."

"But there's nothing new about April? Do you have any leads?"

"The investigation is widespread. We're following up on every logical lead, and everyone is pushing as hard as they can to find her, Mrs. Baldazar."

"I'm sure you are, Mr. Ransom. I'm just so distraught. I feel all wrung out."

"Anyone would. It's a terrible strain on everyone, especially you. But we have to be as strong as we can and persevere. And we'll give it our best, you can be sure of that."

"Thank you, Mr. Ransom. That's all I can ask. Just bring her home, please."

"We'll do it, ma'am," he said, and then hung up.

"What story you got now?" Kathy asked.

"Baldazar left the house the last two nights. Let's talk to Sonny."

* * * * *

When they walked in Jenkins said, "Back again? What's going on?"

"Sonny," Ransom said, "when you were at the Senator's house Sunday night, did he say anything about going out?"

"I don't recall it, if he did."

"What was he wearing?"

"Dark work pants, old loafers, a purple knit shirt with green stripes."

"How about Mrs. Baldazar?"

"A yellow bathrobe, slippers." He smoothed his few strands of hair. "You know, the Senator did seem sort of anxious."

"Anxious?" Kathy said.

"Yeah, rather nervous. And he kept checking his watch."

Ransom said, "Thanks, you haven't lost the touch."

Sonny looked puzzled, but he gave a little wave as they left his office. "Don't mention it."

Ransom hustled to his desk and grabbed up the phone.

Mrs. Baldazar answered, and Ransom asked to speak to

Eduardo.

"*Digame,*" the agent said.

"Just one more question. Answer me in simple Spanish. When Baldazar went out the last two nights, did he just go for a walk, or did he take his Mercedes?"

"*El manejo su carro,*" said Eduardo.

"He drove his car both nights?"

"*Seguro que sí.*"

"That's a big help. *Gracias, amigo.*" He hung up.

Kathy studied him. "You look like you swallowed a canary, to quote someone undoubtedly famous."

"More like a buzzard. Here's what we need: Go find out everything you can about Senator Baldazar's past. Check newspaper morgues, talk to the neighbors again, and try to find out if he's been involved in any scandals. Also, get any financial records you can, and check whether he's ever been sued."

Kathy scribbled notes as fast as she could.

"Let's try to learn," Ransom continued, "who he associates with, and what he does in his spare time. Just answer me this question: Who is this guy? Who is he *really*? You know the routine, give me deep down and dirty."

"And you'll concentrate on Nurse Pettijohn?"

"Absolutely."

In fact, he was beginning to think he'd better learn just exactly what was happening here. Maybe this all meant nothing. But he liked to know what was going on with all the players in every crime drama.

17

"You think she's gonna make it?" Harvey asked, his mouth slack as he stared into the crib at the pale, squirmy baby. She still wouldn't eat, didn't hardly sleep, and cried day and night. Plus, she had the drizzlies. That really stunk up the place. He was about to go outta his skull.

"Hell, I don't know," Lyn replied, hands on her hips, mouth drawn tight. "We've tried a lot of formulas. Unless we get a wet nurse, I don't know what more to do."

Harvey's knees felt shaky, and he waffled down onto a hardback chair where he roosted on the edge and clasped his gnarled hands together.

"Don't start crackin' your knuckles," she warned.

"I wasn't gonna—"

"You always do it when you're jumpy. It drives me right up the wall."

"I wasn't gonna do it, so don't get worked up." He probably was, but he'd be damned if he'd tell her so. It was just something else for her to bitch at him about.

"You know what?" she said, staring out the window.

He blinked. "What?"

"Maybe we should have someone check on her. I mean, something could be bad wrong with her. Just look at those sunken eyes and that puckered little mouth."

"Mebbe so. But I don't see that it makes no diff'rence now."

"You might be right, Harvey. Maybe we'll just wait and see."

Now there was a switch. And, what do you know, the baby was keepin' quiet for a change, too. Aw, she was prob'bly just resting up gettin' ready to throw another fit. He wasn't sure he could take no more.

He stood up and stretched, then edged toward the door. There was a cold beer in the fridge with his name on it. He couldn't get there soon enough.

* * * * *

Ransom was contemplating what to do about Nurse Pettijohn when a young clerk with hair the color of Mars and a galaxy of freckles spritzed across her cheeks walked up to his desk.

"Hi, Betty, how are the kittens?"

"Everywhere all at once, Mr. Ransom. They'll be ready to wean in a few weeks. Are you sure you don't want one? They're real cute."

"Sorry. I can barely keep myself fed. But I'll ask around."

"Great. Oh, here's a fax for you from the lab."

Ah, it was the artist's sketch of the fake nurse done from the candy striper's description. He stared at it, trying to find some clue in the plain face. Betty walked away, and he waved to her, saying, "Good luck with the litter."

Rummaging in his case folder, he hauled out the first drawing. Yes, he thought, the new one looks different. He stared at the latest drawing, thinking the face seemed familiar, but he couldn't place where he'd seen it.

At least it was a new lead. He stuck it in his folder and stood up. Then he grabbed his pistol and his coat and headed for the hospital.

* * * * *

Walking down the hallway, he watched for Nurse Pettijohn, but didn't see her. He ambled into the head nurse's office. She was shuffling papers on her desk.

"Mrs. Blankenship," he greeted her.

She gave him a teasing frown. "It's Winnie. You know that."

"Of course, I'm sorry. May I close the door?"

"Sure, go ahead," she said.

He did, and then he turned back to her.

"You want to know something confidential, I take it?"

"Yes, Winnie, I could use your input on an employee. It might be bending your ethics to talk to me about your personnel, but there are some things I need to know that would be a help in my investigation."

"Oh, my. That sounds serious. Who are you concerned about?"

"It's a nurse. And I'm not implying any guilt by asking questions about her."

"Of course you're not, Mr. Ransom. I understand."

"That's fine. Then what can you tell me about Sheila Pettijohn?"

194

Nurse Blankenship looked startled. "What about her?"

"Tell me about her background, her work habits. Is she a model nurse?"

"She's very proficient at her job. She's always on time, and she handles herself well. Professionally, there's no way I can fault her."

Ransom studied her stoic face. "Winnie, I feel that there's something you're not saying."

Her shoulders slumped, and she gave a half grin. "You sure know how to back someone into a corner, don't you?"

"I'm sorry, that's my job."

"It's hard to put into words, really. I've always felt that being a nurse was all about helping others."

"Yes, it seems like it. But Nurse Pettijohn . . . . ?"

"I have the feeling that something's missing. If I were to label it, I guess I'd say she had a lack of compassion."

"That sounds pretty unusual for a nurse."

"Yes, and her attitude even extends to the babies. I mean, if you don't suffer over a tiny infant who's struggling for life . . . . "

"Then why do you keep her on?"

"It's nothing I could fire her for, and good nurses are difficult to find. But sometimes I wish she'd just move on."

"All right, thanks for your candor. You've been a big help."

She dismissed it with a wave.

Ransom dug into his folder. "Just one more thing. Does this sketch remind you of anyone?"

She studied it for half a minute before speaking. "This woman looks familiar, but there's something different in this drawing from the person I'm trying to match it with."

"And who's that?"

"That's the problem, I can't think who it resembles. Someone I don't know well, I suppose." She stared at the sketch several seconds longer, and then held it out to him.

"That's a copy. Why don't you keep it? Let me know if you recall who it looks like."

She slipped it into her drawer. "That's a deal, Mr. FBI. Is my interrogation over?"

"Yep, I'll turn off the hot lights. You get a reprieve for good behavior."

Before he left, Ransom strolled down the hall to look at the babies in the nursery. He thought about Jester's little guy losing his battle. Then he thought about April Baldazar, and it struck him like a blow to the face: Who on earth could steal an innocent baby? It made no sense. None at all.

* * * * *

Back at the office, Ransom went in to see Jenkins. "Hey, boss, we got any new developments?"

"Nothing," Jenkins said with a grunt. "Still humping the same old leads. You want to get some lunch?"

Ransom's stomach was in knots. He remembered the agent from Quantico saying the successful cases were solved within a week. They had to come up with something quick.

"Thanks, Sonny, but I'm going to hang here and try to think of an angle on this case."

"You shouldn't carry this thing as a personal cross."

"Every man's cross is our own."

"Victor Hugo?"

"No," Ransom sighed, "just a mope named John Elliott Ransom."

After Jenkins left for lunch, Ransom spent an hour going through his case file, searching for clues he might have overlooked in the headlong rush to find April. In the end, he suspected he'd have to unravel the enigma of Nurse Pettijohn and Senator Baldazar. It might not mean anything, but if it did, the FBI needed to know about it right away.

Also, he wondered how the failure of the alarm and the tampering with the video systems were connected. It had to be part of the plan. But why would security guards help with a baby kidnapping from the hospital they work in? It seemed senseless and stupid.

The phone rang, and he picked it up. "You were right," Kathy said. "Something is odd about Baldazar. A couple of neighbors who roam their houses at night said he goes out a lot. They're always hearing that Mercedes fire up."

"'Curioser and curioser,' as Alice said."

"Exactly. So, Jack, did you get anything on our stacked nursie, Sheila Pettijohn?"

"Just that she's no Florence Nightengale. More like a reptile in nurse's clothing."

"You could guess that by looking at her."

"I guess my observations were too shallow. But I'm going to tunnel deeper. Let me know if you dig up anything else."

"Samantha Spade at your service."

"'Bye, Sam."

He got up and headed for the nerve center. It sent a shiver along his spine, but he needed to decipher some computer language. There might be something in the database that would tie it all together. Or, he realized, maybe not.

Cheryl clacked at the computer keys. She paused to twirl a strand of hair, then turned over a page from the stack and began to type again.

"Are you going with the flow, or are you drowning?"

"Oh, Mr. Ransom. I didn't hear you come in. Well, by the end of the day I should be caught up with this." She pointed at the pile of papers. "But then you guys come in and hand me another bunch."

"We're just here to serve the computer."

She flashed a bright smile. Youth could be so intimidating. "I'm the slave to this here machine, mister. 'Course, I don't mind being a slave to the right master, you understand."

"Cheryl, you're miles ahead of me. Which is good, of course. Maybe you can make some sense out of all this."

"Like, how do you mean?"

"Let's fool around a little," he said, adding, "with the machine, I mean."

"Oh, heck." She frowned playfully.

"That is, let's see if we can make a connection. With the computer."

Now she laughed. "I get your drift. Do you have any big ideas? That you feel comfortable tellin' me about, that is."

"I always have ideas, Cheryl. But in this instance, let's see if any of the women getting hysterectomies or having stillbirths or the like can be connected to anyone on the hospital staff."

"Such a serious man. Okay, I can only do that by name, but let's try it."

They came up with seven Martinez women, two ladies named Bishop, and six Jones women whose last names were common to members of Metro's staff.

Now what do we do? Ransom wondered, tapping the eraser of his pencil on the desktop.

Then the two of them noodled around some more with the entries, trying to match up names from the lists of women who'd bought or rented nurse scrubs, women who were registered owners of pertinent vehicles, and people who'd recently gotten birth certificates for infants born at home.

Some matches came up, but mostly on common names, not that the kidnapper couldn't have a common name. Then they ran the lists against the name Sheila Pettijohn, but nothing developed. Ransom began to wonder if maybe this was just an exercise in frustration. Lots of computer beeping was going on, but so far to no avail.

"We need to focus," Cheryl said.

"Hmm?"

"We've got to narrow the field."

"Okay, Cheryl, let's do this. Print out everything you have on Sheila Pettijohn. Maybe I'll see something else for us to try."

"Fair enough," she said, and her fingers became a blur on the keyboard.

In a minute, she ripped off the printout and handed it to him, their hands brushing. It gave him a little tingle. "Thanks, I'll get back to you."

"Don't be a stranger."

Sometimes he wished he were younger. But not more than a dozen times a day. *C'est la vie.*

Next he visited the radio dispatcher, asking her to query the computer for the criminal record, motor vehicle registration, and driver's license information for Nurse Pettijohn. When it was done, he took the handful of printouts back to his desk and dropped into his chair.

Pettijohn had one vehicle: the two-year-old Pontiac. Her driver's license had been issued almost two years ago, valid until her birthday on June 22, two years from now. Her criminal record was of interest: shoplifting, with a fine paid; three speeding tickets; and an assault charge three years ago, dismissed.

Now he turned to information from hospital records, taken from her application for employment, insurance papers, and credit union application. She'd requested three loans from the Medical Employees' Credit Union, the highest amount being five thousand dollars.

He checked the reasons for the loans: To buy furniture, to purchase a washer, dryer, and refrigerator, and to consolidate other loans. The records showed a few late payments, nothing startling. The co-signor on the largest note was Hiram Byron.

"'Roll on, thou deep and dark . . . .'"

Wait a minute.

He rolled the name around in his mind. Then he jumped up and ran to the computer room. Cheryl flinched as the door flew open behind her.

"I'm sorry to startle you, Cheryl. Something important came up." He sat down, a sheaf of computer papers clutched in his hand. "Can you query the computer for the name 'Byron' in connection with this case?"

"Sure, no problem."

As they waited, he scanned the papers in his hand. There, something he hadn't noticed before on Pettijohn's job application: her maiden name was Byron.

The computer printed out a response.

Marilyn Byron, rented nurse's light blue scrubs at the Galaxy Uniform Shop on April 24th; white female, blonde, five feet four or five, mid-thirties, last known address 4130 Eisenhower, Apartment 20, San Antonio, burn marks on carpet, no forwarding address; last employed as a cocktail waitress at Barney's Blue Light Lounge; vehicle owned was a nine-year-old Chevrolet, Texas license BYP 44X.

The vehicle was wrong, but she may have bought a newer one in the past couple of years. He ripped off the printout, turned and kissed Cheryl hard on the cheek, then sprinted from the room. As he left, she touched her hand to the side of her face, her mouth hanging open.

Back in the dispatcher's room, he stood by the NCIC terminal. "Would you query this name: Marilyn Byron," he said to the girl, "for a driver's license registration, vehicle registration, and any wants or warrants?"

The machine whirred into action, but the results were disappointing. The driver's license data showed the same address, which he already knew was stale. The vehicle registration was for the same car, but the license tag had expired. There were no wants or warrants outstanding, and a further check of the Interstate Identification Index showed no criminal history for her. Disgruntled, knowing he was making headway, but now stalled in his latest efforts, Ransom stalked down the hallway, his mind whirling a hundred miles an hour, trying to think what to do next.

* * * * *

Back in the squad room, Ransom's phone rang.

"Mr. Ransom? It's Winnie Blankenship from Metro

Hospital."

"Hello, Winnie." He thought she sounded upset. "What is it?"

"I can't be sure about this. I mean, I only saw her once from a distance, but I think I know who the woman is in your drawing."

"You do? Who?" God, he sounded like a demented owl.

"I was looking at the sketch when Sheila Pettijohn came into my office asking to take some hours off. I couldn't help noticing the resemblance."

"To Nurse Pettijohn?"

"To her, somewhat, but more especially to her sister. I don't remember her name, and she doesn't have short dark hair like in the drawing. That's what was throwing me. Her hair's longer, with bangs, and it's blonde."

"Do you know where she lives, Winnie?"

"All I know is she and her husband live in town somewhere."

Her husband! There was a helpful bit of information. "Do you know his name?'

"I'm afraid not," she said. "I guess I'm not being much help."

"Are you kidding? I owe you a great big hug. And I'm going to collect, so be ready."

In his car, he radioed Kathy.

"Go ahead, five romeo," she answered.

"Are you close to downtown?"

"Close enough to spit."

"Save it for family reunions. Meet me at the Bexar County Courthouse."

"You got something hot?"

"Hotter than your granny's *etouffe.*"

"There's no such animal."

18

The marriage records Ransom sought were stashed in the basement of the ancient Bexar County Courthouse. He could have gone back to the office and had one of the computer operators look them up online, but he was close by and he enjoyed the hands-on investigation in preference to having someone else call up electronic records. That way he knew the checking had been done thoroughly, and he might elicit some ideas about additional information to look for. Besides, he enjoyed visiting the historic building set in a plaza that had originated in 1731, with its two impressive towers, one with a metallic pyramid top, and the other one with a Moorish-derived spire. Such longevity gave him a sense of the continuity of life.

Still, the edifice contained an institution where citizen and criminal alike sweated out the bureaucratic tangle of officialdom. And the air down in the basement brought to mind the musky aroma of some tunneling animal. Ransom soon gave up trying to hold his breath.

He told Kathy what he'd found in the computer records earlier, and what he hoped to find at the courthouse in the subsequent investigation. He undid his tie as he stared at the bulky volumes of marriage and divorce records that filled the floor-to-ceiling bookshelves. The covers were stiff pressed cardboard with heavy metal clasps and had handwritten entries dating back over eighty years. Kathy watched over his shoulder as he searched for the record of the nuptials of Marilyn Byron and her spouse.

Sure enough, in one of the huge volumes, on page 451, was recorded the marriage of Marilyn Eva Byron to Harvey Willard Larkin, on March 29, two years before, in San Antonio, Texas. It gave the bride and groom's dates of birth, so there was no mistake.

"Let's get back to the office," Ransom said.

They met up again in the radio dispatcher's room. Now

Ransom asked for the same computer checks as before, but this time using the name Marilyn Larkin. There was a new driver's license issued in her new name, showing a different address on Hildebrand Avenue.

The vehicle registration was a bombshell. Marilyn had a blue, five-year-old Chevy Cavalier with Texas license FMP 36R.

"I'll be damned," Kathy said as they read it, causing the dispatcher to glance at her oddly, "your Ms. Phoenix was dead right about the vehicle and the tag she saw."

"Looks like it. I'll have to give her a big award."

She snorted. "Oh, right, *Monsieur* Pulitzer."

"No wants or warrants," said the dispatcher as the computer spit out more paper. She smoothed her brunette hair. "The Interstate Identification Index shows no criminal history."

Kathy's big blues glittered. "Let's beat feet to that new address."

"You bet. But first, Brenda, would you run the same checks on our friend Mr. Larkin?" He handed her a slip of paper with Larkin's description.

"Sure, stand by." Her fingers moved quicker than a fly at a picnic.

Larkin had a valid Texas commercial driver's license, owned an older model Ford pickup, and showed an address different from Marilyn's.

"Now we've got two addresses," said Ransom as they walked back into the squad room. "His and hers. And both of them nearly two years old."

Kathy sat in the chair alongside his desk and crossed her legs. "Her newest driver's license was obtained later."

"But it still may be an old address. And they may have moved somewhere else by now."

He picked up a current telephone directory. There was no listing for the Larkins. Then he dialed directory assistance, only to learn they had a non-published number. It could be obtained, but it would take a little time.

Just then, Atherton sailed in and gave them a quizzical look. Ransom waved him over. Kathy tugged down her skirt as Atherton approached. Word was he'd once tried to put a move on her, and she'd closed him down like a clam. Ransom couldn't blame him for trying.

"Hank, we may be closing in on the kidnapper," Ransom said. "Would you contact the phone company and get the unpublished number and the address for these people?" He scribbled the names on a note card and handed it to Atherton. "We're going to check out some addresses. Radio me when you get it."

"Sure, but then I'm on my way to help out with any bust you may make."

"You're welcome to that party, big guy." He smiled. "Oh, and did you interview the security guards at the hospital?"

"Oh, yeah, we had a nice chat," Atherton said. "But it wasn't real informative."

"Aw, hell. Why not?"

"The one guard that was on duty that morning seemed as straight as an arrow. I didn't sense the guy could lie about anything. And he was the one who went for coffee about the time of the kidnapping."

"What about the other guard?"

"That's Rafael Gomez," Atherton said. "Now he's a lot slicker. He answered my questions, but didn't really answer what I was asking, you know?"

"He was avoiding the questions," said Ransom.

"That's it, exactly. I couldn't pin it on him, but I'm suspicious that he could have compromised the alarm."

"Could you think of a motive?"

"No, that's one problem. Why on earth would he jeopardize his job and risk going to jail? I'm going to put the guy under a microscope and see what I can come up with."

"Sounds like a good plan. Give him a good looksee, and we can talk with him again later, maybe at our office where he doesn't feel very comfortable."

"I'm with you. Okay, I'm off to get that information you need."

"Great. We'll be on the radio. Or call my cell."

Atherton strode out of the room with resolve.

"C'mon," Ransom said, and Kathy sprang off her chair like a sprinter out of the blocks.

But before they could escape, Jenkins stormed in. His face was pale, and moisture glistened on his forehead. With a spaced out appearance in his eyes, he looked as if his thoughts were roaming the universe.

Then his gaze fell on Ransom, and he motioned at him, crooking his fingers.

Ransom followed him into his office.

Jenkins said, "A call just came in from the Director. Since

I figured he wasn't calling about my imminent promotion, I told my secretary to say I was out. Then I called a buddy at Headquarters who said the big guy wants to bounce you off the case. That's per the request of our lovable Senator, of course."

"That son-of-a-bitch."

"Right, but personal feelings aside, my nuts are in a vise. And I don't know how long I can stand the squeeze."

"How can I help?" Ransom asked.

"I don't know . . . ." His eyes went vacant for a second. Then he said, "Solve the case, or find the baby. At least come up with a good lead that I can hang my hat on when I face the blast furnace. I'm behind you, but I can't dissuade the Director by shooting blanks."

"Here's some ammo," Ransom said. "Nurse Pettijohn's sister may have done the grab."

"That's super. Brace her right away. Try to get a statement."

When Ransom opened the door, Kathy was there, staring at the ceiling. "We were just on our way, Sonny." And they took off like scalded cats.

As the elevator clanked its way downward, Ransom said, "Did I remember to tell him we had to find her first?"

Kathy wrinkled her brow. "I'm guessing that you might not have mentioned it."

"The memory is always the second thing to go."

Kathy smiled, fox-like. As the Crown Vic squealed around a corner she said, "Where to, O Forgetful One?"

"Barney's Blue Light Lounge is on the way to those other places. We might find her there or get a good address for her."

Kathy crossed her legs. Ransom could definitely see why Atherton had gone for the bait. With that body, she could bring shrimp to a boil.

Fifteen minutes later, they wheeled off the highway. Barney's square building squatted in the middle of a gravel lot filled with dusty pickups. White paint peeled from the walls in dime-sized flakes, and one broken blue light sagged over the door. Two guys in cowboy hats stumbled out as Ransom and Kathy made their way into the murky interior, which was thick with smoke, clamor and misery.

Music with a heavy backbeat blasted from giant speakers suspended from the ceiling. A main stage and three other small platforms featured topless dancers grinding in rhythm, or not, to thudding drums and wailing guitars. Ransom's gaze followed the hazy spotlights that shone upon an auburn-haired girl with impressive silicone implants on center stage.

"Anytime you can break loose, Inspector," Kathy said.

"I'm just looking for the manager."

They settled for the bartender. The manager didn't come on for a couple more hours, she said. Her name was Titania, and she was built like an overweight American Gladiator.

"I figured you guys for cops," she told them. "Feds, at that."

"Titania, we've got something important to ask you," Ransom said, looking down the bar, then into her eyes.

"Sure, doll. Whatever you want."

"We're looking for Marilyn Larkin. Does she work here?"

Titania appeared befuddled, which was not much different from her previous look.

"She's a blonde with bangs," Kathy explained, "about thirty-five, five-feet-four. Drives a blue Chevy?"

"Oh, yeah. Marilyn. She's got pretty big hooters."

"Is she here now?" Ransom asked.

"Nah, she don't work here no more." She glanced down the bar at a guy with a beard who raised his forefinger, then pointed at his empty glass. "Hold on a minute," she told them.

"Sure." Ransom glanced back at center stage as the dancer turned cheeks and pranced.

Kathy gave him another look. "Catchy tune," he said.

Titania came back. "Marilyn got married a couple years ago, and her old man didn't want her workin' here no more."

"Have you got an address for her?"

"Lemme look." She searched through some stacks of papers on a shelf under the cash register, finally pulling out a sheet. "Here's her number . . . but, you know what?" She held her hand to her mouth.

"What?" Kathy said.

"I tried to call her about some clothes she left here, and this number was no good. It was disconnected, you know?"

"Yeah," Ransom said. He pulled the sketch from his pocket and laid it on top of the bar. "Does this look like her?"

She studied the sketch, then nodded and looked up at Ransom. "It could be her. The dark hair threw me at first, 'cause Marilyn's a blonde. But the face is pretty close." She winced, then handed back the sketch.

Ransom thanked her.

"Sure, honey. You come back anytime." She gave him a wink.

As they turned to go, Ransom glimpsed the stage again. The spotlight dimmed, the music faded, and the girl stepped down from the platform. Her stage smile shut off like a power failure. Suddenly, her nakedness and the hollow look in her eyes made her seem as vulnerable and wasted as a broken doll lying in the trash. Sometimes, he thought, the world seemed pretty sad.

* * * * *

As Kathy and Ransom left the lounge, Nurse Pettijohn swiveled toward her red Pontiac in the hospital parking lot. One waiting agent poked another in the ribs. She slid into the sporty car, and the surveillance swung into gear. She pulled out of the lot in a hurry. The agents zipped out after her, radioing the others sitting in a car down the street that the package was headed their way.

* * * * *

Back in the car outside Barney's Blue Light Lounge, Ransom punched the air conditioner on max and said, "Do you think we're on the right trail?"

Kathy pretended to sniff the air. "*Oui,* we're close to *Bouki,* for sure."

He considered the potential. Jenkins had taken a big risk for him, playing a bureaucratic game of Russian roulette, his career at stake. In fact, they could both get fired over this deal.

But more importantly, he sensed they had to find April soon, or it could be too late. He really hoped that this lead would pan out. Pettijohn, her sister, and the Senator—he had the definite feeling that they were an unholy triumvirate.

He still couldn't grasp the significance of the whole scenario, but he hoped they were getting close to figuring it out. He dropped the Ford into drive and pealed out of the lot. The quick departure left another coat of dust on Barney's melancholy building.

* * * * *

Darlene stood beside her desk with her hand stuck into a large metal file cabinet and her slender neck canted to the side, gazing at some figures on her computer screen.

"Hey, big D, what's new in the land of watts and volts?"

"Jack Ransom," she said, striking a pose that made her look like a flamingo. She brushed at her short gray hair. "I haven't seen you since Christmas when you blew out your meter with all those tree lights. Where've you been?"

"Chained to my desk, slaving over mountains of paperwork. I just escaped long enough to have a cup of coffee and to see my favorite gal."

"Hmmph. Last I heard, you were chasing some girl half your age with a figure like a Playboy bunny."

"Idle rumor, doll. Nuttin' to it. You know Kathy?"

"No, nice to meet you." They shook hands, Darlene gave Ransom a "What about her?" look, then she settled in her padded chair.

"Y'all looking for some bad guy again?"

"Now, Darlene, are you still watching those Wanted by Everyone in the Universe programs on TV?"

"Not me. Sitcoms and romance movies suit me fine."

"Well, you're right. I do need some help. I need a current address to go with these names." He handed her a card.

"Sure, no problem." Her fingers punched the keys of her computer as she stared at the card. "Here we are. Harvey and Marilyn Larkin. Their service was established ten months ago at 2784 St. Cloud Road. It's a single family residence. They're a bit of a slow pay, but there's been no interruption in service."

"That's what I love about our friendly electric company—no interruption in service, even when you short-circuit the system with cheap tree lights."

"Anyone but you, Jack, could've opened their presents in the dark."

"And I thought the Grinch was a hard case."

"Listen, when it gets cold, and people have to ante up for the Christmas gifts they charged on VISA, we hear every sob story in the book about why no one can pay their utility bill. I'm as hard-shelled as a turtle. No quarter given."

"I'm sure the Visigoths would tremble before you. Thanks a million, Darlene, I owe you lunch. I'll call you next week."

"That's a date. Don't you forget me, now."

"Not a chance." He waved as he and Kathy went out the door.

They jumped in the car and gunned away from the curb. Five minutes later, Atherton called them on the radio saying, "I've got that address for you. Can you copy?"

It was the same address they'd just gotten from Darlene, on St. Cloud Road.

"Thanks, five alpha. Are you heading that way?"

"I'm on my way. And number five is with me."

"Ten-four. We'll see you guys there."

Immediately, Ransom got another call from Ball Cap.

"It looks like the package we're tracking could be headed for that address you mentioned."

"That's interesting," Ransom said. "Keep us posted on that."

"So Nurse Pettijohn *is* involved," Kathy said.

"If that's where she's going, she's got a lot of explaining to do. God, I hope the baby's all right."

"She just has to be, Jack."

He felt his throat tighten, and he couldn't respond.

Kathy said, "Do you still think Baldazar is in on it?"

"I think if Nurse Pettijohn is a part of it, then so is the Senator. The prick."

"That's just unbelievable. His own daughter, too."

For the next few minutes they said nothing. Ransom turned onto St. Cloud Road. They were getting close.

He radioed Ball Cap. "What's your 10-20?"

"We just turned from Babcock Road onto St. Cloud Road, heading south. The package should be there in a few minutes."

"How many people you got on her?"

"Two vehicles, four agents."

"That's a 10-4. We're going to hang back until you put the package down."

He turned into the parking lot of a shabby burger joint.

Soon, the message came. "The package is out at that location."

Sonny Jenkins came on the air. "Five romeo, we'll be there in about five. Stand by and we'll meet you. What's your 10-20?"

"Ralph's Burger Shack," Ransom said, "corner of 25th and St. Cloud."

It seemed like an hour-long wait. Finally, Atherton and Jenkins rolled up beside them. Ransom described his plan of action.

"Sounds good," Jenkins said. "And just so you know, when this is over I'm calling the Director to fill him in. That's whether we win, lose, or draw."

"Fair enough," Ransom said, and then radioed the surveillance units to hang loose while he and Kathy made a pass by the residence. They rolled by and gave the place a casual look. Yep, he was thinking as they drove: Don't mind us, we're just a normal couple out for a drive.

The house was a dingy wood frame with a sagging porch. A concrete driveway, furrowed with cracks, ran alongside the house to a detached garage at the rear. A rusty pickup, Marilyn's blue Cavalier, and Nurse Pettijohn's sporty red number huddled in the driveway like a cluster of pigeons— or vultures.

Kathy looked at him. "Moment of truth?"

"As Thoreau said, it's 'better than love, money, or fame.'"

She grimaced, and then Ransom picked up the mike and told Ball Cap and the other surveillance units to ease up into the alley behind the house. He'd already asked Atherton and Jenkins to block the driveway once he and Kathy approached the house. No reason to be cozy at this point.

"Let's move in," Ransom said. All units acknowledged.

Ransom paced toward the house, watching the window curtains. The porch squeaked as they stepped up on it, and Ransom sensed the old house sighing. The doorbell didn't work. He pounded on the door with his fist.

No response. The house stayed as silent as a tomb. He glanced at Kathy and thumped again. "Mrs. Larkin," he said.

The air conditioner kicked on at the corner of the house, startling them. Ransom called louder, "Mrs. Larkin, we need to talk to you."

The door swung open, and a string bean guy with greasy hair poking out from under a ball cap stood staring at them. "Yeah, whaddya want?"

"Are you Harvey Larkin?" Ransom asked.

"Uh-huh. That's right. Who are you?"

"We're the FBI." Ransom flashed his credentials. "We need to talk to you and your wife."

"Oh, yeah? What about?"

"About an investigation we're doing. Can we come in?" He edged closer, hoping the screen door wasn't locked.

"You got a warrant?" the man asked, raising his chin and tilting his cap.

"We only want to talk. It will just take a minute, but we need to see both of you."

The man withdrew a bit. "Well, I—"

"Your wife *is* here, isn't she?" He was trying a diversion.

"Uh, no, not right now. But you could come back in a coupla hours. She'll prob'ly be here by then." He reached for the inner door.

Ransom's hand moved to the screen door handle. "Sure, but we still want to talk to *you.*"

"I don't think—"

"Oh, Harvey, let them in, they're not going to bite," said Nurse Pettijohn, appearing beside the man. Her fully packed body made Harvey seem even more like a scarecrow.

"Thanks, Miss Pettijohn," Ransom said, pulling open the screen door and stepping inside. The scarecrow stepped back. Kathy rolled in like a trailing fullback.

"This is a coincidence," Ransom said to Pettijohn. "What are *you* doing here?"

"I came by to see my sister and her husband, but I barely missed Marilyn. I guess I should have called before I just popped in."

The house smelled of musty furniture, rancid garbage, and nervous sweat. Ransom was about to confront them about Marilyn's car in the driveway. But just then from the back of the house came a baby's cry.

Harvey's eyes got as big as platters.

Nurse Pettijohn tried to act as if she hadn't heard a thing. She grabbed up her purse from the sofa. "Anyway, I need to be going."

No one was having any of it.

"Is that your baby?" Ransom asked Harvey, getting in his face.

Harvey blanched. "Well, no . . . we're just baby sittin' for a friend."

"It sounds like you should check on it."

"Nah, that's okay, Marilyn will . . . ." And his partial remark hung there like the Goodyear blimp for a count of two.

Then Ransom stiff-armed Harvey in the chest and skirted Nurse Pettijohn. Kathy slid in front of the door and glared into the nurse's mascara-laden eyes, daring her to move.

"Run, Marilyn!" Harvey yelled.

Ransom sprinted down the hallway.

A rustling sound and another cry, this time muffled, told Ransom which door to try. He crouched, turned the knob, and flung it open. There was no one there. A crib sat against one wall. The acrid smell of dirty diapers hit his nose.

On the far wall, a closet door hung open. Inside was a black wooden altar adorned with a dozen lit candles. The flames flickered, and Ransom's gaze went across the room to where a window was ajar and curtains fluttered.

He crossed the room in three steps, stuck his head out the window, and looked in both directions. There was no one there. But he heard the crunching of small sticks from the front of the house next door, so he clambered out the window and took off running.

Catching a glimpse of one of the surveillance cars in the alley, he yelled at them. Car doors flung open as Ransom ran full bore around the front corner of the house and across the neighbor's yard. Now he heard his prey scurrying along the far side of the house headed toward the alley.

The agents running along the alley came up behind her. She hesitated, and then dashed onto the back patio of the adjacent house. She slowed to a walk, and stopped, her sides heaving, clutching the baby to her chest.

Ransom eased toward her. "It's over, Marilyn. Take it easy. Everything will be all right."

"Get away!" she shrieked.

Ransom noted the purplish bruise under her eye. "We won't hurt you. We're with the FBI. We just want to talk with you."

"No, you can't." The woman's face was flushed, and sweat slicked her forehead.

"Let's go slow, now." He edged closer, ten feet away. "No one will harm you, Marilyn."

"Get back!" she screamed. And with a sudden movement, from under the blanket, she snatched out a stiletto. Ransom and the others stared in shock at the ancient blade. She pressed the point of the dagger to the child's throat. As the atmosphere turned to ice, with human figures frozen in their places, the baby started to wail.

19

With the baby clutched against her breast, Marilyn Larkin retreated across the concrete island of her neighbor's patio. Cushioned patio furniture surrounded her like protective barriers. Overhead, a lattice-work covering softened the sun's glare.

"You're safe here, Marilyn," Ransom said. "Just put the knife down."

"Get away from me, or I'll cut her throat."

"There's no reason for that. You can trust me."

Her eyes shifted left to right, looking for an avenue of escape. "No, I don't know you. I don't know any of you people."

"But you can tell I won't hurt you, right? I'm here to help you and the baby." He signaled for the others to back off. "It's just you and me here. We need to talk about this."

"I don't believe you. You'll grab me and take away my child."

"I won't, I promise. Here . . ." he said, gesturing, "let's sit down."

"No, I want to get out of here." As her voice got louder, so did the baby's shrieks.

"I'm sorry, but I can't let you leave right now. Maybe in a little while, but we need to talk first." He eased down onto a chair. "Please sit down, Marilyn."

Now she studied him. "Anyway, how do you know my—?"

"We know about all of it, Marilyn. About you and Harvey and the baby."

"Then you know the baby must die," she said. She licked her lips, and her eyes narrowed.

"No, that's not going to happen. The baby is fine, and so are you. It will all be okay. We just need to relax and discuss our options." He smiled. "She's really a cutie. Here, Marilyn, let me take a look at her. Let me hold her a minute."

She hugged the screeching baby tighter.

Then he could see the trauma overwhelm her. Her eyes closed, and she began shifting from foot to foot. "No, no, no. She's the Chosen One. She's going to give herself for everyone. An offering—that's it—she'll be an offering to the *orishas*. There'll be new life for all of us." She hung her head and started to sob.

Now the baby stopped wailing and stared at the crying woman, snuffling as her little mouth trembled.

"Sit down, Marilyn. You should rest now. You look very tired."

She sank onto a chair. The dagger dangled in one hand. Her shoulders sagged, and her bangs drooped over her eyes.

"The baby needs to be safe now, Marilyn. No one should hurt it. Just like no one should hurt you anymore."

Her head came up. Tears dribbled from her eyes.

"I know you've been hurt, but it won't happen again. You're safe."

He rose from his chair and stepped over to her, reaching out to touch her shoulder. Then he knelt down on one knee in front of her. "She's really beautiful," he said. "Let me hold her."

She gave him a doubtful look, and she scanned the others around her. Then she took a deep breath, and her body went limp as she sighed. Her gaze dropped, and her taut face relaxed. She handed him the baby.

As he cradled the infant in his arms, Ransom studied the baby's iridescent blue eyes, stunned by the innocence that shone there. He snuggled her against his chest, then reached over to Marilyn's hand and detached the dagger. He slid it behind him across the concrete, and Ball Cap scooped it up.

* * * * *

The baby had a strawberry birthmark on the back of her neck, which was a good sign to begin with. Ransom inked the tiny foot and checked her footprint, which matched the one the hospital had taken at birth. They'd found April Bayless Baldazar.

For her safety's sake, they transported her to the San Antonio Metropolitan Hospital where a pediatrician examined her, pronouncing her colicky, but healthy. Kathy showed the doctor the formula April was getting. He said she needed one without iron. A young agent was dispatched to find some. The doctor also studied the slashes on April's forehead, saying they were healing well and shouldn't leave any scars.

Harvey and Marilyn Larkin and Nurse Pettijohn were transported by the other agents to the FBI office. On Ransom's instructions, they'd been handcuffed behind their backs, a most uncomfortable way to ride in a car. Ransom told the agents not to talk to their prisoners during the trip.

Ransom and Kathy barreled downtown. They rushed into the supervisor's office to meet with Jenkins and Atherton. The two agents looked up questioningly.

"How's the baby?" Jenkins asked, his eyebrows raised.

"The doctor checked her over. She's fine. Molly Jenkins volunteered to watch her. And the head nurse, Winnie, will help take care of the child until we notify Mrs. Baldazar."

"We can't delay too long on that," Jenkins cautioned.

"I know. But we've got to play this hand out."

Ransom looked at Atherton, who was smiling, then back at Jenkins. "Did you call the Director?"

"You bet," Jenkins said. "He was fired up like a blowtorch. I think commendations are in the offing."

"So I can stay on the case?"

"He insisted on it. He said that everything else was water under the bridge."

"Not an original comment, but acceptable," Ransom said. Then he wondered about something else. "Did you tell the Director that we're checking out the Senator?"

"No, I didn't want to rain on his parade right then. Besides, we don't know which way that ball will bounce. We'd better leave ourselves some wiggle room."

"But we'd better find out quick what part, if any, he's been playing in all this. Are the three stooges still handcuffed and in separate rooms? I want to deal with them right away."

"Yep, they're situated just the way you wanted," Atherton said.

"That's fine. Then let's go talk to them. Hank, you go get the SWAT guy with the big arms, Osgood. The two of you interview Harvey. Lean on him, let him know he's in deep shit and sinking fast. I'm betting he'll snap like a twig."

Atherton smirked in a way that sent a shiver along Ransom's spine. "Can do," he said.

"Sonny, I'd like you and one of the other experienced agents to talk to Marilyn. Be a father figure for her. Let her know we realize she's been put upon by someone stronger. Someone we have to stop from hurting people. See if you can get her to help us."

"I like it," Jenkins nodded.

Ransom winked at Kathy. "Let's go visit Nurse Pettijohn."

"She's at the top of my social calendar."

As they walked down the hallway, Ransom said, "Let's push this one to the limit. First, I'll put her in a box, then there's something I want you to try."

Kathy listened and agreed it might work.

Ransom opened the door to the small interview room where Nurse Pettijohn sat squirming in a hardback chair. Her head snapped up, her look at once menacing but also panicked.

"Let's go," Ransom said, lifting her by one arm.

"These handcuffs are cutting into my wrists. Can't you loosen them?"

Ransom glanced behind her back. "There's no blood. That's not so bad."

She glared at him.

"Besides, I'll take them off in a minute—"

"Good, because I—"

"—when I fingerprint you."

"Fingerprint me? It's bad enough you handcuffed me and hauled me down here. All I did was visit my sister, damn it. You're all insane. I'm no criminal."

"Let's go in here," he said, tugging her into a small room with a built-in counter for fingerprinting.

"Most folks consider kidnapping a criminal act," Ransom said. "In fact, you could soon be in the joint keeping company with gals who stuck their old man with a butcher knife, addicts who shake all the time, and women who set fire to their house and kids."

"No, I won't . . . you can't . . . this is crazy!"

He unlocked the cuffs. Before she could rub feeling back into her wrists, he grabbed her hand and pressed her thumb onto a black pad. She wore an expensive-looking white blouse with long sleeves. She cringed as her cuff brushed the inky surface.

"Damn. Now look what you've done." She tried to get a look at the soiled spot, but Ransom rolled her thumb onto a fingerprint card.

"Sorry. I should've warned you. This can get messy."

She bit her lip. Her cheeks were bright red, and anger

radiated off her in waves. Ransom loosened his tie.

When he finished printing her, he handed her some paper towels and cleaning gel. She wiped furiously at the black stains on her hands. They lightened, but the dark discoloration still showed against her chalky skin.

"I'll never get this crap off."

"I wouldn't work at it so hard. They'll print you again when we take you to the Bexar County Jail."

"Jail? What are you talking about? I was just visiting my sister and—"

"Which reminds me," Ransom said, "we can't let you go over to the jail with any weapons or drugs hidden on you. We might as well get that over with."

"Get *what* over with?" Her mouth hung open. She seemed to realize something bad was coming.

Ransom stepped over to the open doorway. "Kathy," he called down the hallway, "can you help me out here?"

She loomed in the doorway, asking what was needed.

"Could you strip search her? Give her a good check for chivs or contraband."

"Chivs? What are you talking about? Contraband? You mean knives or drugs? I don't have anything like that."

Ransom shrugged. "Your sister had a pig sticker that'd go through your heart, and you've got the easiest access to drugs of anyone in town. And don't tell me that nurses and doctors are never junkies or pushers."

"But I haven't done anything. You can't—"

Ransom walked out.

Kathy stepped inside the small enclosure, giving Nurse Pettijohn a cold stare and flexing her rock-hard physique. "Get out of your clothes," she said.

A few minutes later, Pettijohn said, "Are you about through? You must have gotten your jollies by now, you've been over every inch."

"Just one more thing," Kathy fought to keep from grinning. "Bend over and spread 'em."

"Spread 'em? Spread wh—?" Her jaw dropped with the realization, and her milky face drained whiter than ever.

They had some exchanges, getting heated toward the last, and there was almost a scuffle.

But in the end, she bent over and spread 'em.

* * * * *

Ransom leaned against the wall in the hallway, arms

crossed, as Kathy and Nurse Pettijohn emerged from the room. Pettijohn looked like a head of lettuce that'd been left on the kitchen counter overnight. Her blouse was wrinkled and ink-stained at the cuffs. Her skirt was twisted off kilter, and her sheer nylons had disappeared altogether. Ransom figured they were probably in her purse.

"Good, we're right on schedule," he said in his official voice. "Lieutenant Sanchez is due to transport you to the county lockup."

"I thought this was a federal case," Pettijohn said.

"There's been no interstate transportation, so it's a local matter."

"Who cares?" she said, her face sullen. "Nothing could be worse than what you bastards already put me through."

"Sure it could," Kathy said, a sweet smile on her face. "When they do strip searches there, they use a metal probe."

Nurse Pettijohn's eyes widened, and she tried to speak, but no sound came out. She resembled a fish gasping on shore.

Ransom pulled his handcuffs from his belt.

"Turn around, we've got to hold you for Sanchez."

"No, wait." She bit her lip to keep it from trembling. "This isn't fair. I didn't plan this thing."

"You helped carry it out, so you're a co-conspirator. You're just as guilty as the others. You get just as much time in the slammer."

Her eyes stayed scared, but behind them Ransom could see her mind spinning like a slot machine.

"I could . . . ." She paused, sniffed, and then stared hard at him. "Don't you want to know about the leader?"

Ransom puckered his lips as if he were thinking it over. This was the moment they'd worked toward. This was sweet beyond words.

"No, I don't think so," he said. "Turn around."

Her expression was one of total amazement. "What? I can't believe this. You don't want to know who came up with the plan?"

Ransom gave her a cold stare. "I think we already have her."

"Me? What? You can't mean *me.* No way, I just went along with it. But listen, the leader is someone big. You'd be a hero if you got him."

"A hero, huh? Well, maybe. But what's in it for you?"

"Just cut me some . . . I mean, can't you give me a break? If I help you, can't you help me?"

"I don't control the courts. I can't make you any promises. But I'll listen to what you have, and if it's good, maybe it'll impress the judge."

She nodded, a tear chasing down her cheek.

* * * * *

In the interview room, Ransom gave Nurse Pettijohn a typed form with her rights on it. She read it, signed it, and sat forward in her chair. Ransom said for her to tell her story.

She said that they were all members of a *palo Mayombre* cult. The meetings involved invoking *orishas,* or deities, then getting high and having group sex. They dabbled in magick cauldrons filled with animal blood and organs.

In the last few months, their leader had talked of achieving youth and longevity. Recently, he'd claimed they could all achieve eternal life. But to do so, they needed a human sacrifice—and it had to be a baby. The members went along with the idea, afraid not to, and electrified by the thought of such an audacious plan.

"Why did you go for it?" Ransom said.

"At first I didn't. The whole thing sounds crazy, right? I know, it probably is."

"I'd have to agree. So?"

"I did it because I was in love with him."

"In love with who?" asked Kathy.

"The *palero* priest," she said, looking at her hands in her lap. She sniffed again. "I was in love with Pablo Baldazar, the leader. We had dated years ago, then drifted apart, but I never forgot him."

There was a long silence as everyone considered the startling information.

"But killing the baby . . . ." Ransom paused, not sure how to ask the question.

She got it, anyway. "I thought Baldazar's wife would be destroyed by losing the child. I believed that their marriage would break up, and I'd have a chance with Pablo."

Ransom said, "Um hmm. I see."

She continued, saying she'd offered to help Baldazar organize the kidnapping, together with her sister, Lyn, and her brother-in-law, Harvey. She and Pablo were thrown together in the planning sessions, and they soon reignited the old flames. She became sure during their times together that she'd done the right thing.

"What about the key for the outside door, the compromised surveillance camera, and the alarm that failed?" asked Ransom. "Did you have a hand in all that, too?"

Pettijohn swallowed hard. "Well, yes, part of it, anyway. "First, I left a key outside for Lyn. After she got in, she taped it under the towel dispenser in the rest room. Then I retrieved it later."

"Okay, and how were the security bracelet and the alarm compromised?"

"We used aluminum foil to cover the bracelet, so the alarm didn't sound when Lyn went out the door."

"What about the security camera?"

"Rafael Gomez is one of the security guards on the morning shift. He's . . . he's a member of our group. Pablo threatened to get him fired from his job if he didn't co-operate with us. He also told Pablo he'd kick him out of our group. So, Rafael said he'd help. He knew a way to keep the camera from showing the hallway. I didn't ask about the technical part."

Ransom nodded, taking notes. "But in general, how did he pull it off?"

"Rafael came in early and told the other guards they could take off, that he'd punch them out. When the other guard came on duty, he told him he'd pay for donuts and coffee if the guy would go get them."

"And when he did . . . ."

"Like I said, Rafael knows a lot about electrical stuff. He knew how to disable the monitor by doing something with the wiring in the console bank." She sighed. "He was finished and reading a newspaper when the other guard came back with the coffee."

"And then Rafael reversed the wiring he'd done on the camera?"

Pettijohn said, "Yes, when the other guard went to the rest room, he changed the wiring back to normal."

Kathy was horrified. But she was curious, too, and she asked Pettijohn how she and the Senator had gotten involved in the cult in the first place. She wondered to herself how intelligent people could even consider such a thing.

"At first it was just for kicks," said Pettijohn. "We did it for the thrill of doing something wild. Pablo and I were in college, studying a lot, and one of the guys in his dorm told us about this group." She looked at Kathy and shrugged. "We figured we'd check it out as a diversion, something to take our minds off school. Pablo didn't belong to any church, and I was a lapsed Catholic, so we had no religious hang-ups about doing it."

"But you stayed in a branch of the cult, even after college," Ransom said.

"When we started, the whole scene seemed strange, almost funny. It was pretty bizarre, with everyone exhorting the dead, the dark spirits, and all. But when we danced and everyone opened their robes and we had sex with the others, there was an excitement that seemed to grow until we couldn't give it up. We felt rebellious and daring and . . . powerful." There was a distant look in her eyes.

Then she peered at Ransom. "We got into the San Antonio group and found it just as thrilling as the one in Austin. And before long, Pablo said he could see that the higher up you went in the group, the more power you had. That went for everything: more money, more drugs, and more sex."

"So he worked his way up in the cult?" Ransom asked.

"He was smarter than the rest of them, and he had a mean streak that made them afraid of him. A couple of years ago, he became the head priest."

Kathy studied Pettijohn. "Was Baldazar's wife in the cult?"

"No, she never knew about it." She dabbed her reddening eyes. "I never understood what Pablo saw in her. Except that her family had a lot of money, and he was trying to set up a law practice, and maybe go into politics. I suppose that's what enticed him."

Ransom watched her body language. "So, she didn't know about the kidnapping plan?"

"No, that was all Pablo's idea. He hated kids." She nodded as she said it, and her voice was steady and strong. "It was only his wife who wanted them," she continued. "Pablo said they'd get in the way of his being an adult."

"Being an adult?" Ransom asked.

"You know, it would mess up his freedom to do the things he wanted."

No one said anything for several seconds. Then Kathy's brow wrinkled as she looked at Ransom. "Are you all right,

Jack? You look pale."

Ransom wiped drops of sweat from his forehead. "It's just hot in here." But he actually *did* feel light-headed.

Then he stood, pointed at Nurse Pettijohn, and said, "You stay here and behave yourself. Kathy, let's step outside for a minute."

She followed him into the hall.

"Do you think she's ready to do it?" he asked.

"If she's not, you wasted some good SS techniques."

"Kathy, you know this is too important to coddle her. Besides, James Baldwin said that 'Every profession has its ugly side.'"

"So the Ugly American is an FBI agent?"

"Sometimes, my dear."

"And as you said, this is important."

"It's vital."

"Then I'm in it 'til the 'gators get full."

"Okay, let's go make the pitch."

As they got back to the interview room, Ransom approached the disheveled nurse, fixed her with a penetrating look and said, "We appreciate your candor, Miss Pettijohn. The information you've given us has been a big help. I hate to take you to the county jail, but it'll just be for overnight. That's all I can do for you, unless . . . . " And he paused, as though he were seeking the proper words.

"Unless *what?*"

Good, he thought. She's mentally tuned in to the right channel. "I was just thinking out loud. Never mind, we'd better go now."

"No, unless *what*? Can you keep me out of jail? Please?" Her glossy red lips trembled.

"Well, we sometimes make arrangements for co-operative witnesses. You know, people who wear a wire and help us get evidence."

"What do you mean wear a *wire*?"

Didn't this woman watch cop shows on TV? "It's when someone has a concealed microphone and transmitter hidden on their person. When that person talks with the suspect, and he admits his guilt to them, then we can later play the recorded tape for the jury. The good guys win one. But I don't think that you're in that category."

"I could be. I could wear a wire and meet with Pablo, you know, and get him to talk about the kidnapping. You said you didn't know how to nail him for it."

"Yes, I guess I did. Hmm. Do you really think he'd talk with you?"

"Let's just say we're very close. He'll talk."

Ransom smiled, and then they huddled together and discussed the plan. In order to set it up, they'd have get in touch with Baldazar before he left his office. They moved fast, hooking up the telephone recorder, dictating the date, time, and who was being called. There was a moment of silence as they looked at each other in anticipation. Then Nurse Pettijohn punched in the numbers on the phone.

The receptionist transferred the call, and he said, "This is Senator Baldazar."

"Pablo, it's me."

"*Sheila*? What is it?"

"Can you talk?"

"Sure, go ahead. Is something wrong?"

"I'm afraid so. Lyn had an accident."

"An *accident?*"

"Yes, she was in a car wreck. She's in the emergency ward at the hospital. Harvey just called me. He said he had to get to the hospital, and he asked me to come by his house to watch the baby."

"So can you do that?"

"What if someone sees me? I can't explain where I came up with a baby, especially one who's being looked for by every cop in town."

"But there's no one else who . . . wait, let me think. Can you meet me someplace?"

There was a pause. "I don't know."

"It's very important. Please, Sheila, we need to talk about this."

"Well, I guess so. Where should we meet?"

"The same place as last time."

"Okay, I'll see you there," she said.

As the phone was replaced in its cradle, Ransom and Kathy grinned and shook their fists in the air.

"For best actress in a drama . . . ." Kathy said.

"The winner is . . . ." Ransom rejoined.

Then together: "Nurse Pettijohn!"

In spite of herself, Kathy gave the woman a hug. Nurse Pettijohn showed a bit of a smile.

"How fast can you wire her up?" Ransom asked.

"Give me five minutes."

"Here's the transmitter," he said, "go for it." And he left

the room.

Six minutes later, they came out the door. Kathy looked pleased with herself.

As they walked down the hallway, Ransom asked Kathy, "Have any problems with concealment?"

"Nope. The unit is secure. It's located in a belly band. And the microphone's between the two biggest mounds of flesh I ever saw."

"I can appreciate that. So, it should be well-hidden."

"I just hope it's not smothered."

20

Baldazar sat in a back booth in the Rancho Rio saloon, jiggling his knee up and down. He took a gulp of his scotch and checked his watch. The bitch had better show up, he thought, his lips tight, and his face growing hot.

He coughed into his hand. A raucous crowd of losers was fogging up the shitty dive with their smelly cigarettes. He usually didn't smoke, but right now he wished he could fire up a joint, just to relax himself. He reached inside his shirt and fidgeted with the Cross of Nero.

Finally, here she came. She looked nervous. He'd handle this smoothly, but forcefully. No way was he going to let a scared broad queer his triumph. Tonight would be his crowning moment. This would be an epic thrill, the ultimate achievement.

He stood up. "Hi, Sheila. Here, sit down. You want a drink?" He gave her a big smile. He'd get her to calm down. He knew how to handle her.

"White wine, please." She sat down in the booth.

He signaled for a waitress who came over to take the order. She was a nubile thing. Her boobs defied gravity.

As the waitress swished away, he turned to Sheila and said, "So are you all right?" He'd play it real casual.

"Hell, no. I mean, Marilyn's in the hospital, who knows how bad she's hurt? Meanwhile, Harvey's waiting on me, but I don't think I can risk staying there with that baby. Like I said, it would be too dangerous."

"It won't be that bad. Just go watch the kid while Harvey runs to the hospital. If you're not comfortable staying at their place, go check into a motel until tonight. Then if Harvey and Marilyn don't get back in time, you can bring the baby to the ceremony. No one will see you."

"But what if the FBI is watching me?"

"Did you see them?"

"No, but you're not supposed to." She frowned and sat

back, looking perplexed.

"Shit, you've been watching too much TV. Just make a couple of turns and double back. Watch to see if anyone is staying with you."

"That's easy for you to say. You'll be home with the wife. And they would never suspect you, anyway."

"Listen, Goddamn it!" He grabbed her wrist.

"White wine?" the waitress said.

He loosened his grip. "For the lady, please."

She gave him a look, set down the drink with a little dip, and plucked away the twenty he held up between two fingers. "I'll get your change."

"No, keep it."

That changed her attitude. "Yes, sir, thank you." She gave another curtsy, turned, and sashayed away. Man, she'd look good naked.

He glanced back at Sheila, just then noticing her stained cuffs. He asked, "What's that crap on your blouse?"

"Oh, just before I left, I had to change the cartridge on our copy machine. That black shit goes everywhere. It probably ruined my blouse."

"Take it easy, I'll buy you a new one. But you've got to help me here. This is for both of us, you know. Hey, it's for our whole group."

"I know, but I'm scared." She took a big sip of her wine.

He touched her knee under the table. Then he caressed it with a gentle touch. He thought he saw a rise in her. "I understand you're concerned. But just bring the kid to the ceremony, and I'll take it from there."

She stared at the glass of wine, took another sip, and then shuddered as though she'd plunged into cold water. Doubt danced behind her eyes. Then her gaze fixed on him.

"All right, I'll do it, Pablo, but only because I love you and want you so damn much."

"And I want you," he said, squeezing the flesh higher on her leg. He smiled, making sure she'd follow through on the deal. At the same time, he wondered why she wasn't wearing her usual nylons.

* * * * *

Ransom and Kathy escorted Nurse Pettijohn back to the office where they settled her in a room with a muscular agent posted at the door. Then they headed for the supervisor's office. Sonny was talking to Atherton, who lolled in a chair, his long legs stretched out before him and crossed at the ankles.

Ransom told them the story, with some juicy asides by Kathy. The part about placing the unit between the humongous body parts made Atherton sit up and pay attention.

"Super job," Sonny beamed. "You handled that beautifully."

"The whole office made it work," Ransom said.

"How do you see us playing it now?" Sonny asked.

Ransom laid it out. Sonny and Atherton questioned a couple of minor points, but they agreed the plan should work. Then Ransom handed Atherton two twenty-dollar bills and asked him to get some props they'd need later. Atherton gave Kathy a hangdog look, but she didn't volunteer to take over the chore, so he trudged off to get it done.

Kathy smiled as the big agent left. Ransom studied her. She looked like a princess on a golden float gliding down Bourbon Street. Why had those boys in Baton Rouge let her escape? She was a real prize.

They all talked awhile in Sonny's office, and soon Atherton came back clutching a shopping bag. His expression was a mixture of chagrin and forced insouciance. He handed the bag to Ransom in an indifferent manner, then moved over and leaned against a wall.

Checking the contents, Ransom said, "That's perfect, man. Thanks."

"Good," Atherton said. "Now if you've got everything you need, I've got to get into my SWAT gear." He hustled away without another word.

Ransom grinned. Atherton was overcompensating for his embarrassment about the "errand." FBI agents thought of themselves as macho guys. Especially the SWAT team members.

He checked his watch. It was only ten minutes until their meeting with the Bexar County SWAT team. They exchanged glances, then all got up and headed for the conference room.

Ransom hadn't seen the like before. A dozen grown men, some FBI and some deputies, outfitted in black fatigues and jump boots, milled about in the room with weapons of all types strapped on everywhere, their faces smeared with grease paint. It looked like a bivouac where soldiers were about to embark on a serious and deadly mission.

Another twenty agents, in dark-colored casual clothes, sat watching the tugging of belts and straps and harnesses, as the SWAT guys adjusted their gear. Two guys fussed over their sniper rifles for several minutes, and then reverently laid them back in their cases. Ransom checked his Glock to make sure it was loaded, then sat back and relaxed, knowing that tough duty lay ahead.

The preliminaries over with, Sonny told everyone to listen up, and then he yielded the floor to Ransom. Using a white board, Ransom sketched the area in the woods where they needed to set up. Maps of the location were handed out. They arranged radio communications, the pilot said he'd be up over the area by ten o'clock, and Ransom asked if anyone had any questions. He answered a few, and then everyone fell silent.

Ransom knew the realization had set in. In a few hours that drawing on the board they'd been studying would be them, in the woods in the middle of the night, in the midst of a hundred cultists. It could make anyone's blood run cold.

"That's the plan," Sonny said. "Let's go do it."

The SWAT team members with their heavy duty weapons and fatigues and blackened faces moved out as a clattering herd.

Ransom and Kathy held a last session with Nurse Pettijohn, making sure she knew the drill. She looked nervous, but she seemed to be holding together. Maybe, just maybe, Ransom thought, they could pull this off.

It was almost nine o'clock. They needed to get their butts in gear. Ransom drove to the Larkin's house where they picked up Nurse Pettijohn's sporty car, with Kathy driving. Pettijohn would need it to drive to the shindig in the woods.

Forty minutes later, they stopped at a predetermined spot where they met with Nurse Pettijohn. They asked her if she'd thought of any questions. She shook her head. They looked at each other for a long, expectant moment.

"Then here you are," Ransom said, handing her the shopping bag. She took a quick glance inside it. She nodded and gave them a tight smile.

"My robe's in the trunk," she said. "I guess that's everything I need." She exhaled a burst of air and looked Ransom in the eye. "I think I'm ready."

He patted her on the arm, handed her the car keys, and said they'd see her later. Then he and Kathy watched her drive off into the night. Kathy shook her head as she watched the departing car.

"So now she's on her own," she said.

"All by her lonesome," Ransom agreed.

"You sure she won't bolt and run?"

"Kathy, I'm not sure of a damn thing."

* * * * *

Ransom drove to the location where an Air Force bus huddled behind a stand of oak trees just off a country road. An agent guarding the bus said SWAT and the others had deployed fifteen minutes earlier. They'd radioed back that everyone was in place, no guards were encountered, and they didn't think they'd been spotted.

"Let's get over there," Ransom said to Kathy, "before we have to stand in line with the cultists."

They sprinted across the highway and hustled down a dirt and gravel road. It wasn't the road the members would probably take, but it still made them nervous to be so exposed. Then they angled across a field, within view of the clearing where the pentagram was cut into the grass.

* * * * *

Baldazar left his house a little after ten. He'd been antsy all evening, what with Trish wanting to talk, and the fucking FBI guys still hanging around. It was depressing as shit. And then it took forever for Trish to go to sleep. She must be getting immune to those damn pills.

When he was sure she was dead asleep, he walked into the kitchen, told the agents he had to get some coffee at the Quik Shop, and then headed out. If they said anything later about why he'd taken so long, he'd say his car wouldn't start and he'd had to buy a battery. So far, they hadn't asked.

He slid behind the wheel of his Mercedes and fired it up. The engine rumbled with power, and the ride was cushy, plus there was the sensual feeling of luxury. Not many morons out there could afford one of these creampuffs. Being a senator had its advantages.

As he drove, he thought about the money from his senator's pay, plus the campaign contributions, which were pretty "slushy," that is, there were funds available whenever he needed them. And then there were the "bonuses" he skimmed from cult collections. All-in-all, it wasn't a bad set-up. He had plenty of money, and he had power enough to do most of the things he wanted. Besides, after tonight, he'd be all-powerful and untouchable.

He turned off the main highway and bounced down a gravel road. Soon he cut his lights, pulled off the gravel, and wound along a rutted path through the woods until he neared the clearing. Then he angled off the trail and parked under a big cottonwood. Some other cars sat bunched together about fifty yards away.

Reaching into the box in the seat beside him, he pulled out his black robe. For a moment he stared at the four red splotches on the garment, made from the blood of animals. Then he unbuttoned his shirt, his fingers trembling. Tonight would be the ultimate experience. He lived for the excitement of these meetings. And this one would produce a thrill beyond imagination.

He pulled on the robe. Eternity would soon be theirs. A baby sacrifice! The supreme offering was to be made. After that, the spirits could deny them nothing.

* * * * *

The cultists gathered within the meadow, and in the dim moonlight, their dark shapes could just be discerned milling about. Anticipation was high. It was nearing eleven, and the excitement was building. Then, at the edges of the crowd, four torches were ignited. The flames danced and flickered, casting an eerie light across the group. They appeared like an amorphous, writhing organism, or a gathering of ghostly images shimmering upon the grassy field.

A tall figure stepped over beside the pentagram. On his signal, a fleshy red-haired girl dropped her robe and lay back on a small platform. The priest handed her two black candles, which she held upright as she reclined in the midst of the lust swirling through the crowd. The man lit the candles. Then he turned to the throng, which fell silent.

"We are here to contact the spirits of the dead," he said in a booming tone.

A chorus of voices murmured in anticipation.

"The dark spirits of the departed will bring us youth and riches." The priest turned to appraise the altar. "Let us summon them and praise them."

The group rumbled an incantation.

Then the leader spun around, stretched his arms outward, and shouted to the dark sky, "We call upon the spirits of the dead to join us here in life." He paused, and then his feral cry projected over the heads of the black-robed followers.

"Tonight we bring a sacrifice!"

"A sacrifice!" the crowd echoed like a clap of thunder.

Ransom and the SWAT guys watched as the ceremony progressed through various exhortations of the spirits, excited rantings and ravings, and the devouring of boiled cow's eyes and tongues and sex organs. The group drank a red liquid from quart jars. Was it blood? Ransom wondered. But they all seemed too eager to quaff it. It was probably wine laced with drugs.

The crowd grew more agitated. Maybe the stuff was even mixed with some speed. Yeah, that would be great, just great. This situation was turning to shit, Ransom thought. Should they make their move now?

No, they'd better hold off a bit longer.

The priest shrieked, "And now we offer the sacrifice!"

The throng gave out a frenzied cheer that resembled a scream.

"Youth and eternity shall be ours," proclaimed the priest. "We give to the spirits of the dead a living sacrifice." Then he glanced toward the woods and nodded at a figure standing at the edge of the clearing. "The *orishas* will return to us many fold a new life's energy, renewed lust in our loins, and life forever after."

The spaced-out cult members roared their response.

A woman wearing a shiny black robe walked toward the altar. She held a baby swaddled in a blanket. In that moment, the place went so quiet you could hear the stars blink.

Nurse Pettijohn floated across that meadow as if she were a debutante. She halted several feet from the priest. He stared at her and the bundle she held for several long seconds, then turned back toward the altar and clapped his hands.

Two neophytes, a preteen boy and girl, both naked, came forward out of the darkness at the fringe of the mass of robed followers. One of them carried a silver chalice. The other had a cushion with something on top of it. The neophytes stopped on either side of the priest.

"This is Boone One. My shot is blocked," radioed one of the FBI snipers. Ransom touched the microphone in his ear as if he could switch to a channel with better news.

Another message followed: "Boone Two is partially blocked, too. I may be able to get a shot in, but it will be close. Should we change our positions?"

Ransom whispered into his mike. "Negative, stay where you are. It's too quiet right now, they might hear you move. Maybe the kids will step aside in a minute."

"Affirmative," the snipers both said.

"The lifeblood of a babe taken with this ancient dagger," said the priest, lifting the knife from the cushion, "will flow into this ceremonial chalice." He took the cup from the slender girl and held up both gleaming items for inspection. Then an acolyte stepped forward, took the chalice from the leader's hand, and stood by with it at the ready.

"Now I'm totally blocked," said Boone Two.

Ransom said, "Everyone move in when I give the signal."

The priest reached out for the baby. Nurse Pettijohn stayed motionless for a moment, then stepped up to the priest and handed him the bundle. She took a step back, then stood rigid, her hands clasped before her.

He cradled the child in the crook of his arm, gazing out into the blackness, and speaking in a strained, emotional voice. "Dark and departed spirits, your servants deliver you this babe, that you might grant us life for ever and ever."

He raised the dagger over the tiny form.

Then he hesitated, staring at the face of the child nestled in his arm.

"Boone One or Two, do you have a shot?" Ransom asked.

"Negative," they both came back.

The priest swiveled his head to stare at Nurse Pettijohn. She took another step backward. Several of the followers grumbled, impatient for action.

"This is Boone One. Now he's in my scope. I've got a clean head shot."

"Just hold it," whispered Ransom. "Stand by."

The priest hurled the bundle to the ground. The startled group gasped, and the priest yelled curses at the woman. The baby doll lay mute in the dust.

"How dare you defy me and the *orishas?* And on this special night that glorifies the demons of the spirit world." He raised the dagger and stepped toward Nurse Pettijohn. "Now *you* will be our sacrifice!"

"Green light," Ransom radioed to the snipers. Then to the others he said, "When a shot goes off, everyone move in."

As the priest advanced toward Pettijohn, the acolyte shifted his position, forcing the sniper to change his aim just as his finger tightened on the trigger.

The explosion from the hi-powered rifle rocked the

woods. The priest stiffened, and then slumped to the ground. Nurse Pettijohn fell to her knees, reaching out to him.

Then half a dozen agents slapped the bases of illumination flares, which went skyward like rockets, lighting up the entire meadow with bright white blazes of light floating down on tiny parachutes.

Other agents and some deputies tossed concussion grenades as they ran toward the crowd. The brilliant flashes of light, the mortar-like explosions, the engulfing smoke and the dirt thrown up by the stun grenades startled and confused the group. The shock of those "flashbangs," plus the sight of armed warriors charging at them from all sides, froze the cultists into a mass catatonic state.

Then some of the group bolted from the pack. The agents tackled, tripped, or bulldogged them, slamming them to the ground and cuffing them. The other cultists stayed motionless, apparently not wanting some of the same treatment.

The priest staggered to his feet, blood oozing from his temple. He grabbed the front of Nurse Pettijohn's robe and pulled her up to her feet, thrusting the point of the knife against the soft flesh under her chin. She shrieked, but froze in place and stayed as still as a fencepost.

The SWAT team members were almost to the priest, but Ransom held up a hand and said into his mike, "Hold it, everyone. Let me try to talk him down."

Ransom and Atherton stopped five yards from the priest. They were close enough to try a shot, but it would be risky with him pressing the knife against Pettijohn's throat. It would be better if they could get him to drop the dagger.

Then the tall man surprised them all. "This woman, this cheat, who has betrayed the dark spirits and you worshippers here tonight, will still be our sacrifice!"

Ransom was stunned. It was as if the fool believed this mumbo jumbo. He yelled, "No, Baldazar, the charade's over. There'll be no sacrifice. Drop the knife."

Baldazar's head swiveled toward Ransom. Then he spit out the words, "These disciples here tonight will assail your puny forces and trample you. And the unconquerable spirits will strike all of you down with lightning and fiery hailstones."

Ransom glanced up, scanning the sky for red-glowing clouds, but he saw only a few winking stars and a listless moon. Baldazar must've sampled too much of the firewater.

"Attack! Attack!" shrieked the Senator. "Charge them, tear them apart!"

But no one moved. Every cultist in the crowd focused on the guns held by the agents and deputies. Doubt and fear replaced the lust and frenzy they'd felt just moments before.

Baldazar screeched, his face contorting, while both Ransom and Atherton edged a little closer. Kathy snuck up from the other side, her Glock held out straight in front of her. They were all too far away to grab the man, but they were almost within range to rush him, maybe distract him enough to get control of the situation. Also, if necessary, Ransom thought he could make a quick head shot.

When Baldazar took a breath, Ransom said, "Senator, take it easy. Try to be sensible. Let's look at the legal points involved here."

The man got quiet and gazed at him. So, Ransom continued, "We've got you cold for conspiracy to kidnap. You could plead and lighten your sentence on that charge. But if you add murder, you're looking at life in the slammer or maybe even the death penalty."

Ransom thought the logical approach would work. Baldazar was trained in the law—he knew its weaknesses, understood the system, and could figure the angles—so surely this was the key to dealing with him. But Ransom hadn't counted on craziness.

"The spirits of the dead have come among us," the Senator said with chilling conviction. "I can feel their all-powerful presence. All non-believers will die here tonight in agony."

As everyone stared, he grabbed Pettijohn by the hair. "And this traitor will be our sacrificial offering." He pulled her head back, exposing her white throat, then held the blade against it.

This is it, Ransom thought. The idiot's going to cut her throat. He pointed his pistol and squeezed the trigger.

Then a sudden movement paralyzed him, and his finger froze on the trigger.

The acolyte standing near Baldazar had taken a quick step in front of the man. And now, before anyone could react, the acolyte swung the heavy chalice toward the slit in the front of the Senator's robe and rang the tall man's chimes. The metal goblet hit Baldazar square in the crotch with a solid *thunk.* Strong men all around winced and clamped their thighs closed.

Baldazar lost his grip on Nurse Pettijohn as he hunched over, keening in a guttural wail. But he still held the knife, and he glared at the acolyte, whose hood had fallen away from his face.

Ransom's jaw dropped. It was Billy!

Then Baldazar lurched toward the youth. Billy backed away, his hands held out in front of him. Nurse Pettijohn collapsed to the ground.

Ransom aimed for Baldazar's head.

But the man lunged, his arm outstretched, and the sharp steel pierced Billy's chest.

Ransom watched in horror as Billy's eyes grew large, and the youngster groaned, staring in disbelief at the hilt of the dagger protruding from his chest. Billy sank to his knees, gasping for air. In slow motion he shuddered, and then keeled over facedown into the grass. It hit Ransom like a sledgehammer: Billy was gone.

Baldazar stepped over to Billy's body, rolled him over, and yanked out the knife.

Atherton exploded toward him, smashing his shoulder into the Senator's ribs, driving him straight to the ground. They both lay there dazed for a moment, then Baldazar shook his head and raised the knife above Atherton's back.

Kathy fired two quick rounds. Both hit Baldazar's forearm, and the knife dropped into the grass. She pointed the muzzle toward his chest.

Ransom took two steps forward, grabbed Baldazar's wrist, and wrenched his arm behind him, twisting it like a chicken bone. As he rolled the Senator face down in the middle of the pentagram, Ransom cuffed him, saying, "You're under arrest for kidnapping and murder. You have the right to remain silent—"

"Forget that shit, Ransom," Baldazar said with defiance. "My magick is greater than any laws of mortal man."

Ransom jerked him to his feet, and glared into his eyes. "When Hamlet said, 'What a piece of work is man,' he was lauding man's nobility. But in your case, it takes on a different aspect. You're a slimy piece of shit."

Kathy helped up both Atherton and Nurse Pettijohn. Then she picked up the doll and swung it by one arm in front of Baldazar's face. "I doubt your *orishas* will be thrilled with this sacrifice, but maybe you can apologize in court."

21

Night settled in over Ransom's apartment, and he sat at his dining table in a wheelchair, eating spaghetti. He finished the last bite of his dinner, swept the crumbs of Italian bread off the table, and wheeled himself to the sink where he laid his dish, glass, and silverware. As he turned around, he noticed one of the stove burners was still lit.

Then he saw that a dish towel was lying beside it. As though his thoughts had ignited it, the towel suddenly burst into flames. He realized he needed water right away. He wheeled back to the sink and groped for the glass.

But as he filled the glass with water, the flames kindled a roll of paper towels on the counter. Next, a coffee can filled with old grease suddenly lit up like a volcano, and soon an overhead cabinet began to smoke, and then sprouted flames that licked upward like ravenous devil's tongues. He tossed the water toward the blaze, with little effect. The burning towel dropped to the floor, starting up a paper sack full of trash. He filled the glass again and splashed it against the growing flames, causing some sputtering and wisps of black smoke, but not diminishing the conflagration.

He had to get help. This was out-of-control. The phone in the kitchen was only a few feet away, but the smoke was now billowing up dark and thick. He coughed, his throat tickled, and his eyes burned. His cell phone was charging in the living room; he could call from there.

Backing his chair around, he banged into a cabinet. He eased forward, but the right wheel wobbled as he tried to roll away. Grey-black smoke spiraled toward the ceiling and spread wider throughout the kitchen as cabinets, grease, dish towels, trash, and a package of napkins blazed.

With each push the bent wheel got stiffer. Now he could barely make it roll. Then it froze up altogether. Superheated air scorched his throat and lungs as the smoke thickened into a roiling cloud.

From the bedroom came a high-pitched shriek. It was the baby! He lifted his legs from the foot rests and onto the floor, praying for a miracle to put life in them so they could carry him out of this burning hell. He had to walk. He had to run, grab the baby, and get her out of here.

But no miracle happened. His legs remained as dead as two tree trunks. The acrid smoke and searing fire kept growing until it now consumed the kitchen, the living room, the whole apartment, overcoming him. And he realized that both he and the baby would perish.

Then he awoke. He was shaking, perspiring, and coughing. He sat up in bed. His clock showed it was two in the morning. It had only been a nightmare. He was alone in his apartment, and there was no baby with him.

And he realized that in four hours he'd have to slip into his running togs. He was scheduled to race in the San Antonio Marathon. Sure, that was no problem. Except as of now, he felt dead tired, totally spent.

He tried to get back to sleep, but he kept remembering his dream and wondering what it meant. Why were his legs paralyzed and lifeless? And why was the baby even there?

Then it began to make sense to him. Of course, he'd been trying to save a baby for the past week. But still, there was more to it. Somehow, this seemed like his child.

And in the dream, he'd suffered from paralysis. He mulled it over. In dreams, there was usually hidden content. But what could it be? He concentrated harder, knowing it was critical.

Substitution and symbol are often used in dream sequences. Often, one idea is a symbol for something else. There was the wheelchair. That could be a symbol of his inaction or disability, maybe his inability, in regard to something. Not his work, surely, but what?

And then he suffered from paralysis. That might be a substitute for . . . well, maybe parallax—the difference in the perceived direction of an object if it's seen from two different points. He considered that, but could think of no connections.

He walked to the living room bookcase and pulled out a dictionary to look under the letter P. Parallel, parity, parlay. No, nothing there. How about paradox? A statement seems opposed to common sense, but it may be true. Possibly. But that's pretty vague.

Ah, one he missed—parapraxis, which is a slipping of the

pen or tongue or memory. But which one would it be? It had to be his memory. He was blocking out something. Something painful, scorching, burning that might consume him if it came out. But he couldn't bring it to mind or decide how it all might make sense.

It must have something to do with the kidnapping, which had been on his mind, night and day, for a week. Surely, that was it. He'd been afraid of losing the baby, feeling helpless much of the time. He replaced the dictionary and went to the window where he stared outside, his eyes unfocused.

But he hadn't failed, and they hadn't lost the baby. They'd awakened Mrs. Baldazar in the middle of the night to return April to her. April was healthy and safe, and her mother had been overjoyed.

Hearing the truth about her husband was another matter. The Senator had failed his wife and his child. It was a horribly shocking revelation.

And as Ransom thought about it, he realized that Baldazar and he were both men with important personal agendas. The Senator was consumed with his lust for money and power, and maybe he even believed the idea about achieving eternal life. And Ransom knew in that moment that he was not so different from the man he'd arrested. Indeed, he had been overly focused on a search for himself, and on trying to find personal harmony and inner peace.

And what was the cost to each of them as fathers? And to their wives and children?

Parapraxis. A slipping of the memory. Nurse Pettijohn had told him and Kathy that Baldazar said something about his child. It was something that had struck a chord with him personally. Kathy had even asked if something was wrong with him. Baldazar had said that the child was a problem to him. It would keep him from being . . . what?

He tried to think of it as a quotation. The words fit the person. The child would keep Baldazar from being . . . .

An adult! That was it. Baldazar said children would get in the way of his being an adult. And now it crashed down on Ransom from his weak memory banks and dulled conscience. In a sense, he considered his children to be the same burden to him. With them around, he could never find the opportunity to do his precious yoga, meditation, or running. And there wasn't time to read or reflect or think of new concepts about life. He felt as if he was always busy dealing with the kids and their problems or needs or requirements.

And now, as shame and a realization of his folly washed over him, he asked himself an awful question. Was the fact of Beverly's infidelity merely an excuse for him? Could it have been something he'd actually been seeking all along?

Oh, God, yes. In that instant, he knew it had been his escape clause. It had afforded him a way to get out from under his dreary responsibilities, away from the distractions of family life, at liberty to pursue whatever his heart desired. It left him free to indulge his every adult whim. He'd gained his personal liberty, and at what price to his children? What had it cost his family?

He buried his face in his pillow. Tears of bitterness burned in his eyes. He eventually fell asleep, but he could only drowse restlessly until morning.

* * * * *

Ransom struggled awake, feeling depressed, lonely, and confused. The only thing he was certain of was he had to run. He had to sweat, exhaust his muscles, and strain himself to the max—to try to leech himself of the poisons of his stubborn, hard-headed actions. Then maybe he could think more clearly. Maybe he could get some perspective on his situation.

He tugged on his running gear and laced up his shoes. Standing in the kitchen, he drank some orange juice and ate a banana. Then he grabbed his wallet and keys and went outside.

No more terrific morning could have greeted a distance runner at this time of year in San Antonio. The temperature was in the mid-sixties, there was a slight breeze, and the humidity was not too bad. Stringy clouds and morning haze buffered the sun, but the rosy presence warmed his skin. And now he had to go make the run.

He started his car. The low, energetic grumble of the engine seemed to make his legs come alive. He punched on the radio to a pop station and drove to Brackenridge Park drumming the steering wheel in time to the music, his car windows down, with fresh air flowing across his face and arms.

A crowd of brightly-clad runners milled about in the park grounds. People shuffled their feet as they waited in line outside restrooms. Runners stretched their legs in every way imaginable.

He reviewed the race in his mind. The route led out of the park, south on Broadway to downtown, where they'd wind past the Alamo, by Hemisfair Plaza, past the Riverwalk, then east out Houston Street until it hit W. W. White road, where they'd turn south. They'd cut back on Roland Avenue past the South Side Lions Park, loop around it, then run back inside for the finish. That is, if he could make it that far.

* * * * *

The gun sounded, and the race was on. Ransom gladly accepted the challenge, though he knew the recent grueling week at work had taken its toll. For the first five miles he took it easy, loosening up, warming his muscles and getting his stride in a silky groove. He was running shoulder-to-shoulder with a woman about his age and a teenager who was built like a fullback. Then he picked up the pace, pulling ahead of them to the next group of runners.

By mile ten he'd hit a solid gait. They were running out Houston Street, soon to pass the AT&T Center, the stockyards and rodeo center, and the Joe and Harry Freeman Coliseum. All right, he thought, so far, so good.

But by mile fifteen, he was beginning to feel rocky.

He noticed a hint of a cramp in his calf, nothing serious, but it affected his rhythm, and he was worried the muscle might knot up. Plus, now his mouth was getting parched. He hadn't carried a water bottle, figuring he'd grab a cupful at one of the stations along the way.

He'd felt fine as he glided by the ten mile mark, so he hadn't slowed to get a drink. Now he couldn't get one until mile twenty. Where the heck was a Coke machine when you needed one?

His strength began to flag. The strain of last week was hitting him hard. He shortened his stride, trying to loosen the bunched calf muscle. But he felt no change in the stinging pain.

The sun crept higher in the sky, the clouds dispersed, and the breeze dwindled to an occasional warm puff. Now the fireball burned down on his head and shoulders, and he mopped the sweat dripping from his forehead. Several runners he'd passed earlier now caught him and ran on by. He was faltering. His muscles continued to stiffen, and he began to feel weak and jittery.

Now he was coming up on mile twenty.

The park and the water station were not far ahead. He felt as though he could make it. Maybe the water would refresh him enough to slog out the last six miles.

But then he hit the wall.

He'd read about the phenomenon, heard runners speak of it, even tried to anticipate it. But he'd never internalized the message. It was sort of like an auto accident or a heart attack—something that happens to some other guy.

But here it was. And it was as solid as a concrete dam. He could feel his energy drain as if someone had pulled a plug.

With his energy reserves gone, he knew he could only draw on guts and nerve.

Still, he was almost to the park. He could see figures gathered at what must be the water station, and he staggered for it like a man on the desert stumbling in a daze of heat exhaustion toward an oasis. He focused his attention on the table loaded with blue water jugs and dozens of paper cups.

And then he saw her. Standing by the end of the table, cradling a cup of water in her hand, was his daughter, Holly. She spotted him, smiled, and held the cup out toward him.

He stopped and swigged the water, squeezed Holly's arm and told her thanks, then jogged off, taking the last swallow as he moved on. Others racers ran ahead, gulping water as their legs pumped. He watched them crush their cups, and then fling them to the side of the path where they bounced, rolled and curled to a stop.

For a long moment, he stared at the ground that was strewn with so many disfigured cups. He crumpled the cup in his hand. Then, as he ran, he swung his arm to toss the cup aside. But his fingers wouldn't let go. He moved on, but as he pounded the pavement, he began to slow. In a minute, his deliberate jogging dwindled to a walk. And then he stopped.

He unclenched his fist and stared at the balled-up cup. Then he turned his head to gaze again at the stretch of ground littered with debris. In a moment, he glanced back where Holly stood. She was watching, and she gave him a mystified look. She had to be wondering if he was all right. She was probably puzzled as to what in the world he was doing. And, God, she appeared so young and vulnerable and alone.

Then he limped back to where she was standing.

"Thanks for coming to see me," he said.

"But, Daddy, aren't you going to finish the race?"

"I finished what I needed to do," he said. Then he put his arm around her shoulder and strolled with her toward a familiar car he'd spotted minutes before.

"Did your mom drive you here?" he asked.

"Sure, why?"

"She and I have some things to discuss."

THE END

ABOUT THE AUTHOR

The author obtained degrees in sociology and law, then entered the FBI as a Special Agent. He worked criminal cases and terrorism matters for 30 years, stationed in Alabama, New York, Chicago, Puerto Rico, Texas, and Kansas. He nabbed killers, kidnappers, bank robbers, extortionists, and con men, and he played a key role in identifying the Oklahoma City bombers. He is the author of four previous suspense novels and one non-fiction book. He lives on a small horse ranch near St. Mary's, KS, and he's currently at work on another novel.

14290047R00141

Made in the USA
Charleston, SC
01 September 2012